## THE REASON FOR IT ALL

"Where is he, Mrs. McCormack?" Ludlow asked.

"Right here," McCormack said.

They stepped through the doorway behind her, McCormack first and then his two sons. Ludlow could see Pete Daoust in the shadows behind them. Daniel held a pistol in his hand. From the look of it a .38 revolver.

His father had a pistol too, only McCormack's was a .44 magnum. Ludlow had fired one once. It could take down a bear.

This was a family, he thought, that liked its guns.

"You're a goddamn lunatic," McCormack said. "Coming here."

"Maybe."

"My friend, there aren't any maybes about it."

"Sometimes the only way to know a thing is to know it firsthand, Mr. McCormack. See it. Taste it. Smell it. *Then* you know it. Somebody burned my store down last night. A few nights back somebody put a rock through my window. But I'm not here about any of that. I'm here about this."

He set the body down gently on the porch in front of them and unfolded the blankets. . . .

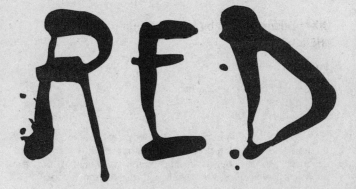

# JACK KETCHUM

LEISURE BOOKS  NEW YORK CITY

A LEISURE BOOK®

August 2002

Published by

Dorchester Publishing Co., Inc.
276 Fifth Avenue
New York, NY 10001

ISBN 0-8439-5040-4

The name "Leisure Books" and the stylized "L" with design are trademarks of Dorchester Publishing Co., Inc.

Printed in the United States of America.

Visit us on the web at www.dorchesterpub.com.

For Neil, Aggie, Beast, Vinni and Zoe – furry friends past and present. Daily tutors in the art of caring. And for the real Red, gone now, who saved my Uncle's life as Sam Berry's dog does here.

## ACKNOWLEDGEMENTS

First, thanks to Gavin Ziegler for his keen eyes and nose for a potential Ketchum story. Then to Paula White, as usual, for her wise editorial readings and to my editor, Mike Bailey, for standing by me on this one – not to mention his concerned and gentlemanly treatment of us writers in general. Many, many thanks to Alice Martell and Stephen King for getting me to the UK in the first place. I'm gratefully indebted to Lowell 'Chip' Woodman for sharing with me his compassionate understanding of Maine law and federal law as regards the rights of animals – or lack of them – in this country, to Bill Tracy for the good fishing tips, and to Fred Christ for all the wacky true stories he's collected for me over the years. Finally, thanks to Neal and Victoria McPheeters. They know why.

'To ache is human, not polite.'
                    Emily Dickinson

'Here I am, Lord, I'm
Knocking at your place of business . . .
I know I got no business here . . .'
                    Paul Simon

# Part One

# LUDLOW

# One

The old man looked at the dog looking at him, watching his hands as they threaded the hook through the brown plastic worm to its bright orange tail, the old dog lying on the riverbank in a patch of late afternoon sunlight filtering through the trees. After all this time the dog was still curious about him and especially curious about his hands. It was as though, to the dog, the hands and what the hands could do were what made them different from one creature to another and that was all.

He heard the boys long before he saw them and so did the dog, knew that someone was approaching and that there were more than one of them cutting down through the woods along the narrow dirt and gravel path from the clearing where the old man had left his pickup, the same way he and the dog had come.

He could hear their feet scuffling the earth and gravel and the crack of branches over the songs of birds and the sounds of the slow-moving river.

The dog's ears rolled forward and up and he turned his big brown scruffy head in the direction of the sounds and then looked back to the old man.

3

The old man said nothing so the dog just sighed and settled in.

The river had been productive for the old man ever since ice-out but now in late June it was almost too easy – he'd been standing on the bank only thirty or forty minutes, no more. And already he had two out of his three-fish legal limit lying headless and gutted in his cooler, both of them four-pounders.

The river flowed wide and deep here. The old man had only to pick a rock or a stump or a fallen tree as he did now – anything the smallmouth could use for cover – and then cast his worm and let it drop. He would retrieve the line in a series of jerks so that down in the brown cloudy water the worm would surge forward and upward and then settle back to the bottom again. Today three or four jerks was all it took and he could feel the tap on the line that told him the fish was interested. He would point the rod at the fish so that the line went slack and the fish could begin to feed on the plastic worm the old man had scented with his spit. Then he would slowly reel the slack back in and when that was finished and he judged the line was tight enough he'd set the hook, pulling the rod up hard over his head, freeing the hook from its swindle of a worm and piercing the fish's mouth.

The bass would want to fight like a demon but the old man wouldn't let him fight, not any more than he had to anyway in order to reel him in.

This was about a fish on his plate and two in the freezer and that was all it was about. His taste for blood sports had fled somewhere between his daughter Alice's wedding and Mary's death. It had never returned.

But he did love the good firm white meat of the fish and so did the dog. Though the dog would eat just about anything, Mary'd said. And over the years since her death he'd found that in this, as in most things his wife chose to speak on, she was right.

He saw the dog raise his head again, his scarred black nose scenting the air.

The old man smelled it too, before the dog in fact. The dog was not what he used to be. When the old man looked at him he could still see the pup inside him the same way he could still see the boy inside himself. But the dog moved much more slowly now, which was probably the onset of arthritis and his eyes were starting to cloud over.

Though there was enough left in him for him to go off chasing Emma Siddon's black mongrel bitch whenever she was in season. He'd caught him at that again just a week ago in the field behind his house. The old man smiling, the dog leaping through the goldenrod stirring up the bees like he was still young and strong.

Still the old man smelled it first.

Gun oil.

Faint, upwind of him, coming off the trail.

The scent of an amateur, the old man thought. Any good hunter would have known to swab it down a whole lot better than this one had. Game would be moving away from them for miles around. Even if they hadn't been coming down the trail as noisy as a herd of goats.

He brought the rod up quickly to just past the vertical and then down hard to the near-horizontal and felt the line whip hissing toward him and then out past him, shooting away across the river to the same half-sunk tree where he'd pulled the first one, the bigger of the two bass, only to the far side of the tree this time where he knew the water was deeper. He let it drift to the bottom and then gave the line a tug.

The dog's head was up again and the old man saw them out of the corner of his eye and turned to glance at them as they stumbled down the hill and then he turned his attention back to the line and tugged once again.

Kids. Seventeen, eighteen maybe.

One shotgun between them carried by the taller of the three, slung over his shoulder like it was a stick or a bat, not a firearm.

'Gettin' any?'

The old man turned to see who was talking to him. It was the one with the shotgun, tall and good-looking and probably aware of that, hair cut short the way they used to cut the old man's hair back in the service, jeans and a teeshirt that read STOLEN FROM MABEL'S WHOREHOUSE, with a drawing of a big-breasted woman in a cowboy hat standing outside some western-style bar.

The boy looked lean, hard, not like the other two. The other two wore jeans and teeshirts as well, one red and one a faded yellow, the kind with pockets cut for cigarettes, but their hair was medium length and brown, not blond and short like the other boy's. The kid in the red shirt had a belly on him.

'Two in the cooler,' he said. 'Have a look if you want.'

The boy in the yellow shirt whose body was just a skinny young boy's body, not a man's yet like the

6

one with the gun, leaned down and flipped the lid
of the cooler. He studied the fish a moment, hands
dug into the pockets of his jeans so that his shoulders
hunched and then stood up again.

'Not bad,' he said. 'Good size.'

The old man grinned. 'You can pull 'em five
pounds or more out of here now and then.' He
tugged the line. 'These'll do though.'

The heavy-set boy in red was scuffling rocks and
gravel with his sneakers. Idle, something sloppy
about him that always seemed to go with a boy
too heavyset for his own good. A fish yards away
underwater could hear what was happening on the
land and the old man wished he'd cut it out.

'This your dog?' said the one with the shotgun.

The old man looked over at the dog and saw that
the dog was looking at the boy the way he did
sometimes. The dog was getting cranky in his old
age and you could tell when he'd taken it into his
head to dislike somebody because he got this kind
of fixed look in his eyes like he wasn't going to blink
or take his eyes off that person for a goddamn
second until that person proved he or she could be
trusted to the dog's complete satisfaction.

The problem with the dog was that you could buy
his trust with a dog biscuit.

He thought about that and thinking about how
easy the dog was made him smile.

'He's mine all right. No need to bother yourself
about him, though. He won't bite.'

Some people were funny about dogs, he thought.
Always figured a dog would want to bite. Whereas
damn few dogs in his experience had ever bitten

7

anybody unless there was major provocation to push the dog and rarely even then. What dogs wanted from people was just the opposite. A dog wanted *not* to bite. To never have reason to bite because they were fed and warm at night with nobody tormenting them and plenty of time to sleep in the sun and run and chase and plenty of room to do the chasing.

'Pretty old, isn't he?' said the boy in red.

He nodded. 'We go back a ways.'

The old man tugged the line. Nothing was biting now. Maybe it was the talk spooking the fish or maybe it was the heavyset boy still kicking up the gravel.

'How old's a dog like that?'

The old man had to think. Mary had given him the dog for his fifty-third birthday when the dog was six or seven weeks old. That was the year before she died. She'd died in '83.

'Thirteen, fourteen.'

'Raggedy old fella.'

The old man had nothing to say to that. He didn't much like the boy's tone, though. He gathered that the boy didn't have much use for animals.

He began reeling in his line.

'What kind of bait you using?' The skinny boy in yellow was looking in his tackle box.

'Worm.'

'Live worm?'

'Plastic. Giving it a try. So far, so good.'

'I like the buzz bait. Ever try that?'

'I never used one. Jitterbug sometimes, hula popper. Generally I like a worm though.'

'Jesus. Cut the crap, Harold,' said the boy with

the shotgun. 'Old man, set down your goddamn rig.'

The old man looked at the boys as the boy took two steps forward along the gravel.

The shotgun was levelled at him, pointed at his belt. *Now what the hell was this about?*

The boy flicked off the safety.

The dog was growling, moving to get up.

'Easy,' he said to the dog. 'Take it easy.'

He held out his hand. The dog could be counted on to heed what the hand had to say even if all his instincts told him not to. He sat back on his haunches again. Growling so low you might have missed it if you didn't know to listen. Right now the dog wanted more than anything to stand up fighting, old and arthritic or not.

'He better take it easy,' said the boy. 'Now set down your goddamn rig.'

Talk sense to him, the old man thought. Keep him rational even if what he was doing wasn't rational at all.

'I set it down I could lose it,' he said. 'Suppose I get a strike out there? They've been biting good today.'

The boy looked at him like he was crazy, then smiled and shook his head.

'Yeah. Shit. All right, reel her in. Then set her down.'

The old man did as he was told. He could see the boy enjoyed holding the shotgun on him a lot more than he ought to. He didn't want to provoke him.

'Gimme your wallet,' said the boy.

The old man shook his head.

'Wallet's in my pickup. In the glove compartment.

You passed it coming down here. Green Chevy pickup, sitting in the clearing.'

'Bullshit,' said the heavyset boy in red.

'It's true. I don't take it with me. I never do. There's not much use for cash down here and if I have to go in after a snagged line or go in to haul out the bass most likely my wallet'll get wet. Or else I have to remember to toss it in the tackle box. Half the time you forget. So I keep it locked up in the glove compartment. There's twenty, thirty dollars in there and I won't say you're welcome to it but I'm not going to argue with a shotgun either. Take it.'

He reached slowly into his pocket.

'You'll want my keys,' he said.

'What's his rig worth?' the boy with the shotgun said to the youngest, the one he'd called Harold.

'Ah, it's pretty old stuff. A couple nice flies. But nothing . . . I mean, nothing really worth bothering with.'

It wasn't an honest appraisal if the boy knew anything about fishing and the old man sensed that he did. The flies were all hand-tied, a good collection. They could have fetched a tidy sum. If the boy saw that, he wasn't saying.

He wondered why.

'Any credit cards in that wallet, old man?'

'I don't use any.'

The boy laughed and shook his head and took a step closer and the old man could see that the shotgun was a Browning Auto-5 12 Gauge, brand new and expensive and he could smell the oil strong as a new-car smell as he dug out his keys and held them out to him. The boy kept laughing but there was no humor in it, only a kind of growing meanness.

As though the laughter was leading the boy on to something.

The old man saw that his face was deeply lined for a boy his age and that the belt he wore was made of very good leather and his jeans were some kind of designer jeans, not Levis, and that the other boys were wearing them too.

They didn't need money. They just wanted it.

Well, they could have it.

He hoped to hell that was all they wanted.

'Here,' he said, holding out the keys. 'Smallest one opens the dash. Wallet's inside.'

Take them and get, he thought.

The boy was still grinning at him, shaking his head.

'You got a beat-up old pickup and a wallet with twenty bucks in it and a rig that's not worth jackshit. You got a couple of fish and a goddamn dog. What the hell you *got*, mister?'

The old man didn't answer. There wasn't any answer. The boy didn't want one.

'You don't have *shit*.'

There was always the chance that the boy wouldn't fire if he moved on him and tried to take the gun away but he doubted it was a good chance because there was a coldness in his voice he hadn't liked right from the very beginning but now it had gone from cold to cold as ice. He glanced at the heavyset boy and saw no help in the bland silly smirk the boy was wearing and then at the youngest one in yellow and saw that this one was scared silent now. And that was not help to him either.

11

Though the boy's being scared might explain the lie about his rig.

He heard the water behind him and the wind in the trees.

He held out the keys.

He waited. Nobody moved.

The boy was building up to something. Calling it off or not, he couldn't tell.

You could die right here, he thought. You ready for that?

He had no answer for that one either.

'What's his name?' said the boy.

'Whose name?'

'The dog. What's his name?'

To the old man the dog was mostly just the dog. He came at a whistle and obeyed the old man's hands, a clap or a wave or a snap of his fingers and probably he hadn't had reason to use the dog's true name in months. But he and Mary had named him as a pup, something simple for his color.

'Red,' he said.

The boy stared at him unsmiling, nodding as though taking this in and for a moment the cold meanness in his eyes jittered in the light reflecting off the river.

'That's good,' he said quietly. 'That's real good. Red.'

The boy took a deep breath and blew it out and seemed calmer and the old man thought it was possible that the storm in the boy was passing though he didn't understand why that should be with just the knowing of a name and then the boy whirled and the dog was getting up out of his crouch, so much slower than he would have just a year ago when he was only that much younger, sensing something beyond the old man's staying hand or his power over events and the boy took one step toward him and the shotgun tore deep through the peace of the river and forest and sunny June day and the peace that had been the life of the old man up to then. And there wasn't even a yelp or a cry because the top of the dog's head wasn't there anymore nor the quick brown eyes nor the cat-scarred nose, all of them blasted into the brush behind the dog like a sudden rain of familiar flesh, the very look of the dog a sudden memory.

The old man stood there stunned.

Why? he thought. Dear god, *why*?

The dog's legs quivered.

'Red!' the boy shouted and laughed. 'Red!'

The shotgun was already pointing back at him. The boy was fast, the old man thought.

It was something to keep in mind.

'He's red now!' said the boy and he laughed again.

The laugh was blood-crazy, dull and stupid. He'd heard them laugh like that during the war, lost to their hearts and souls.

The old man said nothing.

He glanced at the spent shell-casing on the ground and then looked back at the shotgun pointed at him.

'Next time remember to keep a little more cash around, old man. Then stuff like this maybe won't happen to you.'

He glanced behind him at the other two boys.

'Let's get out of here,' he said.

The other two looked more than ready to leave.

The skinny kid had gone white and even the fat one was scowling. The boy with the shotgun didn't seem to notice.

'We don't want your goddamn keys, old man,' he said. 'Twenty bucks isn't even worth our trouble. So today's your lucky day. Just don't get to thinking you should be coming after us, that's all. You'll stay lucky.'

The old man nodded. 'You've still got the shotgun.'

'That's right. I've still got the shotgun.'

The boy looked at the dog and started laughing again. '*Shit! He's red all right!*' he shouted. In a moment the heavyset boy was laughing too, shaking his head like his friend here was crazy. Finally even the boy in yellow, in a shaky kind of way, though he didn't appear to have his heart in it.

That was your second mistake today, son, the old man thought. The first was coming down here, being with them.

He heard them whooping and laughing all the way over the ridge even after they were no longer in sight.

When he was sure they were not coming back he bent over and picked up the shell casing and put it in his pocket.

Then he went to the dog.

He looked down at him for a long moment, thinking. He took off his shirt and draped it across the dog's ruined head and lifted it and tucked the shirt under and wrapped it around. He ran his hand over the back and the warm flanks of the dog. The hand the dog had always watched so carefully and with such great curiosity came away a copper red.

The boy had made a joke of it.

The dog was Mary's gift to him on his fifty-third birthday.

The dog had been a good dog. A damn good dog. His body was still warm.

He got up and closed and locked his tackle box and set his rig, picked them up along with the cooler and walked back to where the dog lay. He tied the arms of his shirt around the dog's neck against the seep of blood and picked him up and tucked him under one arm with the rig and cooler and tackle box all gripped in his other hand and then he started up the path.

The dog grew very heavy.

He had to stop twice to rest but he would not let go of the dog, only sat by the side of the path and put down the cooler and fishing gear and shifted the weight of the dog so that it rested in his lap across his knees, holding him in his arms until he was rested, smelling the familiar scent of his fur and the new smell of his blood.

The second time he stopped he cried at last for the loss of him and for their long fine past together and pounded with his fist at the hardscrabble earth that had brought them here.

And then he went on.

# Two

The old man whose name was Avery Allan Ludlow drove up the hill to the house and thought that the boy was right about one thing.

He didn't have much.

He had the store and the house and the two small parcels of land each of them stood on and that was about all.

The house was over a hundred years old when he and Mary bought it back in 1970 along with an acre and a half for the sum of twenty thousand dollars. The reason it was only twenty thousand was that when it rained the roof leaked in twelve separate locations, leaked all the way through the floor of the attic which bats had colonized by the dozens and down to the kitchen, the three small bedrooms and the living room on the first floor all of which themselves supported a sizeable population of mice. But he'd liked the hand-hewn oak beams across the ceilings and the enormous kitchen, built in the old way so that the pot-bellied stove standing in the middle of it was the center of life in the house. And so did Mary. It took him a year to fix the roof and ceilings to the extent that neither rain nor bats got in any more. A tomcat named Adam, long dead now, handled the mice for them.

His acre and a half of land sloped down a hill through a field of goldenrod, which when Mary was alive had been a seeded lawn, down to a trickle of a stream. There was a woodshed in back and a single huge oak crowning the hill, blackberry patches where he would sometimes see deer feeding at night and a tangled thicket of woods that was somebody else's land beyond. The neighboring land had never been cleared and probably never would be, not in the old man's lifetime. It belonged to a New York lawyer who had bought the seven acres beside him with the notion of building a summer home and then lost interest. Taxes were cheap and the land was appreciating. He kept it but would never use it.

So that the other thing that Ludlow owned was privacy.

He used that now like a wall between him and his anger as he parked the pickup and carried the dog up the hill and laid him down beside the oak tree. He went to the woodshed for his spade and pitchfork. He came back and began to dig.

By the time dusk had fallen he had it deep enough so the bones would stay where he laid them and not rise to the surface through erosion or be dug up by some other dog like Emma Siddons' black mongrel bitch and he lay the dog with his shirt still tied around his head down into the hole. He was never one for saying words over the dead though it was possible that words might have relieved the heaviness in his chest but he didn't say any, just set to work covering him with the rich sweet-smelling earth.

When he was finished he put the spade and pitchfork back in the shed and realized he'd forgotten the fish in the cooler and his fishing gear so he went to the pickup and got them, wondering what it was going to be like to eat the fish he caught the day his dog was shot, wondering how he'd feel about that. He could throw the fish away but that would be like throwing part of the dog away not to mention it was wasteful.

In the kitchen he wrapped the fish in foil and put them in the freezer.

He stowed his gear in the closet.

It was only when he was finished with that and turned to walk back to the stove to heat a cup of coffee that he felt the sudden silence of the house, broken only by his own footfalls and not the accustomed tap-tap-tap-tap of the dog's feet on the wood beside him. He stopped midway across the room as though waiting beside some invisible door that lay there, pausing just a moment before entering into his rage, shaking, as he fingered the spent shell-casing in his pocket.

He took it out and smelled it. The biting scent of powder.

He set it upright on the kitchen counter next to the sink.

He thought that if the boy himself and not his father or someone else had bought the Browning Auto-5 12 Gauge here at Moody Point or in some nearby town he had a very good chance of finding him.

If it was in Portland or even Kennebunkport it was going to be harder.

## Part Two

## FATHERS AND SONS

# Three

He began with what he knew. That Harkness' General Store stocked pretty nearly the same merchandise he did in his own store, which included rifles and shotguns. But the shotguns were mostly side-by-sides and over-and-unders, nothing as fancy as the Browning Auto-5. So he could rule that out. Which left Downtown Guns and Ammo out on the highway and Dean's Sporting Goods over on Ridgefield Road the only shops in Moody Creek proper that might have sold the weapon to the boy.

He called Bill Prine and asked him to come in and cover for him at the store even though today was Monday and Monday was Bill's day off. Bill was good about it. But Bill generally was. He had no more of a life than Ludlow did these days and clerking at Avery's General Store was about as social as he got.

Ludlow showered and shaved and by the time he was done in the bathroom the fog had burned away and the morning was bright. He got in the pickup and drove Stirrup Iron Road past the old Lutheran Church and past his store and saw that the lights were on inside and Bill's Ford was in the driveway.

In town he stopped at Arnie Grohn's restaurant for a cup of coffee. He admired Arnie's waitress Gloria for about the hundredth time that year. Gloria was in her early thirties, red-headed, pretty and married to a drunken schoolteacher from Portland who was rumored to beat her. Which possibly was true because sometimes Ludlow would see bruises on her legs and thighs. He doubted she was just clumsy.

He wondered why she would put up with that.

There were so many hidden realities in the world, so many secret lives. It seemed like nobody lived just one.

He remembered reading in the paper not so long ago about a woman in Florida who had orchestrated a strip-show in her home for some of the local teenage boys, with her fourteen-year-old daughter as the star attraction. She'd turn down the lights and turn on some music and her daughter would take off her clothes and then the woman would leave the room and her daughter would have sex with the boys on a first-come, first-served basis. There didn't even appear to be money involved.

Why anyone would want to do that he didn't know. But then he didn't necessarily believe that age brought wisdom. He didn't understand a lot of things. He figured he never would.

When he finished the coffee he walked across the street and down a block to Dean's Sporting Goods and asked Dean about the shotgun and the boy. He didn't say why and Dean didn't ask. But there wasn't any need for him even to consult the ledger, he said, because Dean's had never stocked the Auto-5. Only the Browning Semi-Auto 12 Gauge. Try Downtown Guns and Ammo, he said, out on 95.

The clerk behind the counter at Downtown Guns and Ammo was a man of about Bill Prine's age, about forty-five, with powerful arms beneath the white short-sleeve shirt and a sallow hangdog look which, along with the beer gut hanging over his belt, told Ludlow that the man spent too many late nights in bars and too few mornings waking to the sun. Behind him a small thin older man in rolled-up shirtsleeves was stocking boxes of standard 2¾" field loads onto the shelves. The clerk didn't smile when he walked in the door, only nodded and said, what can I getcha? The older man just kept stocking.

'I'd like to know if you've sold a Browning Auto-5 to a boy of about eighteen, maybe nineteen, years old recently. Tall boy, on the thin side, short blond hair.'

'You a policeman?' said the clerk.

'No.'

'You don't look like a lawyer or PI either.'

'I'm not.'

'Then why you asking?'

'Say it's a private matter.'

'Private matter?'

'That's right.'

The man smiled and shook his head.

'Sorry. We can't be dealing with private matters here, friend.'

'This boy I'm looking for. He used the Browning on my dog. He didn't have a reason.'

The man stared at him a moment frowning and then shrugged and spread his hands.

'I'm sorry to hear about that, mister,' he said. 'You've got to understand, though, we can't go getting involved in that kind of thing. You were a cop that'd be a whole other matter.'

'I think I can come back with a cop if I need to. But I don't see why you'd want to put us both through the bother. I'm asking you as a personal favor.'

'Sorry, friend. Can't do it.'

'Oh for Chrissakes, Sam,' said the old man working the shelves behind him. 'The kid shot his Goddamn *dog*. Would you just check the damn ledger?'

Ludlow guessed from his tone that these two were not exactly in the habit of walking home arm in arm together after closing time.

'Sure. Great. So suppose he shoots the kid, Clarence?'

'Suppose he does?'

The old man looked at Ludlow, looked him over carefully and then nodded. Ludlow nodded back.

'Hell, he's not going to shoot him, Sam. Check the ledger.'

Sam moved down the counter and opened the ledger.

'I sold it,' he said. 'I remember. Three, four days ago. Boy came in with his father. Real snappy dresser, the father. Kid had a crew cut, right? Cut real short.'

'Right,' said Ludlow.

'Here it is. I sold it to him Tuesday afternoon. Registered to a Daniel C. McCormack, eighteen years of age.'

26

'Got an address there?'

The clerk turned around to the older man.

'Clarence, you sure about this?'

The older man sighed and turned away from his work and looked at Ludlow again. The man was a true downeaster. He had old New England eyes and there wasn't an ounce of harm in them but there wasn't an ounce of forgiveness either.

'Mister,' he said, 'if *anybody* asks you about this . . .'

'I happened to spot him on the street,' Ludlow said. 'I followed him home. I got lucky.'

He nodded. 'That'll do. Sam, show him the address.'

The clerk turned the ledger around and Ludlow wrote down the name and address. The purchase was on an American Express card held by Michael D. McCormack. That would be the father. He wrote that name too.

'Thanks,' he said. 'That's a fine display of weapons by the way,' he said, pointing to the wall racks.

'Why, thank you,' said the older man. 'My little brother here and I do all the ordering. We arranged and hung 'em ourselves. Come by sometime if you ever feel the need of one. Personally I like a good dog. Good luck to you.'

# Four

The McCormack address was in the Northfield section of the Point and Ludlow drove there passing houses he could have fit three of his own into and still have had space for extra bedrooms.

Northfield was mostly a second-home community for rich folks up from New York or Boston who thought these enormous eighteenth- and nineteenth-century homes were the perfect way to get away from it all. Every morning a parade of maids and caretakers got off the buses and trudged the streets to work. Every night at five they herded home again.

The writer Norman Mailer once had a home here and Ludlow knew of at least one CEO in a telecommunications firm who split his time between Northfield, New York City and some small town in Colorado. The man was eccentric enough to prefer to purchase his socks and underwear personally at Ludlow's store which was a good three miles and half a town away from here. Ludlow wondered who he bought his socks from when he was in New York City and out in Colorado.

By Northfield standards the McCormack home was modest. The old man could only have fit two of his inside. He judged it had been built somewhere in the mid-eighteen-hundreds with a second wing added maybe fifty years later. He got out of the truck and smelled fresh-cut grass and passing through the tall hedges and the wrought-iron fence he saw it was the McCormacks' grass he smelled, newly trimmed tight to the earth. He walked the wide grey fieldstone path to the stoop and up the steps past a pair of white fluted columns to the door. The knocker was an inverted brass horseshoe copied right down to the fuller-and-toe grab and he used that.

The maid was a small young black woman with a withered left hand that was discolored white from her wrist to the knuckles. Ludlow tried not to look at the hand but like probably everybody else she met he failed in the attempt. He asked to see Mr McCormack and told her his name.

She smiled politely and turned and walked down the hall past a flight of stairs and disappeared through a door to his left. There was another open door to his right and through it he could see a parlor, plush soft chairs and, hanging over a fireplace, a dark landscape of the stormy coast of Maine. The maid appeared again and said to follow her, please, Mr Ludlow, and he thought it also polite of her to have used his name.

She led him into a study that was wall-to-wall carved oak, nearly as big as his kitchen which was the largest room in his house. And with a good four more feet of space floor-to-ceiling.

The man behind the walnut desk was in his late forties, broad-shouldered, well-muscled and barely greying, not blond like the boy but dark-haired. He wore a white shirt open at the collar and red-and-blue striped suspenders looped to the buttons of baggy beige trousers. The man reminded Ludlow of somebody but he couldn't say who just then. The handshake was firm and the man was smiling in an open good-humoured way and Ludlow distrusted him immediately.

'You're Av Ludlow? Happy to meet you. Have a seat.'

Ludlow eased himself into a chair facing the desk.

'Do you know me, Mr McCormack? The name I told the girl was Avery.'

McCormack laughed. 'I don't know you personally, but I know your store. Ludlow's General. I've been by many a time.'

That still didn't explain the use of his shortened name but Ludlow let it pass.

'I'm here about your boy, Mr McCormack.'

'Call me Michael. Which boy is that, Av?'

'Daniel.'

'Okay, Daniel. What about him?'

'Daniel owns a Browning Auto-5 shotgun. He used it yesterday to shoot my dog.'

'He what?'

'I was fishing Miller's Bend. He came along with two other boys. They wanted money from me. I told them there was twenty or so in the glove compartment of my pickup. Twenty wasn't good enough. So your boy shot my dog.'

The man looked stricken.

'Danny wouldn't do that.'

Ludlow didn't know whether to believe the

stricken look or not. He decided to give him the benefit of the doubt. Once.

'I'm afraid he did, Mr McCormack. I'm sorry. But sometimes a man doesn't know his boy as well as he thinks he does. Daniel was the one who did the shooting. The other two boys just stood by and watched and then laughed when it was over.'

'They *laughed*?'

'That's right. They seemed to think shooting a dog to death was a pretty funny thing.'

McCormack stared at him open-mouthed a moment and then pushed back in his chair.

'So you're telling me what? That the dog went after him or something?'

'The dog was sitting where I told him to sit. He wasn't the kind to disobey.'

McCormack shook his head.

'I'm sorry. That's just not my boy's behavior.'

'As I said, sometimes you just don't know a boy the way you think you do. Does Daniel have a tee-shirt that says STOLEN FROM MABEL'S WHOREHOUSE on it?'

'I don't know.'

'Maybe you'll check for me.'

The man seemed to ponder this. His eyes narrowed.

'What is it, Mr Ludlow? You want money?'

Ludlow noticed he wasn't Av anymore. He was Mr Ludlow now.

'No, sir. I'm after whatever justice I can see coming out of this thing. What I want is to know that the boy admits to what he's done and that he's been made to feel damn sorry that he did it, damn sorry that he ever laid eyes on that dog and me, that he's been punished for it as any decent person would want to see him punished. That would be where you come in, Mr McCormack. He's your boy.'

'Punished? What, are you talking about jail?'

'I'd say a damn good licking for starters. But if I were you, sure, I'd turn him in. Before he gets to thinking he can do this again anytime he likes.'

'You haven't gone to the police yourself?'

'Not yet, no. I was hoping you and Daniel'd want to do that for me. It'd go better for him, don't you think?'

McCormack thought about it and then leaned forward.

'How am I supposed to know you're telling me the truth, here, Ludlow? What proof have you got?'

'I've got a spent shell-casing that the sheriff's office could probably match to the Browning if it needs to come to that. But why not just ask him? Does the boy know I'm here?'

'I don't think so. I doubt it.'

'Call him in. Let's talk to him.'

'These other two, what'd they look like?'

'There was one near your son's age, with too much weight on him. He wore jeans and a red teeshirt. Pack of cigarettes in the teeshirt. The other was younger, thin. He knew a little bit about fishing.'

McCormack glanced at Ludlow and then down to his desk and stared frowning at the blotter for a moment, his hands folded in front of him, then picked up the telephone and pushed a button.

'Carla, where's Danny now?'

He glanced at Ludlow again and tapped the

mahogany desk with his index finger.

'All right, you go on up and tell him to come down here to the study. Harold, too, if he's in his room. Tell them I said right away.'

Ludlow noted the name Harold. He expected that he'd got two birds with one stone.

Fine. It made things easier.

McCormack replaced the phone. Ludlow was aware of the silence in the room and aware of the comfortable chair beneath him and the strong lemon smell of furniture polish.

'You ever consider selling your store, Ludlow?' McCormack said.

'Excuse me?'

'Your store. You ever consider selling it?'

'No. I can't say I ever have.'

'What is it, an acre of land? A little over?'

'That's right. A little over.'

'And you pull in probably about twenty grand a year net, am I right? That's if you don't mind my asking.'

'I don't mind. Twenty's about right, yes.'

'But you've got a real good location there. Not just for a general store but could be for just about anything. If you should ever consider selling, my associates and I might be interested. Could make you a pretty good dollar.'

'I'll keep that in mind.'

'It'd be a lot of work for a man your age, I'd figure. A place like that. A lot of long hours.'

'Is that what you do for a living, Mr McCormack? You buy up people's stores?'

He laughed. 'Among other things. Some friends

34

and I develop property now and then. We just finished a deal for a new Home Depot complex out on Highway One as a matter of fact. I'm afraid in about a year or so they're going to give you some pretty stiff competition.'

'Competition's fine with me. Just so long as they don't manage to run me off the road.'

The door opened and Ludlow was still considering how and why the man knew so much about him and his business when the boys walked in and he saw they knew him right away and knew why he was there. The younger boy had that scared look on his face again and he was struggling with that, trying to contain it. But the face on the one who'd shot his dog had gone from recognition to puzzled-looking in no longer than it took to close the door behind him. Which told Ludlow that this one was sly as well as mean.

He also realized who McCormack reminded him of. It was the younger son, Harold.

'You know this man here?' McCormack said.

Daniel shrugged. 'No. Why?'

Harold was looking at the floor. He shook his head.

'Never seen him before?'

'No.'

'You're absolutely sure?'

'Uh-huh.'

'This is Mr Ludlow, Danny. He's been telling me a pretty amazing story. He says you tried to rob him yesterday. That you shot his dog.'

'Us?'

McCormack nodded.

'Are you kidding?'

'I don't think Mr Ludlow's kidding, no. You say you don't know anything about this?'

'No.'

'Did you take the Browning out yesterday, Danny?'

'No. We drove to Plymouth. Ask Carla. She saw us take the car.'

'With who?' McCormack said.

'Just us and Pete.'

'And you didn't go anywhere else?'

'No.'

'You didn't go to Miller's Bend?'

'Why'd we want to go to Miller's Bend?'

'All right. Do you have a shirt that says PROPERTY OF MABEL'S—'

'STOLEN FROM,' Ludlow corrected him.

'—STOLEN FROM MABEL'S WHOREHOUSE? You own a shirt like that?'

Danny grinned. 'If I did, I'd probably wear it.'

Ludlow had to admit, the boy was good. The nasty little bastard. And because he was good even the younger one looked more confident now.

'But you don't own a shirt like that.'

'No.'

McCormack stared at them a long moment and then swiveled in his seat toward Ludlow and sighed.

'I have to tell you, Av. I thought this was all pretty far-fetched right from the beginning. I've got a couple of good boys here and they wouldn't be involved in something like what you're describing to me. I'm sorry about your dog, I truly am. But I'm afraid you've got the wrong pair of kids, that's all.'

'*Pair* of kids? I didn't say anything about a pair of kids. As I recall the only one I mentioned was Daniel. Seems to me it was you made the connection between what I told you the other two boys looked like and Harold here. Though he was one of them, all right. Danny called him by name.'

He looked at Harold. 'Isn't that so, son?'

'I . . .'

'I want to thank you for lying to your brother about my flies, by the way. Could have brought a couple hundred dollars or so. And you knew that. Nice of you not to mention that to your brother. But suppose you tell your dad about my dog.'

'I don't know *anything* about your dog, mister!'

Even if he didn't know better Ludlow wouldn't have found him convincing. To tell a decent lie you had to believe the lie while you were telling it and make that jump from what was true to what was not with a kind of grace. The boy wasn't capable of grace this time. Though he'd done pretty well about the flies.

Knowing the boy, the father must have seen the lie too. But McCormack wasn't saying.

'The truth would swallow a whole lot easier, son,' Ludlow said quietly.

'I didn't . . .'

He decided to press him.

'I heard all three of you laughing all the way up the hill. Heard you for a long time. You know that?'

The boy was close to crying now.

'I think that'll be enough, Ludlow,' McCormack said.

Ludlow looked at him and for the first time could

see the actual hardness to the man, could hear it in the passionless flat calm of his voice. The man bought land and sold it. Ludlow bet there was iron in every bargain.

What had he expected? He supposed that people like Danny had to come from somewhere.

'If they say they didn't do it then that's that,' McCormack said. 'I'm afraid you're mistaken.'

He stood up.

Ludlow saw that he was dismissed.

He'd learned to swallow what he was feeling during the war. He did that now.

It was never easy.

He got out of the chair and Danny smiled at him as though he'd taken Ludlow's measure and didn't find anything to worry him standing there. He opened the door for Ludlow as probably he would have for any tired old man and then the two brothers moved away into the room nearer to the father and out of the doorway. Ludlow stood a moment looking for something to waver in McCormack's eyes but nothing stirred there so at last he turned away.

'Well,' he said. 'I asked you.'

'Excuse me?'

'I said I asked you.'

'Asked me what?'

'To do the right thing here.'

'It could have been the right thing, maybe. If you'd had the right boys.'

'Oh, I've got the right boys, Mr McCormack. It's you who've got the wrong boys. You've had them all these years and you've still got them and I think you probably know that. I guess I have some work to do. Thank you for your time.'

He paused in the doorway.

'You've been looking at my land for a while now, haven't you? You've been interested. That's how you knew to call me Av. That's why you let me in.'

McCormack smiled. 'That's a fact, to tell the truth. How'd you know?'

'You had to have some reason. I guess you're different from your boy that way. Danny doesn't need one,' he said and stepped out into the hall.

# Five

In the summer of 1950 Ludlow had landed in Korea in a vintage World War II C-54 transport plane so heavy it tore up the runway. He was with the 29th Infantry, troops who arrived during the second week of the shit-storm all the generals back home had thought was going to be such a walk in the park, boys so green yet needed there so urgently that while they'd been promised six weeks of training Stateside, they'd been denied that in favour of what was supposed to be ten days of intensive training once they arrived in Pusan. But they'd not gotten that either. That too was denied them and instead they were allotted a mere three days to draw their equipment and zero in their weapons. Then even this order was rescinded and they were rushed to Chinju right away. A single day in-country and they were headed for the front.

He remembered all of them knowing how unprepared they were. Ludlow aware of how little his own 75 mm recoilless rifle was going to help him against the North Korean T-34 tanks which had already crushed the 24th Division at Osan, all of them scared young men huddled in the transport trucks in the terrible summer heat driving through a country that smelled like human shit because that was what the farmers used for fertilizer.

He remembered shell casings littering the paddy fields like a plague of gleaming locusts, so many casings that the whole field stunk of powder.

He remembered the bodies of South Koreans lying thick as a log-jam in a river, lying all across the mountainsides.

They were in way over their heads at the beginning but they learned quickly or else they died. Korea had taught Ludlow to fight, to obey the rules as you understood them to be and the hard voice of your knowledge and training as best you could. Then when all these were exhausted, to fight however it was you were able to fight with whatever lay at hand.

Otherwise, like the North Korean human sea, the world rolled right on over you.

He sat in Sam Berry's office and said, 'I want to go after them. I was hoping you'd know the best way.'

Sam was a lawyer and Ludlow's friend since their high-school football days together and Ludlow knew he was like-minded on this because Sam's own dog, Buster, a big pure-blood Irish Setter, had once saved Berry's life.

Sam had been a hunter since the age of eleven and he was good at it and always a careful man with a gun. Coming up eight years ago this fall he'd been out for pheasant, alone but for Buster as bad luck would have it, though hunting alone was very rarely his custom. He forgot his safety for the first time in memory and tripped in a tangle of brush, his finger on the trigger of his shotgun.

When he looked down most of his right foot was gone to just above the ankle, hanging by a bloody twist of muscle. He made a torniquet of his jacket but the blood was pumping out of him and he could feel himself going fast into shock all by himself there in the deep woods and so light-headed that he couldn't remember which way the road was.

He could hear the dog barking and saw that the dog would run a few paces and then stop and bark at him, run and stop and bark again.

To Sam, the dog seemed to be encouraging him so he followed, first hopping and then using the shotgun as a crutch and finally crawling through the brush until he found himself in a culvert and knew he couldn't even crawl anymore, much less make it over the hill ahead of him where the dog was, so he just lay there in the trickle of a slow-running stream.

The dog would disappear over the top of the hill and then appear again. Appear and disappear.

Sam kept falling in and out of dreams in which he was warm and cozy.

But Buster had got him back to the road, or almost there. The road was just over the hill right in front of him and his luck was good as well as bad that day because a pair of hunters were driving by and saw this beautiful Irish Setter, a hunting dog, running back and forth across the road peering down into the culvert and barking and they thought, what's a damn fine animal like that doing out here all alone? They pulled over. The dog walked to the top of the hill and howled and the hunters looked and there was Sam lying passed out in the culvert.

He lost the leg at the knee and Sam threw away the Gravy Train and fed the dog top sirloin until the day he died.

So Ludlow knew he was sympathetic. But right from the start he didn't like what he was hearing.

'Okay,' Sam said, 'you can't prove attempted robbery, that's just your word against theirs, so what you've got here is a case of cruelty to animals, maybe reckless conduct with a firearm. Those are Class D crimes in this State. Misdemeanors.'

'*Misdemeanors*? Jesus.'

'That's right. And it gets worse. I hate to tell you this but in god's truth, I don't know that they'd even want to prosecute.'

'Why?'

'First let's assume your boy's eighteen or over. If not, it's a matter of juvenile court and all they're going to give him's a slap on the fanny, not even worth your damn time. But let's assume he is. A crime like this would go before a judge in district court under title 17, section 1031, cruelty to animals. That carries a mandatory fine of a hundred dollars though, theoretically, a prosecutor could go for more. I say theoretically because most prosecutors would be happy with the hundred and some jail time. Under the law the most you could ask for in jail on animal cruelty is three hundred and sixty-four days. And practically speaking, no prosecutor in his right mind would shoot for more than thirty. Fact is, he'd be hoping like hell to get ten.'

'Ten days. And a hundred dollars.'

Sam nodded. 'That's right. You see where I'm going. Hell, Av, it costs the State more than a hundred just to serve him the damn subpoena, never mind the cost of dragging his sorry butt into court.

'I'm sorry. God knows. But the truth is not many prosecutors want to bother with this kind of thing. Not unless they're looking at a repeat offender or a whole lot of dead or damaged livestock. See, I'm talking *property* here, Av. Under the law, an animal's just *property*. Not only here in Maine but in damn near every state in the Union.

'Now what do you suppose old Red was worth on the open market? What do you figure's the going rate on a good old faithful mixed-breed dog these days?'

Ludlow tried to relax his grip on the chair. He felt a sick empty feeling in his stomach like his stomach was telling him he'd forgotten to eat for days. He wanted to hit something. To hurt something.

He wanted to hurt the boy. Somehow.

'Sheriff could arrest him, couldn't he? He could do that much anyhow. Put the fear of god into the little son of a bitch.'

Sam shook his head. 'To arrest the little son of a bitch, the sheriff would have had to have *seen* him pull the trigger.'

'What?'

'That's the law regarding animals. Same with reckless conduct with a firearm. He'd have had to have actually been there. Nope. Best you can get's to serve them a subpoena for a hearing. And as I say, I can't even guarantee you'll wind up getting that.'

'Jesus.'

'I know. It's not fair. Not one damn bit fair. But that's the law.'

'Dammit, Sam. I can *prove* he shot him. What about the shell casing?'

'What about it? Av, look at what you're asking. You're asking a D.A. to go after a search warrant to find and impound the Browning – which they may have got rid of already by the way, since you were kind enough to warn 'em – and then run a ballistics test to match the firearm to the shell casing. You're asking him to issue a subpoena to the boy, then build a case against him and try him in court. All this time, all this work and all this *expense* for an old mongrel dog you already buried.'

He watched Sam shift uncomfortably in his chair. He thought, not for the first time, that his friend was going to have to get rid of some weight. That his discomfort was not entirely due to what they were talking about. Berry was naturally a big man but since the accident he'd got a lot less exercise. He was losing muscle and gaining fat. There weren't many of Ludlow's friends left in Moody Point. He didn't want to lose Sam to a stroke or a heart attack. But it wasn't their way to discuss it.

'Listen,' the lawyer said. 'I wish I could say this was going to be easy but I can't. Still, what I'll do is I'll give the sheriff's office a call and register your complaint with Tom Bridgewater. He'll pass it on to the D.A.'s office. I figure it might have a little more weight if the complaint comes through me. I'll have Tom either call you or drop by the house. What you do is you go home and get yourself some rest.

Meantime I'll put a few feelers out, see what I can find out about Michael McCormack and his family. I don't know if it'll help any, but what the hell, why not? You said they mentioned another boy?'

'Somebody named Pete.'

'And you think he might have been the third one?'

'They said they were with him all day. Said they drove to Plymouth. Stands to reason.'

'All right. Pete.' He wrote it down.

'Thanks, Sam.'

'Thank me if we can make something happen here.' He stared at Ludlow across the desk for a moment. 'Speak to Alice lately?'

'Christmas, I guess.'

'You might want to give her a call, you know. How many daughters have you got, if you get my meaning.'

Sam's only son had died in childbirth. His wife was gone twenty years now. He was alone.

'Red was her dog too once, wasn't he?' he said.

'That's true.'

'Well then.'

Ludlow stood and they shook hands.

'You may have to dig him up again, you know,' he said. 'If they go for this.'

'I'll do what I have to,' Ludlow said.

'I didn't doubt that,' he said.

# Six

He walked in the house through the front door and smelled the familiar scent of burnt wood which never left the fireplace or even the sofa or the easy-chairs. He glanced at the phone on the end table and thought that yes, he would have to call her but not now.

The room had been small to begin with but Ludlow had made it smaller with the heavy sofa and the two overstuffed easychairs and the bookshelves he'd built lining the wallspace so that now the room looked more like a study than it did a living room. There was no television – when its picture died he hadn't bothered to replace it – only a radio on the table by the phone. He considered turning on the radio but instead went into the kitchen.

In the refrigerator there was a little less than half a roasted chicken which he and Red had eaten most of two nights before, so he took that out and put it on a plate and sat down at the table and began to pick it over with his fingers. The room was very quiet. He could hear himself tear the cold moist flesh of the chicken and break the tendons at the joints. He could hear himself lick his fingers.

When he was finished he threw away the remains and went to the sink to do the breakfast dishes and the greasy plate from the chicken. At the window, moths were already gathering in the dusk, leaning toward the light. By full dark the window would be covered with them, lying wing to wing in some unimaginable desire, downy bellies against the cool smooth glass. The big green-and-white lunas would flutter at the window like bats. In the silence of the kitchen he would sometimes hear them and think of Mary and the days before Adam the cat and the repair work when they would hear real bats in the attic and on these nights, like a sudden shadow falling over him, she would appear again only to leave him there once more alone with Red.

It crossed his mind that here in the house he was surrounded by souls.

At eight o'clock Tom Bridgewater phoned. Ludlow told him what he'd told Sam Berry.

Tom listened quietly and then sighed and said, *Jesus, goddamn kids, think they can get away with anything and you know what? Half the time they can.* Ludlow knew that Tom had two teenage boys himself and, sheriff's sons or not, they'd been in trouble now and then, once for stealing copies of *Playboy* and *Penthouse* from D. L. Fleury's drugstore and another time for getting drunk on another kid's father's whiskey and driving around the town that way at two in the morning.

Tom said he should hold onto the shell casing. He'd talk to the D.A.'s office first thing tomorrow and see what he could do.

Ludlow hung up the phone with the feeling that,

like Sam, Tom was squarely on his side but that, again like Sam, Tom was not at all sure about what the District Attorney would want to do.

He took a beer out of the refrigerator and drank it at the table and then another and sat listening to the night sounds and the summer breeze through the screened window behind him. He fell asleep at the table with his head resting on the backs of his hands and dreamed his daughter Alice Ludlow Palmer was a little girl again and that she was out behind the house playing on the swing, long since fallen, which had hung from the oak tree where he'd buried Red.

Over the ridge in the distance he could see two boys, one about eleven and one older, standing in shadows with their backs to him. But he recognized them even so. He felt a great sadness seeing them standing there. He walked over to call Alice in for dinner but she shook her head, *No, not yet*, and glanced at the shadowy boys up on the ridge.

*The dead are home before us, daddy*, she said. *But we have work to do.*

He woke in sudden alarm and the first thing he noticed was the disturbed swarm of moths and insects fluttering at the window over the sink and then he heard the sounds, something scraping across the house back there, something large enough to cause the sudden stir of wings. He got up and walked to the window, hearing his footsteps loud across the wooden floor, eliminating deer in his mind because deer never came to the house, not when they had the berries out by the oak to feed on, eliminating raccoon as too small and then thinking bear though they were rare around here. And then thinking maybe human.

He kept no firearms in the house as a matter of principle but now he thought he might have been better off having one because neither bears nor humans were invariably friendly.

Outside the window he could see nothing but starless dark.

He walked to the back door and turned on the porchlight and as he did so heard the sound of footfalls in the tall grass by the side of the house. He got to the bedroom window in time to see a tall figure run up the side of the hill and disappear behind the stand of trees by the side of the road.

He walked back into the kitchen. He considered the shell casing which remained visible from outside the house on the counter beside the sink and wondered if its presence there had anything to do with the disturbance at the window.

He put the casing in his pocket.

He looked at the clock on the wall and saw it was after twelve which he felt was much too late to phone his daughter.

He went to the living room and got a book off the shelf about the great Rocky Mountain Coalfield Wars in the early 1900s and took it to bed with him but found it was impossible to concentrate on the National Guard and Mother Jones, nor did the book put him back to sleep again so he lay there with the book open on his lap, the weight of it oddly comforting. And that was how he found himself next morning when the heat of the sun through his bedside window burned away his dreams as it burned the mist off the goldenrod.

# Seven

'They're hedging,' Sam said. In Ludlow's hand the old heavy bakelite telephone felt like something you could easily use for smashing. 'They want you to come down to the sheriff's office and sign a statement and they want the shell casing. I asked if that meant they'd be willing to prosecute but all I could get out of 'em was *we'll see*. Which I guess is better than *no way*.'

'I'll drive on over soon as I check with Bill at the store.'

'Fine. Found out a few things about the McCormacks in the meantime. Friend of mine over at the Chamber of Commerce says the father runs with a pretty upscale group these days, though that's sort of a new development. Portland Country Club, that sort of thing. Made his money like his daddy did, in trucking, which kept him out of the social fast-track for a good long while. His daddy was supposedly a mean son of a bitch. Had an arrest record long as your arm, mostly for drunk and disorderly. No arrests on the son.

'Likes to play with real estate. Buys a lot of gold. He married well. Wife's maiden name was Edith

Springer. Her family goes back all the way to the Colonies. You happen to see her out there?'

'No.'

'Word is she's a drunk. A fancy drunk, but a drunk. I wouldn't know.

'Anyway, all in all there's plenty of money and political clout there but underneath McCormack's nothing but redneck, one generation removed. Kind of fancies himself a gentleman farmer nowadays. He owns about a hundred acres of land and a house by the sea up around Cape Elizabeth way, farms fir trees and then horses further inland. All of it's managed for him.'

'What's this land-development business? He damn near made me an offer on the store yesterday.'

'Mostly a hobby, I guess. He sure doesn't need the cash. Just seems to like to buy up nice old tracts of land and turn 'em into shopping malls, chain-store complexes, restaurant complexes. All the joys of modern living, you know what I mean? None of 'em in *his* neighbourhood, of course. He belongs to some Portland-based investors group. They've done a lot of things out this way, but also as far north as Bangor. Oh, I also think I found out who your third boy is.'

'How'd you do that?'

Berry laughed. 'Name Sally Abbot mean anything to you?'

'No.'

'Well, you remember once upon a time I used to be one for the ladies. I mean, before I met Sarah. Had two good legs then and Friday, Saturday nights I was a dancin' fool. One of the ladies I used to spend some time with was Sally. Smart and pretty as they come. If it hadn't been for Sarah I might have married her. She lived out in Old Orchard Beach at the time. Teaches math now over at Moody Point High, has for twenty years or so. Sally knows both the McCormack kids and says they've got a friend named Pete Daoust who's on the chubby side, so probably he's your boy.'

'Daoust. Spell it.'

Berry did.

'She say anything about them?'

'Just what you'd expect. The older boy, Danny, was a troublemaker. Nothing major but she said she had her share of problems with him. Graduated a year ago but he still hangs around the school a lot. Fancies himself a heartbreaker with the girls and Sally says maybe he is. The younger boy, Harold, was never in one of her classes but she had the impression he wasn't nearly as bad as the brother.'

'What about Daoust?'

He laughed again. 'Said with a mouth as big as Pete's and a brain as useless he'd probably run for governor one of these days. Y'know, I'd forgotten how much I liked that woman. I wonder if she still goes dancing now.'

He hung up and dug the phone book out of the drawer and looked up the name Daoust. There was only one listed and the address was Cedar Road. Not nearly as upscale as Northfield, not even close. But it was near Miller's Bend which might explain how the boys had come to be down by the river that day.

He drove to the store and parked next to Bill Prine's Ford. They were the only vehicles on the lot.

Inside, Bill was unpacking a box of hundred-watt lightbulbs and stacking them into a wire rack. He looked up when the cowbell tinkled over the door and smiled.

'Hey, Av.'

'How you doing, Bill?'

Bill kept on working the rack. Ludlow noted that his hands were steady.

By night Bill Prine was a prodigious drinker, some might say he was an alcholic. But by day he was the most reliable man Ludlow'd ever known.

He also thought Bill could probably charm the balls off a snake.

He'd achieved a kind of local fame a few years back when a man from Buxton walked into Ludlow's store one evening just before closing time and tried to rob him. The man was carrying not one gun but two. He was also very drunk. Bill was alone in there, so he did as he was told and emptied the cash register into a paper sack. Then he looked at one of the guns and said, My god, that's a beautiful weapon, what is it? A Smith & Wesson? The man nodded and said, Yes, it's a Smith & Wesson .44 magnum. Bill asked him if he'd like to sell it and after some haggling they agreed upon a price.

Bill paid him out of his pocket and the man set the magnum on the counter.

Then Bill admired the other weapon – a Colt Detective Special. They settled on a somewhat lower price for that and Bill paid him again and then walked to the door and locked it while the man was counting the money in this second transaction and then Bill walked behind the counter and picked up both the weapons and dialed the police.

Ludlow and Prine agreed that the man was probably the stupidest thief in the state of Maine or even in all of America at the time but the incident quickly entered Moody Point history and legend. Bill made the papers and so did Ludlow's General Store and Ludlow thought he was still getting trade on that, three years later.

Why Bill drank he didn't know. He'd never elected to tell him. But it never affected his work and his hands were still steady so, as far as Ludlow was concerned, that was that.

'We get in the Coleman order yet?'

'Came in just this morning. It's in the back. You want to go through it or should I?'

'I've got some business to take care of. You mind holding on here alone again today?'

'Nah. I'll just steal you blind again, is all.'

'You do that. Okay, see you later. Around three maybe.'

'Take your time. I'm fine. You want me to unpack the Coleman?'

'Go ahead.'

He got back into the car and drove through the hills across rolling farmland and into the dark thick pines to Cedar Hill Road.

Number 118 was a small house much like his own except there were neighbors on both sides a few feet apart under thin tired shadetrees and all three places seemed to share an unwillingness to throw things away. At the Daoust's it was a washing-machine leaning rusting along one side of the house next to a mattress and box spring and at the house next door it was a pile of tires and an old V-8 engine sitting on a stump like it had grown there.

Crabgrass covered all three yards unbroken like a single moth-eaten cloak.

He walked up the wooden steps and used the buzzer, waited a while and then knocked. He heard a woman's voice call for somebody named Willie which he guessed would be the *W. Daoust* in the directory.

The man who appeared at the door and stood behind the screen was a good foot shorter than Ludlow, grey and balding, in his fifties and overweight like his son. He wore wire-rim glasses and a pair of trousers with suspenders over a fresh white teeshirt. If you could judge a man by his shoes then this man was both scruffy and conservative. The shoes were old black lace-ups and they'd been cheap to begin with.

'Mr Daoust? I'm Avery Ludlow.'

'I know who you are,' he said.

'I guess you've talked to Mr McCormack, then.'

'McCormack don't talk to any out-of-work carpenter. His boy called my boy.'

'Danny called him?'

'Yeah, Danny.'

'And?'

'And what? Listen, Ludlow. Pete says they drove to Plymouth. Hung out at a mall there, even bought a couple of CDs there. A goddamn *expensive* couple of CDs. Didn't say anything about any shotgun or anybody's dog.'

'Maybe they did drive to Plymouth. Before or after. I wouldn't know about that. But at about four in the afternoon they were at Miller's Bend and, when they didn't get the money they wanted from me, Danny McCormack shot my dog and your son stood there with him laughing about it.'

The man looked uncomfortable then and Ludlow thought that maybe Daoust could actually just manage to see Pete doing something like that. Laughing.

'Look . . .' he said.

A woman appeared behind him and he guessed the whole family tended to weight because her jeans were too tight for someone her size and so was the horizontal-striped blue-and-white shirt. She carried a dustpan and handbroom and she gestured at him with the broom like a schoolteacher shaking a pencil at an errant student.

'Mr Ludlow, I've heard every word of this,' she said, 'and I want to know just what you think you're doing coming out here like this. If you have a complaint with the McCormacks then you take it up with them. But as I understand it, even if the boys *aren't* telling the truth about this – and I'm not saying that, not for a minute – then the one you have a quarrel with is Danny McCormack. So why don't you just leave us all the hell out of this, okay?'

'I'm sorry. But if you heard what I said, ma'am, then you heard that your boy was party to an attempted robbery. That he thought it was funny that his friend shot my animal. Why would that kind of thing make me want to leave him out of it?'

'He didn't shoot your dog.'

'He was there. And he saw the boy who did. I want him to say that.'

'Maybe he's sorry. Ever think of that?'

'Excuse me, but how can he be sorry? If he denies it happened?'

The woman looked to her husband and then back at Ludlow and Ludlow knew that at least for the moment, he had them.

'Listen,' he said, 'I'd be willing to forgive your boy if he shows the nerve and the decency to own up to his part in it and tell the sheriff what happened, what Danny McCormack did. You're right. It wasn't your son who fired the weapon. And I know that a boy can be hard in his heart sometimes and then regret it later on. I only want the truth from him. You talk to him for me. Tell him to do what's right. That's all I'm asking.'

He took a pen and pad out of his shirt pocket and wrote down his home phone number and his number at the store, then tore out the page and held it out to them and, when the man opened the screen door to take it, he opened it just a crack as though he were worried about a swarm of hornets getting in there.

'Thanks,' he said. 'I'd appreciate hearing from you soon as you can talk to him.'

As he got into the truck he heard shouting inside but couldn't make out what they were saying. There were three voices though, and the third was Pete's, high and whiny. He wondered if they'd be able to shout some sense into him.

Clouds were rolling in from the north off Sabago Lake as he drove to town. There was a coppery electric taste in his mouth that told him they were in for a summer storm. By the time he pulled up to the courthouse the first few drops of rain were falling big as dimes across his windshield. He rolled up the driver-side window and stepped outside into the still dark air.

He found Tom Bridgewater seated at his desk in the sheriff's office eating a cruller from Arnie Grohn's restaurant down the street and reading and drinking coffee. The book in front of him was *La Bête Humaine* by Emile Zola and Tom looked to be about three-quarters through it.

'Slow day, Tom?'

Tom smiled and put the book down on a stack of papers. His left central incisor was capped with gold and hung lower in his mouth than the right incisor, which was not capped. The gold tooth gave him the look of a hick. But Tom wasn't a hick. He had a degree in criminology from some university down south and had read through most of Moody Point Public Library. He raised honeybees and probably knew more about them than anybody in the state. Ludlow thought this was normal. That, again, people were rarely what they appeared to be. Tom was just lazy, both about getting ahead in his profession and about getting the tooth capped properly.

'Nah,' Tom said. 'Paperwork up the butt. You hear about this woman yesterday? She's at a service station over on 91, paying for gas, sees a guy outside trying to steal her car. See, she's left the keys in there. She's also left her six-year-old kid, her daughter, asleep in the back seat. So the guy pulls out of the service station. But by then the woman's got the driver's-side door open, wraps one arm around the steering wheel, tries to scratch him, pound him, with

61

the other. The guy's trying to shove her out. She reaches under the front seat and pulls out the Club. You know, the steering-wheel lock? And she's pounding him with *that*. The guy's got her halfway in, halfway out of the car. Anyway, he drags her a quarter of a mile and plows them into a Roy Rogers restaurant. She pulls the guy out of the car and takes the Club and bashes him in the head, then she breaks both the guy's legs! The guy's begging for mercy. Ever hear such a thing? We got him on robbery and abduction. He didn't even know the kid was in there.'

He held up the book. 'But this Zola's terrific,' he said. 'You ever read him?'

'No.'

'You should. This one's about a guy sees a murder through the window of a passing train. He's always wanted to kill somebody but he hasn't got the guts, so he attaches himself to these two people who actually did it, like some sort of leech. Drives them nuts. You never read *Nana*, either?'

'No.'

'You should try him sometime, Av. I wish I could get the boys to read, or even Evelyn for that matter. All Evelyn reads is the damn newspaper. And the kids are worse than that. I'm lucky if they look at a TV Guide. Sorry about your dog. You got that shell casing for me?'

Ludlow handed it over.

Tom looked at the casing and sniffed it, pocketed it and finished the last bite of cruller, picked up his styrofoam coffee cup and got up from his chair.

'Let's go see Phil Jackman.'

Sam Berry had mentioned the assistant D.A.'s name over the phone but Ludlow had never met the man. They walked down the hall to his office and a pretty brunette receptionist announced them and Tom opened the frosted glass door and they went inside.

The office was cluttered with books and papers. Worse than Tom's was if that was possible.

Jackman sat behind his desk in his shirtsleeves, the perfect Windsor knot of his tie pulled low. He looked up from a typed sheet of paper, first out the windows where thunder rolled and then at Tom and Ludlow. He stood, much taller than he looked sitting down. He extended his hand.

'Mr Ludlow?'

His wrist below the shirtsleeve was thin like all the rest of him but the grip was firm.

'Ay,' Ludlow said.

He handed Ludlow the paper off his desk.

'Tom's prepared a statement for you, a complaint against the McCormack boy. I'd like you to look it over and see if it's accurate or if we've missed anything. If you have anything to add, let us know.'

'This mean you're going ahead?'

'It means the office is considering charges.'

'Considering.'

'I have to consult the District Attorney. It's his decision.'

'But you, Mr Jackman, what would you like to do?'

'I don't know. So far it's your word against theirs. Then again, they're three kids and you're a respected businessman. Did you bring the casing?'

'I've got it right here,' Tom said.

'Good.'

Ludlow read the document. Tom had done a good job with it. It was dry and clinical but it was all there and he'd written it better than Ludlow could have managed to do. He guessed all that reading was worth something.

'Looks fine to me.'

Jackman handed him a pen. He leaned over to the desk and signed where it said *complainant* and as he stood felt something pinch in his lower back. It was the same familiar pull at his nerve-ends that he'd felt every now and then ever since the war. It ran straight down his leg. Some muscular conspiracy inside him that didn't want him standing upright again. He winced and straightened and forced the issue.

Tom Bridgewater noticed.

'You okay, Av?'

'Just my back. Gets cranky on me sometimes.'

He turned to Jackman. 'So what happens now?'

'I'll be talking to D.A. Phelps this afternoon. Soon as we've discussed it, we'll get back to you. Meanwhile, no further visits to the McCormack's. And no contact with the Daoust boy, either.'

'I already contacted him.'

'You what?'

'Not the boy, actually. I talked to the mother and father just before I came here. I had the feeling they might be willing to help us. I don't know.'

Jackman wasn't a man good at concealing his annoyance. The bright red splotches in his cheeks gave him away. He probably wasn't much of a poker-player either.

'That wasn't very smart, Mr Ludlow. They could sue for slander. I wouldn't do it again if I were you.'

'I don't intend to. I just wanted them to see that there's a person involved here, somebody real and not just some fellow by the name of Ludlow. If they call I'll pass them right on to you. That's assuming you decide to go ahead. If not . . .'

'If not what?'

'If not then I don't know what I do. If you've got any ideas I'd like to hear them.'

Jackman's handshake was more tentative this time.

Ludlow walked Tom back to his office and left him sipping cold coffee there and then walked out into the driving rain.

# Eight

The widow Emma Siddons was in his store with a box of ten-penny nails and a box of eight-penny nails on the counter in front of her and Bill was ringing up the sale when he came through the door. Emma was older than god but she still did all her own carpentry work and repairs. A pair of summer people, a middle-aged man and woman, were going through the camping gear in back.

Emma smiled at him and said hello and then as he passed said, 'I haven't seen that old dog of yours sniffing around my Evangeline the last few days.'

'He's gone, Emma,' Ludlow said.

'Gone?'

'Boy shot him. Back by Miller's Bend on Sunday.'

'Oh my lord. Why would—?'

'There wasn't any sense to it. Just meanness.'

He saw Bill staring at him.

'Shot him? Old Red? Jeez, Av,' he said, 'why didn't you say something?'

'I don't know. I buried him back of the house. I went to the boy's father but I don't think it bothers him much.'

'What are you going to do?'

67

'I filed a complaint. Hope the law does its job, I guess.'

'You saw Tom Bridgewater?'

He nodded. 'And Sam. And just now the assistant D.A. Fellow named Jackman. I signed the papers. Now I'll just have to wait and see.'

Bill shook his head.

'Jesus. Kid would do a thing like that ought to be horsewhipped, if you ask me,' he said. It was loud enough for the couple in back to hear. They turned and then hastily looked away.

Ludlow bagged the nails for Emma and handed them to her. Bill gave her change out of a twenty.

She turned to Ludlow and put a hand on his arm. Emma had a bad case of arthritis but the hand felt soft and smooth as butterfly wings.

'I'm sorry, Av. For all my complaining when 'vengline was in season, Red was a good old dog. I'll miss him.'

'Thanks, Emma. That's good of you to say.'

'You know my advice to you?'

'What's that?'

'Go out and get yourself another dog. Get yourself a pup and get him right away. You'll feel a whole lot better for it, believe me.'

'I don't know, Emma. I might do that. We'll see.'

She gave his arm a pat and then removed her hand and turned toward the door.

'Meantime,' she said, 'I hope Tom Bridgewater jails that little son of a bitch and throws away the key.'

Ludlow smiled.

It was the first time that day.

# Nine

Business was slow so they were mostly caught up with their inventory by day's end. He was about to let Bill go on home when Sam Berry walked in. Berry was holding the door for a slim, attractive young woman with dark hair and wearing a grey business suit who smiled at Sam and swung her attaché case through the doorway ahead of her. She threw back her hair with a toss of the head and walked to the counter. The smile was trained on Ludlow now.

'Av,' Sam said, 'I want you to meet Carrie Donnel from WCAP News over in Portland.'

'Mr Ludlow.' She held out her hand.

Ludlow took it, thinking it was a rare thing indeed that he'd felt the touch of two female hands in the course of a single day.

'Miss Donnel.'

'Carrie's our secret weapon,' Sam said. 'And it looks as though we'll need one.'

'I don't follow you.'

'Jackman's declined to prosecute. McCormack's already got a lawyer, fellow by the name of Cummings. I know him well and he's got plenty of clout,

69

believe me. They've been in touch with D.A. Phelps. Got to him quick too, not much after you talked to Jackman. They're arguing you could have picked up that shell casing anywhere, even if it does match. You could have shot your own dog for all they know. There's no way you can match the load itself to *any* gun in particular.'

'Oh, for god's sake. Why would I want to do that?'

'You wouldn't. Point is, with all three boys denying it Phelps doesn't think the case is strong enough to be bothered with. Especially not with this Cummings character making noises about slander. You ever throw Danny McCormack out of your store, Av?'

'I never laid eyes on him before Sunday.'

''Course not. But what they're saying is, you did. Threw him out for trying to steal a penknife a few months back or some damn thing. Trying to make out like you're some kind of crank. Somebody with a grudge against the boy.'

Ludlow shook his head. 'I guess I've heard it all now.'

'Not quite. Remember you telling me the boy denied knowing you in front of his father? Well, McCormack's lawyer says that both boys are now saying they *did* know you. Knew you from here, right here from the store. And that's all. Said they told you that right to your face in McCormack's office. And McCormack's backing them. Lying all the way. They've closed ranks, Av. *Tight*.'

'Pete Daoust too?'

'Him too.'

'I thought his parents might pull him around.'

'McCormack works fast. It wouldn't surprise me

if there was money involved. The father's out of work, you know.'

He was aware of the woman's eyes. The eyes hadn't left him for a second. Through all of this she hadn't so much as glanced in Sam's direction. He was also aware of Bill's silence behind him, standing so still that not so much as a board creaked beneath his feet. Ludlow didn't like being the focus of all this attention. Sympathetic or not, it was making his anger burn just that much brighter. These people on him like a steady driving wind. He wanted to throw them all out of the store and start breaking things. That it would be his own things he was breaking didn't matter.

'I think maybe we can turn it around, though,' Sam said. 'Anyway, I think we've got a shot at it.'

'How?'

'Miss Donnel here.'

'There was a case in Lagrange last winter,' she said. 'A man owned a trailer just outside of town. The trailer lay on his *brother's* property, though the trailer itself belonged to him. The man also had a house *in town*.

'Apparently the man was away from his trailer for three weeks during one of the worst cold snaps of the year. He was staying at the house. Somebody, very possibly his brother actually, put in an anonymous call to the animal welfare people. A cruelty complaint. The sheriff's office went out to investigate.

'They found two dogs, barely alive, chained outside in the yard. One had neither food nor water and the other's waterdish was nothing but a block of ice. They found a dead goose with a string around its neck lying beside the steps and a dead rabbit in a collar and chain out by a shed, both of them frozen solid. *Inside* they found six starving cats, three starving dogs and a parakeet dead in a cage in the bedroom. There was urine and feces everywhere. On the couch, on the bed, in the sink. Everywhere.'

He watched her. He noticed the clipped speech, the restless movement of her hands, the wide brown eyes that barely blinked and gazed steady and businesslike into his own.

'At first the man claimed he'd been coming up every two or three days to feed them. Then he claimed that his *brother* was supposed to. His lawyer argued that the sheriff's office had no case, that they had to show possession. And that the animals weren't *in* this man's possession at the time because he was living elsewhere, consequently they weren't his responsibility. The property was his brother's. So the animals were *his* responsibility.'

'But the animals belonged to him. Not to the brother.'

'That's right.'

'What happened?'

'I guess the D.A.'s office didn't feel like getting involved in a family squabble over a few starved animals. They decided to drop the charges. At least until the papers got hold of it and then the local TV station. That's the point we're making here, Mr Ludlow. It was the press and public opinion that forced them to prosecute. Once it hit the news they *had* to go ahead.'

'And?'

She sighed. 'And the guy was acquitted. The judge ruled for the defense. He said that the animals weren't in the man's possession so they weren't his responsibility.'

'And I bet they didn't charge the brother either, am I right?'

'No. They didn't.'

'So whose possession *were* they in?'

'Nobody's, I guess. In the law's eyes, at least.'

'Look, Av,' Sam interrupted. 'The bad guy got away that time. That's not saying it's got to happen here. At least this way we've got a chance of getting them into court. Carrie's a damn good reporter. That's why I wanted her on this.'

'You're telling me you want to report all this on television?'

'I want *you* to report it, Mr Ludlow. I want to take a film crew down to where it happened and interview you right there at Miller's Bend. No naming names. Because at this point naming names is arguably slander. Just you, telling your story. What the boys did and then what the District Attorney's Office isn't willing to do. I want to *piss people off about this*! Excuse me,' she said.

Now he knew where the clipped speech pattern came from. She had the slower cadence down very well but the original had just come through like trumpets over a string quartet.

'You're not from around here, are you, Miss Donnel?'

'I'm from New York, originally.'

'I thought you might be.'

'I'm an outsider? Is that it?'

'Not at all.'

'Will you do it, then?'

'Go on television? I don't know as I'd do very well at it, tell you the truth.'

'You'll be fine. I'd help you every inch of the way. We'd run it through until you were comfortable. I won't just leave you hanging in the wind. I promise.'

Ludlow thought about it. He didn't even own a working TV anymore.

'I don't suppose you've got a dog, do you, Miss Donnel?'

'Cats,' she said. 'Three of them.'

'Cats.'

'Three of them.'

He nodded. 'All right. I'll do it.'

# Ten

Two nights later he was watching himself on the six o'clock news on a set Carrie Donnel borrowed for him from the station.

He saw a stiff, gruff old man in a wrinkled shirt and jeans whose hands were the only graceful part about him gesture toward the river and then point up the trail while the camera circled around him and he heard himself talk about the boys and the dog, responding to Carrie Donnel's question about how the dog was a birthday present from his wife, Mary. She's gone now, isn't she? she said and the old man in the picture nodded. And so is Red now, she said and the old man nodded.

He thought he looked a little bewildered on the screen, also that you could clearly see the anger, which surprised him. Especially you could see it when he spoke of the prosecutor's decision not to charge the boy. Ludlow thought he'd been good at concealing his anger all along but the camera didn't lie and there it was, just as he had to suppose it always had been, clean and visible.

At the end of the story she stood before the camera and said that nationwide, for the killing or violent abuse of animals, offenders were fined on average only 32% of the maximum fine possible and spent only 14% of the maximum jail time. Most offenders, she said, never even came to trial. She quoted Ghandi to the effect that the greatness of a nation and its moral progress could be measured by the way it treats its animals.

In York County, she said, it might also be measured by the justice it seeks for Avery Allan Ludlow and his dog, Red.

They'd shot that speech after he'd gone and Ludlow was moved by it now and respectful of the soft aggression of her delivery. He resolved to thank her in some way although at the moment he did not know how.

The phone lay off its cradle. He'd taken it off in case someone should try to call him during the broadcast but now the handset lying beside the cradle seemed both a reproach and an invitation to him. He still hadn't phoned his daughter yet. Now half the county knew about Red. It was high time that she did too. In fact it was long past time but first he wanted to get some food inside him and a beer or two.

After he'd finished his steak and eggs and a second beer and cleaned off the dishes he looked up her number in Mary's old address book. He found it there in Mary's small neat script. He dialed and then put his finger down on the connect plunger thinking what do I want to say to her and slowly dialed again. The phone rang twice. Then he heard her voice.

'Hi, Allie,' he said.

'Dad?'

'Am I interrupting dinner?'

'No. Dick and I are going out to eat tonight. I was just getting ready. There's a new seafood restaurant by the government center we want to try. How are you, dad?'

'I'm fine.'

'I've been meaning to call.'

'Me too. How's Dick doing?'

'He's fine. Overworked as usual. Every Fourth of July he just goes crazy here. He's got the parade to deal with, the concerts at the Shell, the fireworks over the river and more fireworks in the Commons. All of that plus, you know?'

'I could see where he'd be busy, all right.'

'Life at the Mayor's office. Business as usual.'

'How about you, Allie?'

'I quit my job at the V.A. Hospital. We're ... I've been wanting to tell you, dad ... we're trying to have a baby.'

'Really?'

'For four months now. So far, no luck. We may have to go for some tests once Dick's work lets up. I don't know.'

'That'd be good, Allie. A baby, I mean. Your mom would have—'

'I know. Wouldn't she have loved that?'

'Yes.'

'Are you really sure you're okay, dad?'

'Red died,' he said.

'Oh, god. When?'

'Sunday.'

'Oh god.'

For a moment neither of them said anything, the

silence stretching from Moody Point to Boston as though nothing existed between.

'You loved that old dog,' she said. 'What hap—?'

He didn't want to tell her.

'He was a damn good animal,' he said.

'Get another, dad. You really should. I know you think maybe it's too soon, but—'

'People say that. I'm thinking about it.'

'I think it would be a good idea. You shouldn't be up there all alone. In the meantime, listen, you could come visit us for a while if you wanted. We'd love to have you.'

'You haven't got the room, Allie. And Dick's got his work. I'd just be in the way.'

'No, you wouldn't.'

'Sure I would. And you know I would. Don't worry. I'm fine here.'

'How's grampa?'

'Your grandfather's the original Comeback Kid. Every time his body floors him again he comes back meaner than ever. Hospitals and nursing homes kill people half his age all the time. Not him.'

She laughed. Then there was a silence.

'Listen, dad, you haven't—'

He knew what she was going to say. He just hoped she wouldn't just this once.

But he guessed that in a way she had to.

'I don't suppose you've spoken to Billy.'

'No.'

'And you won't, will you? Not even feeling lonely the way you are.'

'Who says I'm feeling lonely?'

'Dad, I just don't think this is good for you. Billy's—'

Behind him the window exploded.

He dropped off his armchair to the floor, instincts kicking in, glass flying all over and around him. He felt it pepper his bare arms and face and neck and heard her shriek come at him small and far away through the phone line, the phone clutched in his hand exactly like a club now, heard her yelling, *Dad! Dad!* as the rock rolled across the boards and stopped in front of him. He saw a white sheet of paper fastened to the rock by four elastic bands.

He got to his feet saying, *It's all right, baby, I'm fine, I'm okay* into the phone as he went to the window and heard the car screech away kicking up road dust, a dark sedan with no headlights or taillights heading fast down Stirrup Iron Road toward the main road below.

There was an inch-long triangle-shaped sliver of glass sunk deep in the palm of his hand. He could hear his blood dripping on the wooden floor.

'Hang on a minute,' he said into the phone and heard her voice wanting to question him, frightened. 'Hang on,' he said. 'Everything's all right. I'll be right back.'

He went to the kitchen listening to the glass crack and splinter beneath his shoes and rinsed his hand in the sink and then carefully removed the shard of glass. He tossed it into the sink and ran his hand under the water again, took a handful of paper towels and clutched it tight to stop the bleeding.

Then he went back to the phone to lie to her.

'My god, dad, what the hell *was* that?'

'We have been having a little trouble. Some kids up this way've been throwing rocks, breaking windows nights. They just broke mine. I'm okay. Little cut on the palm of my hand I ought to attend to, though. Nothing to worry about. But it looks like I'm going to have to vacuum the living room. I'd better get off the phone. You go on and have a good time at dinner and don't you worry about me. It's just a prank. Just kids. That's all.'

'Some prank! Jesus!'

'I won't argue with you there.'

'You sure you're all right?'

'I promise.'

When he was able to reassure her and get her off the phone he looked down at his hand and saw that the ball of toweling was soaked through. He was going to have to do better than that. In the medicine cabinet he found gauze pads and iodine and adhesive tape. He was shaking. He cleaned and bandaged the wound and walked back into the living room. The cool wind through the window billowed his drapes so that they reached out to him as he stooped to pick the rock up off the floor.

He pulled away the elastic bands. Beneath the sheet of paper the rock was roughly the size of a baseball and he saw that it had come from a stream or a river, it was clean and worn smooth yet had no scent that would indicate the sea. He uncrimped the paper and turned it over. The words and letters were out of a magazine, pasted there.

YOU LOOKED GOOD ON TV YOU OLD FUCK
YOUR ONE
AND ONLY APEARANCE
HA HA

He noted the misspelling of the word and wondered if that was on purpose. He wondered if *your one and only apearance* was supposed to be some kind of threat. He put the paper on the kitchen table, weighted it with the stone and went to work on his broken window.

# Eleven

'I can tell you what the note means,' Carrie said.

She had driven down from Portland and they were sitting in Arnie Grohn's place having dinner. Her station was picking up the tab and she'd wanted to take him somewhere fancier but Ludlow felt at home here.

'The note means that as far as the station's concerned, the story ended with last night's broadcast. And whoever threw your rock knew all about it.'

She stabbed at her Porterhouse steak as though it were a living thing.

'No follow-up you mean? Nothing?'

She leaned forward, her eyes intense. From the moment they'd sat down he could see she was angry, as unsuccessful in her own way as apparently he was at trying to hold it inside.

'I wanted to go out to the McCormack house today,' she said. 'That would be the natural thing to do at this point, perfectly normal, get the story from Danny's point of view or at least get his or his father's "no comment" on videotape. Get them closing the door on our faces, whatever. I had the camera crew set and ready to go when the senior editor walks in looking like someone's just told him he'd been smiling all day with a piece of spinach in his teeth. He says he's sorry – and he *is* sorry, Av, I can see he is – but we're going out to cover some apartment-building fire instead. A goddamn fire. Nobody's even *killed* in this fire, Av. There aren't even any injuries to speak of. You see where I'm going with this?'

'He got ordered off.'

'You're damn right he did. And this is a decent guy. He's one of the reasons I still work at this toytown station. He was embarrassed as hell. He knew that *we* knew exactly what was happening.'

'Who could do that? Make him back off that way?'

She shrugged. 'Had to be one of the station owners. It could have been somebody's own idea, or it could have been pressure from a sponsor. If the sponsor was big enough. I don't know who applied the screws. But there's some kind of old-boy thing going on here.'

'Your editor wouldn't tell you?'

'Believe me, Av, I asked him. I damn near walked off the job today and he knew it. But Phil's a buck-stops-here kind of guy. What he's got to do to keep his station going, he does, even if it means doing something he doesn't like, something as shitty as this. If it was his decision to knuckle under, and it was, he's willing to take the flak from us and so be it.

'I'm morally certain he fought as hard for this story as I would have,' she said. 'But sometimes in this business you're just up against it. You do what the money boys say you do or you walk. Period.'

'I wouldn't want you to walk over this, Miss Donnel.'

'No. I didn't think you would. And it's Carrie, for god's sake. I wouldn't want Phil to walk either. So I let him off the hook. I covered the goddamn fire.'

She speared another piece of steak and then set the fork down on the plate and finished her beer instead. His own beer was already gone so he caught Gloria's eye and ordered another round for both of them. His pork chop sat untouched on the plate.

'I want to thank you for what you've done,' he said. 'What you've tried to do. Not everybody would have bothered.'

'I'm not through with this, Av. Not yet. I just have to find some sort of angle. Something big enough so that they can't *afford* to ignore it. I just can't think right now what that could be.'

The beers arrived and he drank some.

'Sam Berry told me that we can sue even if they refuse to prosecute,' he said. 'Hire our own forensics man and subpoena the shotgun and maybe get to him that way. The money'd be nothing but ... it's something I guess.'

Saying it out loud made Ludlow feel practically helpless. It was so damn little against the dog's life and against the meanness in the boy. Not even the boy's name on a criminal record.

He could see she felt the same.

'A lawsuit's not enough,' she said. 'Too many people sue other people every day. It's not news. It's nothing.'

She was right. It *was* nothing.

He was not going to find his justice here, not

where he'd always looked for it, under the law and in the common decency afforded by human being to human being. Ludlow thought about what she'd said about something they couldn't afford to ignore and looked down at the plate in front of him, the wasted chop he had no heart to eat. And days later he thought that maybe it was the pork chop and the rest of his meal sitting untouched on the plate that finally moved him to do what he did. So small a thing.

'Miss Donnel . . .'

She gave him a look, reproachful.

'Carrie. I think I'd like it if we could just pay the check and get out of here. If that's all right with you. I want to thank you again. You've been very kind.'

'Sure,' she said.

He called for the check and she paid it on a credit card.

'Why don't you buy me a nightcap, Avery? A real drink in a real bar. I could use one. Maybe we can just sit and talk a while. Not about any of this.'

She leaned forward. Confidential. Something mischievous in her look.

'By the way,' she said. 'I think our waitress likes you. You notice?'

'Gloria?'

He looked around. Gloria was two tables down, putting beers in front of Sid and Nancy Pierce. She turned and gave him a smile.

'Hell, I'm old enough to be her grandfather,' he said.

She laughed. 'Stardom, Av. You were on television

last night. You're glamorous now.'
   'Sure,' he said. 'And Nixon's in the White House.'

# Twelve

It was the simplest of motions. A turn toward him in the parking lot of the bar as he opened the door for her, her hands going to his shoulders and then her mouth on his.

He couldn't have been more surprised if she'd pulled a gun and shot him.

# Thirteen

He watched her dress in the pale bright moonlight through the window, amazed that there was a woman in his bedroom again after all these years, more amazed that it should be this woman so much younger and smarter than he was who had wanted him. It saddened him to see her nakedness disappear into the clothing, like the passage of birds through the autumn sky. She was looking at a photo framed on his dresser, tucking in her blouse and then picking up the photo, turning it toward the moonlight.

'This is Mary?'

'Yes.'

'She was beautiful.'

'She never thought so.'

'Well, she was wrong, then.'

She placed the photo down and picked up the one beside it.

'And this is your daughter.'

'That's Alice, yes.'

'What is she here, twenty?'

'That's the year before she married. She's twenty-three there.'

'She looks younger. Takes after you I guess.'

91

He laughed. 'My god. I hope not.'

'She could do worse. How old *are* you, Av?'

'Did I ever ask you that?'

'No.'

'Well, then.'

'I wouldn't have imagined vanity.'

'Hell, I'm sixty-seven. I'll be sixty-eight in August.'

She put the second photo down beside the first.

'What about your sons?' she said. 'There aren't any photos here.'

'I don't have any sons.'

She sat down beside him on the bed and placed her hand on top of his and leaned toward him. The blouse was still unbuttoned and he could see the narrow breastbone and even more than the hand on his it was the sight of her soft pale flesh that was a comfort to him and went a ways to stop the sudden trembling.

'Yes, you do,' she said. 'Sam told me.'

'He shouldn't have.'

'If you don't want to talk about it, I won't press you. But don't blame Sam. I'm a reporter. I find out things. Sam's a good friend to you.'

He nodded. 'Back then, when it happened, a man couldn't have asked for better.'

He sighed and lifted himself up on the pillows.

'You want to know about my boys?'

'If you want to tell me.'

'All right. Tim was eleven, the older boy was twenty-four—'

'Billy.'

'That's right. I don't use his name much. Just when I talk to Alice. And then she's the one who always

92

manages to bring him up. So that I don't call Allie too often either. I know that's wrong, but . . .'

'You don't want to keep on going over and over it again. And here I am asking you to. I'm sorry.'

'It's all right. I don't mind you asking. I would have once. But it's different with Allie. She has this idea in her head that I should be in touch with him. That it'll make things better for me somehow. I don't agree. Only problem I'm having with you is, I don't know where to start on it.'

'Start with Tim.'

'We had him late. I was forty-eight and Mary was forty-two. So that he was kind of a surprise to both of us. We had to fix up the attic in order to give him a bedroom, got rid of all the stuff we'd stored up there. He turned out to be a good boy, an easy boy. Favored Allie that way and his mother.

'Billy'd been different right from the start. And we probably loved him all the more because of it. You know how that can be. You see a boy struggling to get hold of what other kids seem to come by so easy, your heart goes out to him. It seems to me he always had a way of turning a good thing sour on himself. He went out for baseball his sophomore year and I coached him. He made the team easily too. Shortstop. Then broke his leg stepping off a curb in the parking lot right after the second game, which his team lost, by the way, when he tried to sidestep a hard line-drive. So they weren't even real unhappy to see him go.

'We knew he had a problem with lying. He was always making up things. Told us once he'd seen a dead man down by the bank of the stream behind the house here. This was when he was just a young boy, maybe seven or eight. But we took him serious enough. And of course there was nothing there.

'He dropped out of school when they kept him back junior year. Went to work at Clover's Hardware here in town. Got to work late half the time, stayed out nights. Made up lies about why. We were too easy on him, Mary and I, but there was always this way about him, it was like he couldn't help himself. Everybody gave him leeway. Old man Clover too. But they had to fire him after a while.

'I got this idea into my head that he might work things out for himself in the service, get some discipline into his life, you know? It'd worked for me. And maybe he wanted to get out of the house by then anyway because it was one of the few times he listened to me and did what I told him to do. He joined the Navy. Nine months later he was out on a section eight. You know what that is?'

She nodded. 'Mentally unstable.'

'I think *unfit* is the word they use. Anyhow, I made the mistake of taking him in again. I think we both knew it was wrong at the time. But the boy *was* unfit. You'd think about what it was he could do in the world, *be* in the world – and you'd come up bone dry. He did odd jobs for a while, went to work for a filling station out on highway 202, got fired from that for stealing parts for his old Buick which he never did admit to stealing. We think he may have broken into Tom Hardin's house one night. There was no way to prove it. But the house was broken into all right and all of a sudden Billy had money in his pocket. Said he won it in a card game. I didn't believe him.'

'God. Terrific. How'd you deal with all this?'

'Me? Badly. Hell, I'd have thrown him out half a dozen times if it hadn't been for Mary. He was her first-born, she couldn't see us doing that. But there was more shouting than talking going on in this house back then. It didn't make a damn bit of difference to Billy. He'd just lie in your face and stare you down. Like he believed the lie himself. And I think probably half the time he did.

'I think he was living mostly in a fantasy world by then. He'd got himself involved with a local girl, Cathy Lee Stutz, who was crazy as he was. They'd drive up to Portland and come back with all these books about black magic, the occult, whatever. Wore chains around their necks, burned black candles in his room. I don't know where they got the money to buy it all. He wasn't working. Tom Bridgewater told me later he'd heard she was turning tricks up there in Portland. I didn't disbelieve him.

'But with the Stutz girl around at least Billy wasn't here so much. Mostly he was staying out at her place. I came in one afternoon and they were sitting in the middle of a white chalk circle they'd drawn out there on the living-room floor. I told them to take their nonsense elsewhere and they did. So after that at least there was a little peace and quiet around here for a while. You want a glass of water?'

'I'll get you one.'

'No, I'll get it.'

He got up and walked naked into the kitchen, a little surprised that he wasn't embarrassed doing that in front of her, thinking that he could almost feel the moonlight through the window cool against his skin, bluing the walls, filling the shadows with its dark cool color. He ran water from the tap and filled his glass, drank some and filled it again and carried it into the bedroom. She was sitting where he'd left her. His shorts were beside her on the bed. She reached out to him for the glass, changing her mind. He handed it to her. He pulled on his shorts and watched her drink. She smiled at him and handed back the glass, his thumb grazing hers.

'You have to get back real soon?' he said.

'Soon. Not just yet.'

'Don't take this wrong. Lord knows I'm not complaining. But what are you doing here, Carrie? With a man like me?'

'You mean with an *old* man like you. With a man old enough to be my father.'

'And then some.'

'When I could be with a much, much younger man. Any man I wanted, right?'

'Probably you could be, yes.'

She laughed and shook her head. 'Av, the only problem with a man your age is that sometimes he starts thinking just like a young fool again.'

'Pardon?'

'Never mind. Sit down. Tell me the rest.'

Despite what he'd said to her this was what he didn't like to speak about even now, so many years later. What had happened was a weight upon his heart from the very beginning and it was one that would never go away no matter how many times he told it or how long he refused to tell it. The words had a weight of their own. You only found out how heavy it was going to be this time around as you went along.

He sat down on the bed beside her.

'Cathy Lee, this girlfriend of his, started seeing somebody else after a while. I guess it was somebody with more money than Billy because after that he was always after money. For a while he even went back to work for it. Everything he made went right back into Cathy Lee. To take her places, buy her things.

'I was with Bill Prine over at the store the night it happened, taking our six-month inventory. Allie was with us too. She'd always had a good head for figures and she liked helping us out come inventory time. It was dead of winter. Tim was home asleep in the bedroom upstairs. Mary was reading in the kitchen. It was about eleven thirty by the time we finished up the inventory.

'We hadn't seen Billy in a few days.'

He drank what was left of the water and set the glass on the windowsill behind her. He felt her breath on his cheek, smelled her hair. She was leaning close. He didn't want to look at her. Not now.

'When he told the story later, he'd lie. But it was *confused* lying. Not what he usually did. He'd lie about one thing and then maybe he'd tell the truth about that and lie about something else and then tell the truth about whatever the hell *that* was and then go back and lie about the first thing again, or something completely different. It just went on that way.

'But how we pieced it together was that Billy had come around the house earlier that night looking for some money. Mary told him no, that if he wanted money he'd have to come down to the store and talk to me. Well, he knew he wasn't going to get anything out of me. I'd had it by then. So they argued. Eventually he left.

'Then just before eleven he came back to the house again. He still wanted money and Mary told him no again.

'I don't know why, but he locked Red up in the bedroom here. Here in this room. Maybe he was barking. I don't know.

'Then he came back out to the kitchen and started hitting her, beating her. Maybe he thought he'd get money out of her that way or maybe it was just one of his crazy rages. But he hurt her. He hurt her so bad I guess he thought he'd killed her. Because then he . . . he decided . . . *jesus!*'

'It's all right, Av.' She took his hand again.

He could see it all. Everything he'd come home to that night.

He gripped her hand.

'He decided he'd have to cover it up. He went out to the woodshed. He got the can of fuel for the Coleman lantern I used to keep out there and then he went up to the attic bedroom and threw the lantern oil all over Tim. All over my son, who was sleeping.

'He lit a match and threw it and closed the bedroom door and locked it behind him. He burned Tim to death. Up there in his bedroom.

'But oil doesn't burn as hot as kerosine or gasoline. He'd killed Tim all right. He was saturated with the stuff. But all that burned up there was my boy and the mattress he was lying on. Not even the drapes caught fire.

'He waited outside the attic door until my son stopped screaming. Until it was quiet.

'Then he went downstairs. He threw the oil over Mary lying there on the kitchen floor and then he lit another match and threw that on her and then he got into his car and drove away.

'But . . . she . . . my wife wasn't dead. She was still alive. He'd beaten her but he hadn't killed her. *He was wrong*. Wrong about that. Like he was wrong about the oil burning the house down and covering up what he did. He was wrong on *everything*. All of it . . . it was all for nothing.

'I guess the pain woke her.

'She got outside somehow and rolled across the ground, in the dirt, on the grass, till the flames were out. And then she still had enough left in her to crawl back into the house and dial nine-one-one.

'They found her on the stairs halfway up to Tim's bedroom. Red was in a panic. The robe she was wearing had been burned right into her body. I wonder sometimes if she knew Tim was dead back there at the end. If that was what stopped her.

'She lived for five more days. Never came out of the coma. I think that was a blessing. The burns were so bad they wouldn't even let me hold her.

'In the end, I did anyway.'

He got up and walked to the dresser and opened the bottom drawer. He took out a picture in a wooden frame. He handed it to her.

'That was Tim,' he said. 'That was my son.'

She held the picture in her lap and looked down at it awhile and when she looked up at him again he saw there were tears in her eyes.

'I don't understand,' she said. 'My god, Av. How can you go on living in this place? With what happened here?'

He sat down beside her.

'The walls are painted over,' he said. 'The floors are all sanded. You'd never know there was any fire here. Not in the kitchen and not up in the attic. But I can still see the fires, the marks they left. I know their exact shape and size. I see them every day.

'But this was our place. Mary's and mine. Allie's. Tim's. They grew up here. Hell, it was even Red's place. I won't let him take that away from me too.'

They sat quiet for a while.

'So what happened to him?' she said. 'To Billy, I mean.'

He sighed. 'Oh, he tried to say it was another boy. Friend of his. Even that it was Cathy Lee Stutz. Never would admit to it. But by then he'd gone ahead and said so much that they had a case against him. They had his prints all over the Coleman can.

'I said I'd stand by him even after what he did if he'd just admit it and stop his damn lying and tell me *why* he did it, why he had to go and kill them. That he was flesh and blood and I'd do what I could for him. But he wouldn't do it. He wouldn't stop lying. His lawyer convinced him to take a guilty plea but as soon as he did he started right in again, saying he never did it, that it was just a plea, that it meant nothing. To this day he tries to convince Allie of that whatever she calls him, even though she damn well knows better. I washed my hands of him. Years ago. He got two consecutive sentences of thirty years to life each.

100

'It's not enough.'

She nodded. 'So you have no son.'

'That's right. I lost him that night too, I guess.'

She gazed down at the photo of Tim again.

'What a handsome boy,' she said.

'He was a happy boy.'

She handed the photo back to him.

'You feel guilty, don't you, because you weren't there?'

'I don't know what I feel.'

He turned and put the photo back inside the drawer and closed it.

'You have to go to work tomorrow, don't you?' he said.

'Yes.'

'You have time for a beer before you go?'

'Sure I do.'

'I'll get us some from the kitchen.'

He walked out and there beside the table climbing the kitchen wall like streaks of black lightning were the scars which only he could see to mark where she had fallen.

# *Fourteen*

At noon the next day he was at the store. Business was slow because of the rain. Sam Berry called.

'This McCormack son of a bitch has got one long reach. Or maybe it's his lawyer, I don't know. But Phelps is still declining to prosecute and I can't shake him. I got the call this morning.'

'Despite the story.'

'Despite the story.'

'The rock through my window? The note?'

'No prints on either of them. You can't identify the thrower or the car. Anybody could have done it.'

'Nobody else had reason to.'

'I know that and you know that. The court's a different story. I'm sorry.'

'So am I, Sam.'

Through the misted rain-flecked window he saw a car pull into his lot, a new white Lincoln Continental, low beams on and windshield wipers moving fast as the car sat on idle. He couldn't see inside.

'You want to go ahead with the lawsuit?'

'Of course I do,' he said.

He thought it was probably the first time he'd lied to Sam about anything.

103

The car door opened and a woman stepped outside. She wore a brown belted raincoat pulled tight around a trim figure and a clear plastic scarf over her head. Her face was obscured by the window. The woman stood by the open car door a moment looking in at the store and then quickly got back into the Lincoln again and closed the door.

'I'll get things started then,' Sam said. 'You know that I can't do this for free, Av. But I'll try to keep costs down. I know you're not made of money.'

'That's fine, Sam. You do what you have to do.'

'I'll be in touch.'

'Thanks, Sam.'

He put down the phone and stared out through the window watching the Lincoln pull out of the parking lot into the rain and thought how dry the summer had been and how they could use this, the grass and trees all comfortably drinking in the light warm rain that would not wash away the topsoil or drown the vegetation but instead would get things growing again, a boost to the soul of the land as last night the woman Carrie had been to his own soul.

There were ways to go about this other than a lawsuit. Sam said that despite McCormack's money he was just a good ol' boy at heart. A wolf in sheep's clothing.

Good ol' boys could be pushed. Wolves could be made to snap.

It was time he started pushing.

# *Fifteen*

'Don't tell me,' McCormack said smiling. He was sitting in the study this time in one of the plush leather chairs facing the fireplace. There was a newspaper open on his lap. Behind him mounted on the wall which Ludlow had not been able to see on his first visit here were a five-point white-tail buck, a coyote, a timberwolf and a small black bear.

The crippled maid had shown him in and now he was standing there.

'Don't tell me. You've thought about it. You want to sell the place,' he said.

'No,' Ludlow said. 'The store's fine as is.'

'You should think about it. You don't take much out of it.'

'Enough for me.'

McCormack sighed, the smile fading and folded the paper neatly and reached over and set it down on the red leather couch.

'I hear you're suing me.'

'I'd rather not.'

'I don't know why you'd want to bother. It won't be worth either your time or your money.'

'I don't suppose it would be about money.'

105

'What, then?'

'I guess it would be about word getting around as to what the boy did and what you're doing.'

'What am I doing?'

'I'll tell you what you're *not* doing. You're not setting him straight about this. I bet he's still got the gun, doesn't he? I bet you haven't even taken the damn thing away from him.'

'That's none of your business.'

'I saw him over at the high school day before yesterday. Drove by, and there he was. I didn't see any bruises on him. None that I could notice. I don't suppose you strapped his butt instead?'

'We don't go in for that, Ludlow. I don't know where you come from. But it doesn't happen here.'

'It doesn't.'

'No.'

'I guess you're more civilized than me.'

'I guess that's a possibility.'

Ludlow turned and looked at the mounted heads on the wall and then looked back at McCormack.

'You shoot these all by yourself, did you?'

'Uh-huh.'

'You figure you're a good shot, Mr McCormack?'

'Damned right I am.'

'I guess you learned in the service, then. You look to be about the right age for Vietnam.'

'I never went. Just lucky I guess. No, I learned to shoot on my own. What's this got to do with anything?'

'I was in Korea myself. They call that one The Forgotten War. Though I don't think anybody who was there forgot much about it. Or their families.

106

When I came home my daddy threw me a party. Invited half the town. He was proud of me. Hard to say why. I didn't do anything special over there but he was proud anyhow.

'I'm wondering if you're proud of Daniel, Mr McCormack, because if you're not then something's wrong between you and the boy. Something maybe you can still do something about if you care to. While he's still here with you. Before he goes out on his own to do god knows what to who. Instead of just hiring your lawyers and covering up for him.'

McCormack stood and reached in his pocket for a cigarette and lit it with a heavy silver lighter from the table. Ludlow was aware of the smoke and wondered if they ever used the fireplace because there was no woodsmoke smell in the room, only the smell of tobacco now.

'Look,' McCormack said. 'I don't need any lectures from you. My boys are my boys and I'll handle them any damn way I see fit. The bottom line is this. You go ahead and sue if you want to. It might cause me a little embarrassment in some places but not very much, I promise you. Because you can't win. I promise you that too. And even if you could, Ludlow, what would you get out of it? The value of the dog. A goddamn dog from the goddamn dog pound. Even if you did win, which you won't, I couldn't care less. Do you understand that?'

He nodded. 'I guess I do.'

'You guess you do. Good. Don't come back here. And don't go snooping around after my boys anymore or I'll have the sheriff on your tired old ass before you know what hit you. Have yourself a *real* nice day, Ludlow. You know where the door is.'

As he walked out into the hall he saw a woman stopped midway down the stairs and he paused and looked at her and he guessed that the woman was McCormack's wife, the boys' mother, and that she'd heard at least that last part of what they'd said because she looked at Ludlow as though Ludlow were a thief slipping away with some precious thing that she owned, as though somehow Ludlow were breaking her heart. A pretty woman once, he thought, though not anymore despite the expensive clothes and jewelry. And he wondered about the woman in the Lincoln Continental that afternoon. And he wondered if he should feel bad for her as he walked toward the door.

# Sixteen

There were times after Mary's and Tim's death he'd drink himself to sleep. He allowed himself permission to do that for quite some time.

He'd rise late those mornings and the dog was used to eating early. The dog had a clock in his belly unfixed to Ludlow's sorrow. The dog had come up with strategies to wake him, heavy head or not, and these were progressively more insistent. He would begin by licking Ludlow's face and much of the time the warm wet tongue was enough. If Ludlow turned his face to the pillow and continued to pursue his troubled sleep the dog would burrow beneath the covers and with his cold wet nose seek out the back of Ludlow's neck.

If he still would not relent the dog would walk on him.

There would be dreams he would not wish to part with in favor of the furious empty day ahead of him or else the ache in his head was fierce enough so that he would sometimes rise and smack the dog hard across the rump and send him yelping off the bed. Those mornings he would wake up angry at the dog and at himself. The dog would cower until he was reassured. It would rarely be long before he would do so. He couldn't stay angry at the dog. There was no meanness in the dog, only an innocent hunger. The dog looked forward to the day even if Ludlow didn't.

And in the long run Ludlow believed those mornings and those strategies had brought him back. The dog would not permit Ludlow his indulgences and self-pity and finally neither would he. It was a matter of fairness to the animal and an affront to simple pride that the dog should know so much more of life than he did. He stopped drinking and stopped relying on Bill Prine so much and got himself back to work. He took Red fishing on the weekends or they would go for a drive and hike up into the mountains or they would do what he was doing now here in Ogunquit. Alone without the dog for the first time.

His father, Avery Allan Ludlow Sr, was four months shy of ninety. He had endured angioplasty and a double bypass yet still insisted on his pack a day, the directors and nurses of the Pinewood Home be damned. His father was smoking now, sitting on the porch-swing with Ludlow and Ludlow watched his hand move away from his mouth with the cigarette half finished. The hand he watched had held an axe or a two-handed saw or a tool of some sort practically all his father's working life. He had been in the bucking and logging industry up in Somerset County ever since he was a boy and the hands were still the most vital parts about him save his eyes and his thinking and his sharp tongue. With illness and inactivity the muscles of his legs and arms and trunk had withered inside him so that his flesh hung on him, outsized for his body.

Ludlow thought him still a handsome man. So, he gathered, did the ladies of the Pinewood Home.

'Pop,' he said. 'I think I might be going to do something stupid.'

Ludlow told him about Red and the shooting and the rest of it and what he was thinking of doing and by the time he was finished his father had smoked two more Winstons and flicked them off the porch into the hedges. They rocked back and forth on the swing listening to the chains creak and ladies laughing behind them in the house and his father nodded and his eyes swept over the fresh-cut lawn in front of them and then across the hill to the road that led through town and past that, to the sea.

'It's not stupid,' he said. 'Hell, blood's blood. You ever taste an animal's blood? It tastes exactly like your own does. You tell me why's a man's blood is any better or any more precious than a dog's blood? It sure ain't to the dog. Me, I could never see the sense in it. Red was family to you. I figure you owe something to family. And you do too or else you wouldn't be out here wanting to talk to me.'

'I've been thinking. I don't talk to Billy though, do I? Never.'

'Billy who.'

'Your grandson.'

'I know who he is. I also know what he did. And that what he did damn near *broke* you. Red ever do anything like that to you? Or me? Or Allie?'

'No.'

'So don't go getting all guilty and stupid on me.

We're your family. Like your mother and Tim and Mary were your family. Hell, you've sorted this out for yourself already. Or else . . .'

'Or else I wouldn't be here.'

'Right. You only need somebody to tell you you're not just howling at the moon right now. Well, you're not. Or else I am too. And so's pretty much everybody else I like or ever did like and as far as I'm concerned, we can go right on doing it just for the pretty sound it makes. To hell with what people think.'

He stood and the weight of him missing off the porch swing on the other side was hardly any weight at all. He put his hand on Ludlow's shoulder and for all its wide mass that too seemed lighter than it ought to have been.

'Go on about your business, son,' he said. 'Come see me again sometime before my birthday. You can be a worrisome difficult son of a bitch but I don't mind your company, not at all.'

# Seventeen

It took him nearly a week to find the boy the way he needed to find him, in the situation he needed. It was costing him at the store but Bill Prine didn't seem to mind the extra time and there was no other way he could think of to do it. He spent his days haunting the boy, parking a block or two back from the house until he came out in the morning or afternoon and climbed into his car and drove off.

He didn't worry too much about being seen. He was figuring seeing the truck would rattle the boy and that was how he wanted him.

Many days, the younger boy, Harold, was with his brother and they would drive to Cedar Hill Road and pick up Pete and the three of them together would take the highway out to Portland and once to Yarmouth and the time they went to Yarmouth three young girls got in the car with them in the center of town by a drugstore and they drove to a mall and hung around all day at the arcades and ate pizza and at night they went to a movie. The girls spent most of their time laughing and talking together in secret and so did the boys but the boys seemed to aim for more subtlety, feigning the assured stance of adulthood, though with none of its tired wisdom.

Portland was no good to Ludlow nor was Yarmouth. He needed the boy in Moody Point. He needed him there under specific circumstances and he began to despair it would ever happen. The boy would stop at a store for cigarettes and then pass through town on his way somewhere else or the three of them would stop at a MacDonald's outside of town and then drive on. But a pack of cigarettes was not what he needed to see in Danny McCormack's hand.

On the morning of the fifth day into this he was coming out of Bill Brockett's bakery with a cup of coffee and a cheese danish and saw Harold McCormack leaning with his back to Ludlow's truck near the driver-side door, his skinny arms folded across his bony chest half-obscuring the MacIntosh Computer logo on his teeshirt. He walked over.

He set the coffee on the hood of the truck to let it cool a while and took a bite out of the danish. The boy looked skittish, scuffling his feet and moving back and forth across the truck's door like he was scratching an itch.

'I saw you parked here,' he said finally. 'Danny didn't.'

'Where is he?'

'Down the street at Bowman's Auto.'

'He know you're here?'

He shook his head. 'I told him I needed cigarettes. He'd be pretty damn mad if he knew I was talking to you.'

'Would he?'

'Hell, yes.'

'He get mad a lot, your brother?'

He took another bite of the danish and then sipped the coffee. It was still too hot so he put it back up on the hood again.

The boy sighed and shook his head. 'Listen, Mr Ludlow. I'm not gonna say everything's all buddy-buddy between Danny and me. But that's not the point.'

'What is the point, then?'

He shifted against the truck. Ludlow thought that what he really wanted was to be allowed to climb inside there and have Ludlow on the outside so they could quit talking altogether. But the boy had called this.

He took another bite and looked at him.

'I wanted ... I wanted to tell you that I'm sorry. About your dog. For what we did. That's why I'm here. To say that.'

Ludlow just looked at him a while. Letting him listen to his own words hanging in the still air. Then he nodded.

'I'm glad to hear it,' he said. 'Of course, the one I need to hear it from most's your brother. I'm still glad to hear it from you, though. The question is, what now?'

'Huh?'

'You going to keep on lying for him?'

'God! What do you expect me to do? You ask me in front of my *father*! You get this on *TV*!'

'I expect you to tell the truth, son. Just like you're doing now. I expect you to tell your father and I expect you to tell the police if it comes to that.'

The boy shook his head again. 'You don't get it,'

he said. 'You don't understand. That's just not gonna happen.'

'Then suppose you make me understand.'

He stood there, calm in front of him and sipped the coffee. The boy kept shaking his head, moving back and forth against the truck. It was something to hear this from the boy. Something but not enough.

'Listen,' he said. 'I gotta go. If Danny sees me here . . .'

He started to move away.

'Who're you afraid of, Harold? Your brother? Your father? You were man enough to come down here and say what you just said to me. I figure that already makes you a bigger man than your brother. Maybe your father too. I don't think you have all that much to worry about from either of them. Do you?'

Harold smiled. It wasn't a good smile.

'Mr Ludlow, believe me, you haven't got a clue.'

Ludlow watched the boy walk off down the street swinging his lanky arms and wondered if he wasn't maybe right about that. He was only seeing part of the picture, he was aware. For all he could tell the boy's home life might be a nightmare or it might be the same as most people's lives, some good, some bad, mostly neither one. But you went on what you did know no matter how little and you tried to find out the rest if possible. It was all you could do.

He finished the danish and opened the car door, still watching the boy and saw him stop and turn around and then walk back to the truck again. The boy looked hurt and angry now.

'You saw Carla?' he said. 'You saw our maid?'

He nodded.

'You saw her hand?'

'Sure.'

'I want you to consider why my father would hire a maid with a crippled hand, Mr Ludlow. Out of all the help available around here, my father chooses her.'

'I figure she must be pretty good. Despite the hand.'

'Oh, she's good enough, all right. But it's not that. It has nothing to do with that. And it's not out of the kindness of his heart, either. Just think about it, Mr Ludlow.'

He spun on his heel and walked away.

Ludlow picked up his coffee, got in and started the truck, wondering what the boy was talking about. Trying to tell him something about the maid that was important to him.

*Power*, he thought. Something about power. Had to be.

He wondered how often McCormack found some way to remind the woman about her withered hand or even how he might choose to go about it. If with regard to McCormack he was dealing with the ordinary smug superiority of the rich or whether it was cruelty.

In either case he'd take what the boy said in the spirit in which it was given.

He'd take it as a warning.

Though he guessed it didn't change anything.

The following day he followed them to the high school playground. It was late afternoon.

The three of them were playing baseball with five

other boys Ludlow didn't recognize, four men to a team. He watched them in the distance from his truck for over an hour and then went to Arnie Grohn's to have himself a late lunch and when he came back they were still playing as he had thought they would be. He thought that Harold wasn't a bad batter for his size nor was Pete Daoust. Though Pete had a tendency to go for pitches that were high and outside, he had a home-run heft to him and he used it effectively.

The real surprise was Danny.

As a pitcher he was fine. He had a strong right arm and he was accurate and he fielded the ball with ease. But at bat he swung with ever-increasing passion at pitches Ludlow thought no one with any sense would even want to think about, high and low and inside and outside, whatever was thrown to him. It was as though he couldn't stand to see the ball get by him.

A group of teenage girls had gathered watching them and at first Danny was showing off for them, grinning from the pitcher's mound and frowning and shaking his head when he missed one in the batter's box as though he were just having a real bad day, inexplicably, like he really couldn't understand what had suddenly come over him. As things grew worse he seemed to forget about the girls completely.

He seemed to have no eye for the thing at all. Of the eight times Ludlow watched him he struck out four times, popped out twice and got a pair of singles distinguished only by how hard he had to run in order to reach base before the ball did. The veins stood out in his neck as he swung.

It was better than Ludlow had dared hope for. At

118

bat Danny McCormack appeared like a man with a mission, the nature of which he barely understood and who could fill the gaps of his understanding only with will and fury.

No one laughed at him, though they might have. Not even the girls, who grew more and more silent as the game went on. He was bigger than all but two of the players on the other team and perhaps he was older but Ludlow thought that would not necessarily account for their deference to him. He thought that Danny was not a boy you laughed at. And that the others knew it. He wondered how much pleasure that subtracted from the game and why these boys would even want to engage him.

Perhaps it was a way of getting even, he thought, a judicious humiliation he was watching, played out on the neutral ground of a ball field where the game itself permitted his rage to go only so far and no further.

After a time, the fourth man on Danny's team looked at his wristwatch and shook his head. It was over. The girls had already drifted away.

He watched Danny take two of the metal bats out of the dirt behind the backstop and toss them into the rear seat of his car. He got in on the driver's side with Pete Daoust beside him and Harold in the back. They turned out of the lot and drove towards town.

Ludlow waited, then followed.

In town they pulled up in front of the Anchor Restaurant across from Fleury's drugstore and Ludlow knew he had them now, if Danny would take the bait.

He stopped his truck beside the driver-side door

just as Harold was getting out the back and cut his engine and said, 'Hey.'

Danny was closing his door and he turned and Pete Daoust looked up over the roof at him and scowled and slammed his door.

'You,' Danny said. 'This goddamn old man again. You been following us, haven't you?'

'Why would I want to do that?'

'We've seen your truck.'

'It's a small town. I suppose you would now and then.'

He got out of the truck and closed the door and walked to the curb and stood there in the sun.

'We saw you over in Portland.'

'That's possible too.'

'You better cut it out.'

'Cut it out?'

'Following me. You know what I'm talking about. I'm telling you right now to cut it out.'

A pair of men in overalls and old Boston Celtics caps walked out of the Anchor and looked at the old man and the three boys standing by the curb, two of the boys standing well behind the other, and then they crossed the street.

'Are you threatening me, son?'

'I'm telling you.'

The two men turned midway and glanced back at them and then continued on.

'I wouldn't be threatening anyone if I were you. Not unless you can fight a whole lot better than you can swing one of these things.'

He nodded toward the bats on the car seat,

bringing them to the boy's attention. He let his gaze stay there a while.

'You stupid old son of a bitch. What are you doing out there watching us? *Spying* on us? Who the hell do you think you are?'

'Let's just take off, Danny,' Harold said. 'Let dad handle things.'

'Yeah. Fuck this jerk,' Pete said.

Ludlow heard the uncertainty in Pete's voice. It was what he'd been hoping for. The heavyset boy was the wild card. Now he knew it was a card that wasn't going to get played.

'You've got a nice swing, Pete,' he said. 'Good eye too. Not like Miss McCormack here.'

'You *fuck*!'

And then Danny was diving through the open window reaching in and the other two boys stepped back as he came out with the metal bat clutched in his fist. Ludlow almost smiled it had been so easy but knew it would not do to smile. Plus, for all he knew the boy might be better at this than he looked.

He moved fast up onto the open sidewalk in front of the restaurant with his back to the boy as though he were trying to get away from him, retreating, knowing that the sight of his back would encourage him as it would almost always encourage a coward. When he felt the boy close enough behind he spun into the bat as it arced down and let it have the outside of his upper arm halfway through the swing.

The boy was off balance, his other hand fisted, held wide away from his body and though the pain in Ludlow's arm was sudden and intense he knew nothing was broken nor any muscle sufficiently

121

bruised to hinder him. It had been important to let the boy strike the first blow but now he had to finish quickly.

He came in low as Danny tried to plant his weight equally on both feet again, and hit him just beneath the ribcage. The boy woofed and doubled over. Ludlow slid his bruised arm midway up the length of the bat to raise the boy's arm further and give himself a second opening and then hit him in the ribs and felt and heard one crack.

The boy screamed and dropped the bat and doubled over to the sidewalk.

Ludlow looked around. Pete had moved away, not toward him, standing with Harold. That was good. He didn't want to involve them. A woman pushing a baby carriage had stopped and was watching him wide-eyed from half a block away. D. L. Fleury was standing in the door of his drugstore across the street, a customer behind him. Ludlow watched his look of astonishment resolve itself gradually into a wide smile. He guessed that word had got around and D. L. knew all about this.

He kicked the baseball bat away from the boy, heard it ringing in the gutter.

A car passed by.

He leaned down and whispered close into Danny's ear and saw and smelled mucus and tears.

'You've just been suckered, boy. I've got witnesses all over this street who saw that you went at me first, with a weapon. Some of them are old friends of mine. So don't go trying to make a fuss over this. I just gave you what your father should have given you and wouldn't. But you damn well had to have it one way or another. It's not going to bring my dog back but maybe you'll think twice and maybe you'll think of me and Red before you let that mean streak out again.'

He nodded to the woman with the baby carriage and then across the street to D. L., who nodded back gravely, and then he went to his truck. He opened the door and turned to Harold and Pete.

'I think he hurt his ribs a little,' he said. 'You'd better give him a hand.'

Driving through the hills up Stirrup Iron Road a small black cat darted out in front of him, chasing a rabbit across the road like a sudden message from the unknown living world and he slammed on the brakes and stopped just inches from the cat's haunches and then sat trembling in the cab of the truck holding onto the wheel and staring into the tangled mass of scrub where cat and rabbit had disappeared unharmed until his trembling stopped.

He put his truck in gear again and, with far more care, drove on.

# *Eighteen*

Sam Berry's office smelled of pipe smoke and old books. Outside his second-floor window a wind had come up on the street buffeting and bending the trees, and leaves were blowing but inside the office was silent. He watched Sam tap the dead ashes out of his briar pipe into the metal garbage pail and then turn the bowl over and tap it, hollow-sounding, on the calf of his artificial leg and then turn and tap it into the garbage pail again. Sam smiled and shook his head and began to fill his pipe with tobacco from the hide pouch on his desk.

'You're saying this'll do for you then,' he said. 'Am I right?'

'Yes.'

'So forget about the lawsuit. It stops here.'

'That's right. I don't see as it would get me anywhere anyway, do you?'

'Good chance it wouldn't, no. I told you that right off.'

Sam looked at him and smiled. 'You been pulling on my good leg so to speak, haven't you, Av? You never did intend to sue them. You just thought you'd distract me, so I wouldn't see what was going on.'

'You'd have tried to talk me out of it.'

'I would indeed. You know that kid could've killed you out there.'

'My feeling was that people like him don't usually kill people my size unless they've got a gun. Old man or not. The boy's a hothead. He's a coward and a bully. I was counting on that.'

'But this is the end of it now, right?'

'This is the end of it.'

'Just so long as it is. You know you were on pretty shaky ground with the law going after him that way.'

'I know it.'

Berry tamped in the tobacco with the tip of a yellow-stained thumb.

'You ever eat Chinese, Av?'

'Not much.'

'I like it now and then. Moo goo gai pan. Ribs. Egg rolls. I even like the weak tea they serve and the fortune cookie at the end. Only thing is, most times you open up the damn cookie and the fortune's silly. You know, "*Your wishes will be granted.*" "*You would do well to expand your business now.*" That sort of thing. Only once I ever got one that made any sense to me. "Nothing in the world is accomplished without passion," it said. How about that? In a *fortune cookie*. I thought it was pretty damn good.'

Ludlow nodded.

'But I figure passion's like the wind in the trees out there. Blows hard for a while and feels strong and clean while it's blowing and maybe it even blows so long and hard that you start living with it. It feels like the wind's a part of you, like it's essential, if

126

you know what I mean, something you can hardly imagine life without. But it's got to pass. So you can get on with things without all the confusion of that wind in your hair.'

He sat back and struck a match and held it to the bowl of pipe.

'You can't even light your pipe in a heavy wind,' he said.

# Nineteen

'Dad? Are you all right? Your voice sounds funny.'

'I'm tired, hon. Hell, I'm an old man and I'm tired. What can you expect? But don't you worry about me. I'm fine.'

It was late for her to call. Eleven o'clock. He wondered what had prompted her. She seemed to have no news to speak of.

Just a call, he thought. Don't go attaching any significance to it. It's nothing.

There was no way she could know what had happened today with the boy.

'You should get some sleep,' he said. 'I should too.'

They said their goodnights.

He went to bed but sleep evaded him. He kept seeing the cat dart out in front of his truck. An event the world had put in motion and of which he was not a part until that very instant when things died or didn't die according to the nature of their meeting.

According to their collision.

# Twenty

The night his store burned down he'd done an unusual thing.

Instead of going home after closing he'd gone to Arnie Grohn's restaurant and ate Arnie's meatloaf with mashed potatoes and green beans and then walked two blocks down through the clear warm summer breeze to the Birch Tree Inn.

He sat at the long polished wood bar drinking beer with a dozen strangers or near-strangers, a few of the faces familiar to him but no more than that. He drank three beers over the course of an hour and listened to the laughter of the men and their voices rising over the country songs on the jukebox. It was as though the men were speaking in another language because he could make out none of what they said. He felt a sadness he hadn't felt since the night he'd told Carrie Donnel about his family and he didn't know where it came from or what he should do about it. The barman was a young man with glasses and sandy hair who spoke with a southern accent which Ludlow could not place exactly. He was polite and friendly and told him that his third beer was on the house. Ludlow thought that

131

even a young man was able to recognize sadness when he was staring pure into the face of it.

He supposed everything was showing now.

When he finished he set the price of the buyback on the bar and thanked the barman. He walked up the street to his truck thinking that in just this single hour the air had started to chill.

When he got to his truck Luke Wallingford was standing in front of it. 'Jesus, Av,' he said. 'Everybody's out looking for you.'

With three beers in him it did not make sense right away. Wallingford ran his own small hunting lodge and bought traps and supplies from him. Why he should be out on the street looking for Ludlow at this hour, or why anybody should, was a mystery.

'Av,' he said, 'I don't know how to tell you this. But the store's burned all to hell. Jesus, Av, I'm sorry.'

It occurred to Ludlow that people kept telling him they were sorry these days.

'The store? My store?'

'It's burned. They're out there now. Some of us came looking for you and I saw your truck. I mean, all the ammunition you had in there? All that fuel? The store's a damn disaster. I don't even know if they've got the fire out yet. You want me to drive you over?'

'I'll go myself. Thanks, Luke.'

'I'll follow you.'

'All right.'

Driving up the mountain he could see the smoke in the night sky. Then he could smell it through his open window. Cresting the hill, he saw the mars lights and spotlights and warning lights and the fire's golden yellow glow and then he saw the fire engines and the volunteers at their hoses pouring water in through the broken front window and down onto the roof. The fire was still burning.

He knew most of them. Store-owners and managers, workers, professional men. Ludlow's own accountant was there. Yet displaced from all contexts familiar to him, here in this place and at this sudden strange activity, they took on the character of men working in a dream. It was a dream of heat and acrid smoke, of darkness and flickering light gleaming in the water on the street, of realms of hell in which he saw once more his wife and son each of them alight with flame.

He felt the same familiar ache at such senseless waste break over him again. To stand and watch what he'd worked for, what Mary had worked for too, destroyed seemed to destroy her yet again. The life he'd known now seemed capable of multiple, even infinite shatterings. What was the loss of the dog but another loss of them, his wife and son? What was the loss of this but the loss of the dog again?

He heard timbers crack and saw a leap of flame and burning cinders pour from the suddenly crumbled roof like a clawing hand set free and reaching far into the pure night air. Water poured through the opening and smoke plumed and billowed.

He turned his back to it and set his hand down on the cold bed of the truck.

Luke Wallingford asked was he all right. He said he was.

'You've got insurance, don't you?'
'Uh-huh.'
'Thank god for that.'
'You hear anything?'
'About what?'
'About how it got started.'
'Not yet. I guess they'll know in time, though.'
'I guess I already do,' he said.

# *Twenty-one*

She rolled away from him in the starless night and
he reached around her seeking the soft weight of her
breast and cupped it in his hand. Her hair smelled of
smoke from the blaze. She brought her own hand
up to his and held it there.

'I only see you when something disappears,' he
said.

'I know.'

'Tell me the truth. You say you can fight for it.
But they're not going to use this story either, are
they?'

She sighed. 'The truth is, no. Probably not.'

'Nobody died, am I right?'

'That's right. Nobody died.'

He felt his heart trip in his chest like a young wolf
slamming at the bars of its cage.

'So. Was this in the nature of a consolation prize?'

'Jesus, Av. Don't be small. It doesn't suit you.'

'I'm sorry.'

'I know. You were sorry as soon as you said it.
Forgiven.'

She squeezed his hand. The breeze blew over
them from the window.

'I'm damned if I know what to do,' he said. 'I feel like every time I turn around the world shrinks a little.'

She nodded.

'You want to know why I'm working up here, Av?' she said. 'Up here in the boondocks? For eighteen years my dad was a New York City cop. Rode a prowl car through the upper west side. The safest precinct in Manhattan. Other cops used to kid him about what a cushy assignment he had. But nothing's cushy if it's against your nature.

'After eighteen years and two months my dad had a nervous breakdown. Nothing dramatic. I mean, he didn't try to eat his pistol or anything like that. My mother just found him sobbing in the living room late one night and she sat with him watching him staring into the dark and sobbing into his hands until morning. And then he wouldn't go to work again. Said he *couldn't* go to work again. He took a job as a night watchman for the Jamaica Savings Bank instead. Scraping away in order to put me through college.

'But even that seemed to get to him after a year or so. Or maybe it was the city that got to him. Or both, I don't know. He'd never been out of New York in his life. But my senior year they decided to move up here to Standish because my mother had a sister living here. It was the last time he ever saw a uniform. My father went to work as a clerk in a grocery store and my mother got a job as a waitress in a bar. And the summer I graduated my father had a heart attack and died. He was forty-eight. They'd been up here all of eight months. And then he died.

'I think my father became a cop because *his* dad was a cop. I think he drifted into it, not chose it. And it broke him. He was a good man and a kind man but he never knew what he wanted. I think that eventually it killed him.

'I'm not like that. I was suited for this job from the beginning and I'm good at it. Most of the time I know exactly what I want and where I want to be.'

She turned beneath his arm and pale and still she looked at him.

'What about you, Av? What do you want? There must be something.'

He thought at first that she was expecting him to say that it was her he wanted. But he looked at her and saw that it was not that, that her question was more serious than that. He thought that she had seen correctly into his aloneness. He had no answer for her, none that he could say. Except one.

'The truth,' he said.

# Twenty-two

He dreamt of men and wolves.

He saw them first in moonlight in a clearing in the woods, saw them from a distance, not knowing what they were. Only shapes moving close to the ground, prowling back and forth amid the great oaks.

He approached warily. Heard growling and the snapping of teeth. Closer he saw that they were men, yet not men. Shape-shifters dressed in the bloody pelts of wolves and then the wolves themselves, the one bleeding seamlessly into the other and then back again.

He smelled musk, fur that was damp with rain. Blood. Urine.

They moved in a rough circle, in pairs and alone. On four feet and on two. He pressed tight to a tree and watched as the circle widened, as more seemed to join them out of nowhere. Twenty, thirty of them. More. The moon overhead was bright and full. One passed within three feet of him, this one standing upright and unmindful of its path through the trees, knowing its way exactly, staring up at the moon instead. In its eyes he thought he saw a madness linger and then calm.

How one should follow directly from the other he did not know.

He moved closer, drawn to them, curious. Unafraid, yet still keeping to the trees. And then suddenly they were all around him. A dozen of them standing upright. Wolves now, not men, nothing of the man about them, grey-bellied and hugely muscled with claws sharp as the talons of eagles, jaws wide, ears pointed and pale tongues lolling. He saw that like the other they were staring straight up at the moon.

They glanced at him as with one mind.

And then they turned away.

He looked down at his hands and saw that he was one of them.

He looked up to the moon as they had done. In its flat round surface he saw his own unblinking eye.

He woke. He lay in silent stillness on the bed for a very long time, remembering.

# Twenty-three

In the morning he drove to town to see Tom Bridge-water. It was early and the sheriff's office was deserted but for Tom at his coffee machine. He offered Ludlow a cup of coffee and Ludlow declined. They sat down at his desk and he offered him a sugar doughnut and Ludlow declined again. He noticed that Tom didn't take one for himself either.

'I dunno,' Tom said. He shook his head. 'It's hard to figure. Maybe it wasn't them.'

'No? Who then?'

'Damned if I know. Listen, Av, they weren't even in town. We checked. They were out at the house at Cape Elizabeth throwing a big eighteenth birth-day party for their kid The young one, Harold. Couple dozen witnesses and every one of them reliable. Nobody left there all night long.'

'What about Pete?'

'He was up there with them for the party, stayed with them overnight.'

'So they hired somebody.'

'Who did? The boy? Danny? Come on, Av.'

'The father did.'

'Why'd he want to do that? Why'd he want to risk that?'

'I beat his boy.'

'Yeah, Av. I know.'

He looked at Ludlow disapprovingly. Ludlow didn't much care.

'Don't go doing that again, all right?'

'What'd you find at the store, Tom?'

'Gasoline cans. Two of 'em. Somebody torched it, all right. Didn't even try to cover it up.'

'And no prints on the cans, right?'

'Nope.'

'And nobody saw anything.'

'Nobody we've turned up. We were out on this practically all night.'

'So who'd want to do that to me? Other than these people? Name somebody.'

'I don't know. A man makes enemies. Some crazy customer of yours, didn't like your service maybe. Some twisted kid who likes to play with fire.'

'You're stretching. There's no such person and you know it.'

Tom sighed. 'Listen, Av. I'm not trying to stonewall you. You know I wouldn't do that. We've been friends a damn long time. I'll be driving out there personally later this afternoon to have a talk with them. I'd be out now but there's a four-car wreck on 91, goddamn tanker involved, so we're pretty shorthanded here at the moment. All I'm saying is right now we haven't got much to work with. If I could, I'd bring 'em in here one by one and run at them as hard and as long as it takes. But Jackman's already said no to that. No probable cause. So unless one of 'em confesses, gets drunk, says something, does something stupid that I can use, I mean unless one of them slips up somehow . . .'

He spread his hands. Ludlow looked at him a moment and nodded. He got up out of his chair.

'Okay, Tom. You be in touch with me if you get anything, all right?'

'Av, please stay out of this. That's a warning, friend to a friend. For your own good I'm warning you. If you're right about this, which god knows you probably are, then these folks are playing hardball. If you're not, they can sue your butt into the ground.'

'Sure, Tom. I understand.'

'I mean it.'

'What's the book these days?'

'The book?'

'Yeah.'

'Oh. Elmore Leonard. *Hombre*. Great.'

'Yeah. I read that one. You take care, Tom.'

'Remember what I said, Av.'

'I will.'

He left the office, stepping out into the cool morning air.

He drove to Northfield, past the McCormack place, noting that there were lights on inside in the den. He pulled into a driveway up the road and turned around and drove by again more slowly this time. He saw no cars in the driveway nor any activity outside or in. He parked the truck a block down and walked back to the house and up the path to the stairs. The grass was freshly mown again. The smell of it was a pleasure he could not deny himself nor did he try.

He walked up the stairs and used the horseshoe knocker. The young black maid with the withered hand opened the door and looked at him, puzzled, frowning.

'It's Carla, I believe, isn't it?'

She nodded. 'Yes.'

'Do you remember me?'

''Course I do, Mr Ludlow.'

Her voice was soft and deep. Half purr, half growl. Ludlow thought the voice suited her well. He thought she was a very pretty woman, the withered hand be damned. Her face was fine-boned and petite, almond-shaped, with high pronounced cheekbones and wide dark eyes, her skin the color of black coffee and free of any blemish he could see.

'Could I talk to you a moment?' he said.

She looked around him at the street left and right. Her good hand fluttered nervously on the doorknob. The street was quiet.

'Is anybody home?'

'No,' she said.

'Then do you think I could come in a moment? Just a moment.'

'You're gonna get me some trouble, Mr Ludlow.'

'Are they due back any time soon?'

She shook her head. 'Not till tomorrow.'

'Then nobody will ever know. I surely won't tell them. And my truck's parked a block away. I don't think anybody's going to connect it up with my being here.'

She hesitated, looked around again, and then motioned him inside. She shut the door behind him. He smelled a light strawberry-scented perfume. He

144

thought that suited her too. She turned and faced him.

'Do you live here full-time, Carla?'

'Yessir. Small room at the top of the stairs there.'

'You were home last night?'

'Yessir, I was.'

'Anybody else?'

'Just me. Everybody else's up at the farm. For the party. Mr Harold's birthday party.'

'And nobody came back last night? All night long?'

She shook her head. 'No. Nobody.'

It was what he'd expected to hear and what he'd been afraid he'd hear. He guessed she could see that.

'I already talked to the police, y'know,' she said. 'Called me early this morning. They asked me pretty much what you been asking. I'm sorry about your store, Mr Ludlow. I truly am. It's a terrible thing.'

'Thank you.'

He didn't know anything more to ask her. She looked down toward the polished wooden floor, clutching the forearm above her crippled pale white hand with her good hand and then looked back at him again.

'Can I say something to you, Mr Ludlow?'

'Sure. Call me Av, though, will you. Mr father's Mr Ludlow.'

She smiled. She was one of those people who smiled with their entire faces and not just with their mouths. He almost managed to smile back at her. Then she looked serious again.

'It's not my place to say, but I think you should

145

know that this is a home, I mean a family, with a whole lot of bad troubles in it. I think Miss Edith tries her best, but ... well, you know, Mr McCormack's a pretty hard man. And the boys've got their problems too. I wish I knew how deep they run in those boys. I wish I did.'

She shook her head and he could see her honest concern, as though against all reason she might bear some responsibility for this herself, share some complicity, as though over time she had seen and heard what she would not have wished ever to see or hear yet wanted somehow to set it right anyway, against all probability and with almost no real power to do so. He felt suddenly sorry for her. He thought that he was talking to a good young woman here. They were not her problems by a long shot but out of loyalty or character or affection she had taken them on anyway in her fashion.

He wished he could reassure her. But he couldn't.

'Believe me, Carla,' he said, 'in the older boy at least, the problem runs deep. I'm sorry.'

'He did what they say he did, then. Shot your dog.'

'Yes. He did.'

She nodded sadly. 'I wish I could say you were surprising me. You know, I been here going on six years now. I've been tempted to leave, many times. I stay on I guess 'cause I figure Mrs McCormack needs me. I know she sure needs somebody. But I wonder sometimes if it's worth it. Mr McCormack and Daniel, I take a lot from those two. More than I sure need to. Mr Harold too, sometimes. And there's some not so nice folks coming through here now and then. I could get other jobs, other places.'

She held up her withered hand, the fingers like pale thin claws, the wrist mottled brown and white. He saw that she was unashamed of the hand and liked her even more for it.

'This don't hold me back. It's not like having two good hands to work with but it's not like having just one hand either. And you know, I manage fine. My mother taught me that nothing should hold a person back and I believed her. But sometimes I don't know whether to stay or go, go or stay.'

He nodded. 'I can't tell you what to do, Carla.'

'I know. I guess I'll just wait a while, see what happens.'

He turned to leave. 'Thanks, Carla. Thanks for your time, thanks for talking to me.'

At the landing he turned back again just as she was about to shut the door.

'Those not so nice people you mentioned coming through here, you seen any lately?'

She laughed. 'I see 'em *all* the time,' she said. 'I see 'em and I don't see 'em, if you know what I mean. I figure it's better that way, don't you? But not last night, if that's what you mean. And not the last day or so, no. 'Course, I don't hear every phone call everybody made out of this house, either.'

He thanked her again and walked back to the truck and drove to the Daoust place on Cedar Hill Road. He felt like a honey bee buzzing some dark dead garden of flowers. He parked in front this time and got out of the truck and noticed that the mattress and box spring were gone from the side of the house though the rusted washer remained. There was a brand new power-mower in their place, the kind you sit on, and the scruffy grass had been cut and seeded recently. He remembered that the buzzer hadn't worked last time but he tried it anyway. This time it did.

The inner door opened and as before Daoust stood behind the screen, a grey man-shape against the dark interior. As before, he wore a teeshirt and suspenders clamped to dark shapeless slacks, his drab uniform.

'You again,' he said.

'Is Peter around, Mr Daoust?'

'No. He's up the Cape. Why?'

'Went up for the party last night, did he?'

'For the party, yeah. Why?'

'I guess you didn't hear. My store burned down last night. Somebody set fire to it.'

'I hope you're not saying what I think you're saying, Ludlow. Because Pete was up there all night long with the McCormacks and dozens of other people. My boy didn't have anything to do with it. Couldn't have.'

'He stays with them pretty often up there? The boys being such good friends and all?'

Daoust shook his head. 'No. First time.' *Like he was insulted, still carrying a grudge against McCormack money and power.* 'First time they invited him,' he said. 'Special, for the party. Why? So what?'

He was tiring of this surly fat man and his whys. He was also seeing clearly what was going on here. The invitation to Pete was to cover him just as the party'd been conveniently set to cover the rest of them. There was no way of proving it, of course. No way in hell. As Carla'd indicated, all McCormack would need was to make a couple of phone calls. To somebody who was *not* going to be at the party.

'I see you've been making a few home improvements,' he said.

He glanced toward the mower. Daoust looked at him blankly. He pressed the buzzer and heard it go off inside.

The man looked uncomfortable, shifting behind the screen.

'Yeah. Well, it was about time. You know.'

'Sure. I know. Only I was wondering, mower like that doesn't come cheap. And what I'd heard was, you were out of work these days.'

'Oh yeah? Well, you heard damn *wrong*.'

Daoust was angry now, all puffed up with himself and guilty too. The guilt was easy to read. But he wasn't the sort of man to let conscience eat at him for long. Not when there was cash involved. Ludlow would have liked to put his fist right through the screen, right into his face.

'Don't tell me,' he said. 'McCormack put you onto something, gave you a job, didn't he? And maybe a little on the side as well.'

'*Fuck you*, Ludlow,' he said. He slammed the door.

Ludlow went back to his truck. He felt helpless again and angry. He thought that the burnt store didn't matter. The burnt store was just a way to get at him and one that hadn't worked.

What mattered was all the rest of it, what he'd seen in the fire the night before, and finally it was the dog that mattered and how the dog had died. He knew what he needed to do, it was perhaps what some part of him needed to do all along. If it might seem to others to have no reason to it, he saw the reason clear as day.

And what reason had the boy needed. Or his father.

He got into his truck and drove on home.

# Part Three

# RED

# Twenty-four

He walked to the base of the tree with the spade in his hand and the blankets under his arm.

He dropped the blankets and began to dig.

The earth was still soft where he'd turned it. In a short time he came to the body of the dog. He dropped the spade and squatted to clear away the dirt with gloved hands. The smell of the dog was high with a terrible sweetness which stunned the scent of fresh-turned earth.

In decay the dog had shrunken its skin. Grub worms had found the body along the burst stomach and ribcage and he brushed them off the muddy red fur as best he could. His shirt still shrouded the ruined head but even the shirt seemed thinner to him and less substantial. It was as though all that had happened by the river that day had happened to them years ago and this was what was left, a carcass almost strange to him from which the dog inside had long since fled.

He spread the blankets and lifted him from the hole and laid him down. The earth the dog had been lying in inside the hole was wet and black and teemed with insects furiously feeding. He wrapped the dog in the blankets and then picked up the spade and threw earth back into the hole, enough to cover the sight of it which was somehow too much to think of or to look upon. He carried the dog down the hill. His back ached with the effort of digging.

When he came to the truck he saw Emma Siddon's shaggy black mongrel bitch staring at him from across the road like some mournful harbinger or witness. He watched her scent the air. Ludlow wondered what idea she had of what lay beneath the blankets he carried. It was clear she had some notion for at any other time she would have approached him looking for Red or even a scratch behind the ear. But here the scent of death was on them, he thought. Death kept her rooted at a distance. He wondered if the bitch knew whose death and supposed she didn't, yet it was impossible to say what call of blood to blood truly might be heard.

He lay the dog down in the bed of the truck.

The black bitch stood and whined. He thought Emma was feeding her too much these days or else she missed her chases with Red. He wondered who would chase her now. He got into the truck and started the engine and watched her slink away into the tall brown grass by the side of the road and then turn and glance at him with her brow furrowed and liquid eyes and then move further into the grass until she disappeared.

He drove his truck down the mountain.

# Twenty-five

On the highway he passed the Home Depot complex McCormack said he'd built, a three-quarter circle of buildings behind a vast macadam parking-lot with the Depot one quarter of the circle and the rest composed of a K-Mart, an IGA, two restaurants, a dry-cleaner, travel agency, beauty parlor, Pac Mail and fitness club. He felt curiously dated by all of them, even by the enormous parking-lot, as though he were stepped out of some simpler age and seeing all these things for the first time and did not know what to make of them.

Turning off into the quiet tree-lined streets of Cape Elizabeth Town he drove and turned around and drove and turned again until he felt it had become clear to him by style and decor which of the few restaurants there McCormack would be most likely to frequent. He parked the truck in front of it and went inside.

It was not yet lunchtime. He ordered a beer at the bar and paid for it and asked the bartender if the manager was around. The bartender pointed him toward a door in back.

He knocked at the door and a voice said, Come

on in. The manager sat at a cluttered desk in a cluttered room with bulletin boards on two sides filled with posted scraps of paper, a trim middle-aged man with a narrow tanned face and his tie undone. He looked at Ludlow and smiled.

'What can I do for you?' he said.

Ludlow told him he was a friend of the McCormack family and that he'd been on his way to the Cape house coming down from Portland and had almost got to town when he realized that he'd left his directions and Mike's phone number lying on his kitchen sink. But then he remembered Mike saying he ate here at The Captain's Table fairly often. He thought that maybe somebody here might help him.

'Sure,' said the man, 'the McCormacks are good customers' and he gave Ludlow directions. Ludlow shook his hand and thanked him and walked back through the bar and outside to his truck.

A mile out of town, he turned and drove up along a narrow road that led first along a high jagged coastline with the blue-black of the sea to the right of him and houses perched on cliffs above it and then through a forest dense with fir and pine trees and stands of birch and finally through farmland where he could see horses grazing. The paved road gave way to hard-packed dirt as the manager had said it would. He disappeared into forest again.

He crested a hill and the house lay beyond a bend in the road. It was white clapboard, three stories high, with black shutters newly painted. Beyond the weathered wooden fence and mailbox the long wide lawn was neatly kept.

He parked at the gate and waited.

Nobody came out to greet him.

He got out of the truck and walked around back and lifted the dog out of the bed of the truck. Once again the dog's lack of weight surprised him. He thought of his father's diminished weight getting off the porch swing.

He remembered that before Mary died the dog had slept on a throw-rug at the foot of the bed but then after she was gone, he'd come up to sleep on the bed beside him. The dog farted in his sleep but Ludlow didn't mind. Sometimes he'd get to running, chasing cats or rabbits through his dreams, he guessed. Or perhaps running next to Mary or Tim. And that Ludlow did mind because it would wake him and many nights sleep was hard to come by. The dog certainly felt substantial then. He remembered the dog yawning, tossing, his troubled movements on the bed much like Ludlow's own.

He remembered nights holding him, his face pressed into the thick red fur at the back of his neck and that the dog would sometimes turn to lick the salt wash of tears off his face. But then other times he would only lie very still waiting for Ludlow to finish, as though in some secret shared knowledge that finally this was necessary. Even the dog's musky unwashed smell was solace to him.

He walked toward the house.

The wind blew the scent of evergreen through the trees. It bore the smell of death away from him. He carried the dog up the hill not knowing exactly what he would do once he got there but knowing that he needed them to see.

He heard his own footsteps on the wooden steps, an old man's shuffling.

He saw a lace curtain flutter at the window to his

left. He was two steps from the wide grey landing when the door opened behind an ornate scrolled screen door and then that opened too.

He stopped. The woman stood in the doorway. Her long hair was tied back into a bun. She wore jeans and a denim shirt rolled at the sleeves and she was wiping her hands with a hand towel as though she'd been cleaning. He saw the frightened look in her eyes, the same one he'd seen on the stairway that day only it was puzzled now as well.

He saw her glance at his burden and then at him and then at the blankets again. Her eyes widened and skittered side to side as she realized what lay beneath them.

'Oh, my god,' she said.

'I need to speak with your husband, ma'am.'

'Oh, my god.'

Her hand moved to her mouth. He saw she was crying.

'I'm sorry. It's your husband who needs to see this. Not you.'

She shook her head.

'Why are you doing this to us? *I don't understand*.'

'I don't mean any disrespect but I'm afraid you've got that wrong, ma'am. I mean about who's done what to who.'

She stepped toward him urgently and turned her head.

'Do you see this?'

Beneath the stray ringlets of hair that framed her face the bruise on her cheekbone was an ugly blue and yellow.

'I got this last night, Mr Ludlow. We were getting

ready for bed. All I did was *ask* about you. Do you understand me? All I did was mention your name and ask Michael what on earth was going on. This was my answer.'

'He did that to you often?'

'No. Never.'

'Never?'

'Once. A very long time ago. He'd had much too much to drink.'

'A man hits you one time, he'll probably hit you again.'

'*This wouldn't have happened except for you!* Don't you see that? Can't you please just leave us alone?'

'I didn't start this, ma'am. I'm sorry you have to be here seeing this. It's not what I was after. To trouble you.'

She looked at the blankets again. 'My god,' she said. He saw her face turn pale. Her hand went to her mouth. For a moment he thought she was going to be sick. The wind had died down. The smell of the dog was high again, wrapping them in the scent of death.

'Where is he, Mrs McCormack?'

'Right here,' McCormack said.

They stepped through the doorway behind her, McCormack first and then his two sons. He could see Pete Daoust in the shadows behind them. Danny held a pistol in his hand. From the look of it a .38 revolver.

His father had a pistol too, only McCormack's was a .44 magnum. Ludlow had fired one once. It could take down a bear.

This was a family, he thought, that liked its guns.

'You're a goddamn lunatic,' McCormack said. 'Coming here.'

'Maybe.'

'My friend, there aren't any maybes about it.'

'Sometimes the only way to know a thing is to know it first hand, Mr McCormack. See it. Taste it. Smell it. *Then* you know it. Somebody burned my store down last night. A few nights back somebody put a rock through my window. But I'm not here about any of that. I'm here about this.'

He set the body down gently on the porch in front of them and unfolded the blankets.

'It still all comes down to this,' he said.

'Jesus H. Christ.'

He pulled the shirt free of what remained of the dog's head. The shirt tore, it's fibres thinned. Maggots squirmed in the sudden light.

'Get that goddamn thing out of here. *Now*, Ludlow.'

'Sure I will, in a minute. When you tell me what you're going to do about it.'

'I'm not going to do shit about it. You're trespassing.'

'I know that.'

'Then you also know I could damn well shoot you.'

'I know that too.'

He saw Danny step around his father in two long strides and then he was down the steps to Ludlow and the gun was pressed to Ludlow's ear.

'You old stupid fuck,' he said. 'You don't fucking *listen*.'

He reached for the boy's forearm and had it in
both his hands and heard McCormack yell, *No, goddammit Danny!* when the gun roared against him
and he felt a sudden wet shock where his ear had
been, the gun still pressed there so that he could
smell the powder and feel the cold wet bloody barrel
against his cheek as he fell back down the steps,
falling away from a vision of man and boys and
woman all open-mouthed leaning toward him down
from the porch. His hands still gripped the forearm
so that he took the boy with him, tumbling down on
top of him, head to chest onto the lawn.

He wrenched at the arm and slammed it against
the first wooden step and heard the boy scream dim
and far away beneath a torrent of black sound.

The gun dropped to the grass. Ludlow rolled the
boy over and reached for the gun and lay there
pressing it hard against the boy's head, his other
arm wrapped around his neck and squeezing. The
boy tried to twist away and then felt the gun at his
head and went still.

His back was out again and it was bad this time.
He could feel the pain shoot down all through his
leg. Blood from his ear was dripping into Danny's
face, onto his cheek and into his open mouth as he
gasped for breath, the taste of blood making him
sputter up a fine spray of red.

'You got more damn mistakes in you than any kid
I ever knew,' he said.

He cocked the trigger.

'You're going to shoot a man, you kill him. Or
he's going to think hard about killing you.'

McCormack was shouting something. He couldn't

make it out for the ringing in his head.

He looked up and saw the .44 magnum pointed at him.

'Put it down,' he said. 'You can't shoot me without me shooting the boy. That simple.'

He saw the woman mouth the word *Please*, whether to him or to her husband he didn't know, her face gone suddenly old and drawn. McCormack glared at him for a moment, then lowered the gun to his side. Ludlow watched him a second or two, getting his breath and then turned to Danny.

'Here's what we're going to do. We're going to get up, Daniel. Together, real slowly. Knees first and then the rest of the way.'

The boy did as he was told. Ludlow's back hurt so bad it almost doubled him over. He didn't let it. He felt blood running down his neck and wondered if there was anything left of the ear at all.

'Ma'am?' he said. 'Would you throw me that hand towel you're holding there?'

She was gripping it in her hand, her knuckles angry red. She stepped forward, shaking. Her face was white. She handed him the towel and Ludlow nodded and pressed it to his ear.

The gun never left Danny's temple. He told the woman, Thank you.

'I'm taking him into town,' he said. 'Trespass is one thing and I guess I'm guilty there but weapons assault's another. I never knew anybody to shoot a suspected intruder in the ear at point-blank range in broad daylight. I don't think the police have either. I think they'll want to talk with Danny. We might even make the papers this time, Mr McCormack. You never know.'

McCormack shouted something, his mouth an angry snarl.

'I can't hear you,' Ludlow said. 'Sorry.'

He put the gun to Danny's ribs and started walking him down the hill, then told him to stop and turned and looked at the woman, McCormack's wife, standing frozen in front of the porch.

'I'd appreciate it very much if you'd cover up my dog for me again, ma'am,' he said. 'I'll be back for him.'

# Twenty-six

'You drive,' he said. He handed Danny the keys.

He held the gun on him while Danny got behind the wheel and then walked to the passenger side. He groaned getting in and saw the boy turn and look at him. The boy was hoping.

'Go on,' he said.

The boy put the keys in the ignition and started it.

'Go easy. It's a damn bumpy road.'

'Something wrong?'

'Yeah, something.'

'You wouldn't fire that thing.'

'Were you expecting me up here today?'

'No.'

'Than how do you know what I'd do?'

'You're crazy, old man.'

The boys voice was coming from very far away through a high steady whine of sound.

'Maybe,' he said. 'But in that case you'd better do as I tell you, hadn't you?'

The boy put the truck in gear and they started down the road. Ludlow turned the blood-soaked towel to its clean side and pressed it to his ear and then removed it and looked at it. It came away bloody but less so than he'd expected. He guessed the bleeding was slowing down. He turned the rear-view mirror toward him so he could see.

The whole upper portion of the auricle was gone as though somebody had spooned it away with a jagged spoon. He saw shattered cartilage poking through bloody shreds of skin. There was a glistening line about an inch in length and a quarter-inch wide along the side of his head just behind the ear where the hair was gone. It was seeping blood. A slightly different angle and he'd have been a dead man. He turned away the mirror and pressed the towel to the wound again.

'Would it help if I said I was sorry about the dog?'

'It might have once. Some. If I thought you meant it. Which right now, I don't. Your brother already told me, did you know that? No. I bet you didn't. But I think you're pretty damn late with your apology. I think we're way beyond that now.'

'Mister . . .'

'Just drive,' he said.

Where the forest ended, the paved road began and they drove that through the wide green rolling farmland. Ludlow noted that Danny wasn't pushing the truck to more than thirty even out here on the straightaways, trying to prolong this he supposed, trying to think of something to say or something to do that would change Ludlow's mind about taking him in. Well, thirty miles an hour was fine with him. His back had eased up but it was still hurting bad and the headache from the bullet throbbed like the steady rythmic blows of a hammer. The slower they went, the better.

It was only when they passed into forest land again that he realized the error in his thinking.

Suddenly the truck was jolted from behind. He glanced over and saw that Danny was braced for it, knew then that he'd been watching them coming up behind them through the rear-view mirror. Ludlow slapped his right hand against the dash. His shoulder hit the door. He saw Danny glance at the gun.

*No way, boy,* he thought. He held it steady.

He turned and saw McCormack behind the wheel of the big black Lincoln, a boy silouetted in the passenger seat beside him who Ludlow thought would probably be Pete because of his size, and another passenger in back. He guessed that would be Harold. He wondered if Harold had volunteered for this duty.

The car shot forward and rammed again. This time he was braced and ready. The truck veered up the hill but held the road.

He saw Danny take his foot off the accelerator.

'No,' he said. 'You keep going.'

The boy frowned but did as he said.

*They were going to run them into a goddamn tree. McCormack's own son was driving.*

And McCormack said that *he* was crazy.

He tried to think. The headache pounded interference.

He could tell the boy to stop, get out of the truck and confront them. But that was most likely what they wanted him to do. McCormack had the .44 magnum and he'd bragged about his shooting. While Ludlow hadn't shot in years, hadn't shot seriously since the war and hardly ever with a handgun. He could use the boy to bargain with again as before but the boy was right, even if he didn't know it. Ludlow had no intention of killing him. Or anybody else for that matter. Which ruled out firing out the goddamn window. McCormack might have guessed that about him by now. That he didn't want any killing. Maybe that was why he was out here.

Banking on that.

No. It was better to keep driving, to take the chance that McCormack wouldn't come at them hard enough to risk his own son's life in a collision. Once they were out of the forest they were on the open coast road after that. There were homes and people living in the homes. Witnesses. Beyond there, the highway and town.

They had only to get out of here. Another two miles, maybe.

The Lincoln hit them again, harder this time.

The truck swerved onto the narrow shoulder, skidded and then righted itself back onto the road.

'Jesus! Can't we stop this thing? You're gonna get us killed!'

'Just go on. Just the way you been going. No faster.'

'He's not going to stop, I'm telling you.'

'He'd better stop.'

'I know him. He won't.'

'Maybe you know him and maybe you don't.'

'I'm fucking telling you! We got to stop this truck!'

'You forget. *I don't listen*. This gun says you keep on driving.'

The boy was sweating, fists clenched tight at the wheel.

168

He felt a moment's doubt. Ludlow knew the boy was a liar and a damn good liar at that. But what he didn't know, what he *couldn't* know was just *how* good. Whether what he said about his father was true or wasn't true.

And then he had his answer.

He turned and saw that the Lincoln had fallen six or seven yards behind them.

Suddenly, horribly, he saw it surge.

When it hit, the Lincoln was probably doing seventy. It took the bed of the truck on the passenger side and Ludlow heard breaking glass and the screech of metal on metal and Danny screaming something beside him. For a moment they were weightless, frozen together in time. Passengers in a sudden void. And then they were down over an embankment pounding through scrub and rocks and fallen logs headed for the pine trees and birch trees dense ahead of them and he saw the windshield go on his side, webbed and shattered by some fatal heavy limb hanging across their path and felt a fine dust of glass fall across his face and hands as the truck lurched sideways and tumbled, rolled once and then righted itself and rolled again, so that he was on the roof and then on the seat and then on the roof again with the passenger door flung open, though he had no idea when that had happened.

He felt Danny slam into him as something jarred them to a sudden stop. And the last thing he thought was errant nonsense.

*Get behind the razor*, he thought. *Get behind the razor.*

# Twenty-seven

At first he couldn't see, he could only hear.

Rough voices, anger in them. Anxiety and maybe fear. For a moment the sounds themselves made no sense to him, only gradually resolving themselves into words and language though for some reason the emotions they expressed were clear to him from the moment he awoke. It was as though for a moment on awakening he were listening to a foreign tongue or as though he were an animal with no language at all yet with senses necessarily alert to all the nuances of human feeling.

'Well, find the fucking goddamn thing, will you?'

*McCormack's voice.* He thought that a man should not be using such words around his boys.

'We're looking, dad!'

*Harold's voice. Shaky, scared.* Close by. Somewhere to the left of him. He could hear the boy's feet dragging through heavy leaves, scuffling over the surface of a rock. Then in the leaves again further on.

He was lying on a bed of pine needles. He could smell them, feel them pricking at the back of his hands. The thick root of a tree lay directly beneath his head. Whether he'd been thrown here from the truck or been dragged here he couldn't say.

'Try over that way. Did you double-check the truck?'

A sigh. 'Jesus. Yes, dad.'

*Danny this time*. Sullen-sounding. Like his father was just one great big annoyance to him. So that Danny was alive. Danny was well. He could hear his shoes in the pine needles just beside him.

There was no justice anywhere.

'I want that goddamn gun. You find it.'

Slowly his vision cleared. It would not be wise, he thought, to let them know he was awake. He lay motionless and kept his eyes slitted nearly shut so that he was able to see them only darkly. He would've liked to have moved around some to see if anything was broken. But he didn't dare. He could hear them shuffling back and forth, searching the ground.

*For what?* For the gun, the .38, the one he had in the truck with him. He could not remember letting go of it. He risked moving his fingers. It wasn't there. Of course it wasn't.

'Look, dad. If *we* can't find it, what makes you think *they* will?'

*Danny again*. Impatient. He wants to get out of here, Ludlow thought.

'They're cops, you fool.'

'*Town* cops. I mean, we're not talking FBI here, y'know? This is just gonna be an accident to them, that's all. I mean, these guys are not a bunch of geniuses. They're gonna write it off as an accident, for god sakes.'

Not as confident as he was trying to sound. A dim grey shadow standing above him a few feet away, waving his arms at his father. This time Ludlow could hear the nervousness in his voice, the brittle tension. So the crash had shaken him at least. It wasn't much but it was something. He guessed the boy was just like anybody else to that extent. He could fear his own death in a truck plunging headlong into trees. He could fear the law.

The knowledge didn't help him much. Not right now.

'I gotta agree with your dad, Dan.'

*Pete Daoust.* The farthest away from him, somewhere out of his field of vision. This boy definitely scared, his voice on the edge of breaking.

'The gun's *evidence*, man,' he said. 'The gun *belongs* to you guys. So if they find it, what's it doing out here? Jesus! We *gotta* find it.'

'We don't *gotta* do anything, shit-for-brains. Like I said, we don't find it, they won't find it.'

'Hey. You two. Shut up. Just find the fucking gun.'

*McCormack again.* He saw the man pass by him walking left to right. The .44 magnum glinting in the light through the trees. A moment later Pete Daoust walked by. There was a rifle or a shotgun in his hands. Ludlow couldn't tell which without further opening his eyes. He didn't want to do that. He guessed it didn't matter much one way or another.

For a long while the searched in silence.

He heard only footfalls and birds above and beyond him and the wind rustling the pines and scrub.

'Jesus. Damn,' Pete whispered.

The silence lengthened.

A while later McCormack sighed.

'All right. I don't think it's a good idea for us to be out here too damn long. Not with the Lincoln sitting up there. I guess it got thrown way clear of us when his door opened up. So we'll just have to hope for the fucking best. I don't like it much but we can't stay out here the rest of the day looking.'

He sighed again and then stood silent as though considering something.

'Pete, Harold, get some branches, scuffle up the leaves. Nobody was anywhere around here, right? Danny? Here. Do like we said, son.'

In Ludlow's peripheral vision he saw something long and dark pass from hand to hand between them.

'Dad . . .'

*Harold's voice. Pleading* with him.

And it wasn't just the pleading, there was something in McCormack's voice just then that warned him, a tiredness and a grim resignation and he opened his eyes and started to roll. He saw Danny standing over him and saw the heavy broken limb of the tree come down across his head exactly where the ear had been, understanding in just that too-late instant what they were thinking, that they were covering the bullet-wound with something infinitely worse. He felt a sudden jolt throughout every nerve in his body and he thought, oh my god, so this is what it's like, this is what Red must have felt suddenly and forever and then he was falling into blackness again so deep it seemed to burn his eyes.

# Twenty-eight

When he woke the second time it was dusk. Nearly night.

He woke utterly lost to himself.

He did not know who or even exactly what he was. He might have been some spirit of the woods, newborn of earth and pine needles on the first day of creation. Not flesh at all. He might have been anything.

He tried to sit up but he couldn't. The trees were moving overhead as though he lay in the center of a huge vernal carousel set absurdly in the forest by some fool maker's hand.

He moved like an infant unsure of his limbs. First one foot and then the other, one hand and then the other. Then his arms and legs. He blinked to slow the whirling. He blinked again.

When he judged it might be possible, he tried to sit up a second time and this time he could. Pain raced through him, immense and angry, and then just as suddenly disappeared, a phantom pain hiding somewhere inside a phantom numbness. He put his hand to the back of his head and felt a strange damp softness there. The back of his head transformed to spongy moss. The hand came away a sticky brown, red and black to which dead pine needles clung.

He wondered how he'd got here.

He saw the truck in the shadows a few feet away, lying upside down and wrapped around the trunk of a tree like a finger curled tightly around a pencil.

The truck was familiar to him.

He tried to stand. He could get to his knees but no further so he crawled to the tree that was nearest him and, with his arms around the trunk, he hauled himself slowly up. Until the shaking in his legs grew tolerable he was content to embrace the tree like a lover, with his cheek pressed softly to its rough fragrant flesh, breathing deeply of the scent of it and then after a while he let go and tried to walk.

His goal was the truck. The truck was very familiar.

It might even have belonged to him.

He kept close to the trees and stumbled once and caught himself on a limb and held himself up. Pain darted through him and then vanished. The forest swam.

When he reached the truck he bent down and peered through the driver's side window. He looked at the debris scattered on the ceiling. A crushed paper cut. A torn map half open. An empty soda can. A window-scraper. Gum-wrappers. The contents of an ashtray dusting all the rest with a fine grey powder that mingled with bright shards and pebbles of broken glass. He did know what he was looking for here or what these things should mean to him, so he turned away.

It was getting dark. He knew he should not be out here in the dark.

In the dark he would lose his way.

He thought that he should try to climb the hill. He wasn't sure why. It was enough to feel he ought to.

He followed the path of broken undergrowth, stopping often to cling to what few saplings the truck had left standing, seeming to remember the truck's dark passage, catching his breath and regaining his balance and then moving on. Halfway up the hill he felt a queer sensation, a tingling up his backbone which his mother used to say was somebody walking over his grave, or perhaps it was his father.

His father was alive in a nursing home. His father's name was Avery Allan Ludlow, Sr.

He looked down at his feet and saw the gun lying in the leaves in front of him.

It was as though the gun had called to him.

Like him, the gun did not belong there. He thought it would be wrong to leave it lying there.

He stooped carefully and picked it up, dusted off leaves and dirt and with difficulty put it in his pocket. Standing up the pain lanced through him again like a bolt of lightning and then was gone.

It was dark when he crested the hill. Moonlight bleached the trees beside him. Behind him, the way he'd come, the forest was black and dense. He stared at the road and wondered which way to go.

He thought that there was something he was supposed to do.

He sat down to think with his back to a birch tree. The gun stretched the leg of his trousers. Inexplicably he had begun to cry.

After a while he looked up from his lap and saw a pair of eyes glinting low at the edge of the scrub directly across the road. The eyes moved back and forth, up and down the road and then settled on him and stared.

A moment later he saw them move tentatively forward.

Then more aggressively, moving through the startled brush.

The dog who stepped out onto the shoulder had gone a long time without proper feeding. He could see its ribs through the thin white fur, could see its skinny haunches. A farm dog probably, a mutt with a lot of beagle in him, neither young nor old yet nearly feral now, the kind of dog who was left outside to scrounge for itself in every kind of weather. Closer now he saw it was a male. The eyes were large and did not seem hostile but only curious about him sitting there alone.

'C'mere,' he whispered.

He sounded strange, his voice a hoarse gurgle he barely recognized. He tasted blood in his mouth and licked his dry cracked lips.

He held out his hand.

The dog's nose twitched, scenting him. The dog's head held low.

'I won't hurt you.'

The dog raised his head and looked at him and barked. The voice was high and clear and echoed in the still night. He barked once more and then fell silent. For a moment the dog continued staring, resigned and empty of hope for this encounter as perhaps for most encounters with the human animal and then turned and walked slowly back into the scrub. He saw the brush move as the dog passed through and then could only hear it move and then finally the dog was gone.

He sat listening to the silence, listening to scraps of memory inside him like pages fluttering in a wind.

When he stood up again he had found his direction.

He stepped out on the road and headed up the mountain.

# Twenty-Nine

The sky was filled with stars. A half moon bright above. A Janus moon, he thought. *A half moon was a Janus moon.*

Janus, the god of doors and gates.

Had a month named after him.

January.

*January, February, June or July.*

*Shine on, shine on harvest moon.*

*Up inna da sky.*

Strange what he was remembering.

In the war one summer night under just such a sky, he'd shot a North Korean sniper out of a tree. Or else Phil DeAngelo had, they never knew which. They were sharing guard duty that night and both had fired on him at once.

In the morning they went out to look for him.

They were puzzled at first at what they found. Apparently the bullet had hit the rifle, not the man. The rifle had fallen from his hands and then the man had fallen after. He fell upon his weapon, which was pointing upwards. The barrel broke away from the stock and pierced his right calf muscle and his left thigh, impaling the man like a bug on a collector's setting-board. The fall had broken his neck and immobilized him. Yet this would not have been fatal to the man except for the fact that the barrel had pierced the femoral artery of his thigh. His blood had drained out of him through the broken barrel like rainwater through a drainpipe and by morning he was long dead.

*Their first year in the house they had to put pots and pans out all along the floor to catch the rain. Then he'd fixed the roof.*

The blood beneath the North Korean sniper was a black sticky pool crusted over by the heat and swarming with bloated flies.

*Sticky. Like his mossy head.*

He touched it.

*Allie's head and Billy's.* Both of theirs had popped out fine. But Tim's was looking like a breech-birth and Doc Jaffe had to get his hand in there, into Mary's insides and turn him around inside her.

They'd almost lost him.

He'd been present at all three births and at Tim's he almost fainted.

*The summer heat in Korea. You could almost faint. You couldn't breathe.*

And then they *had* lost him.

His own breathing was a thin rasping sound, the only sound out here except for the scrape of wind through the trees and brush and the sound of crickets everywhere and frogs somewhere down below over the embankment, in a stream probably, and his scuffling feet moving in short awkward steps along the tarmac.

He saw the headlights from a car coming up

behind him, saw them dim in the distance and then watched them grow steadily brighter, yet he didn't turn but merely moved on and when the lights swept over him and disappeared over the hill like the wings of a great white bird passing, all its passing meant to him was not a lost opportunity for rescue or aid but that, in the glare of headlights, he had seen ahead to the edge of the forest where the road began cutting through farmland.

He was closer.

He was aware that the angle of his walk was wrong.

He kept veering off to the left and had to correct to the right every six steps or so. He thought of the four steps up to the porch of his father's nursing home which were so hard for his father to climb. He needed a hand getting up and down these days. He wondered if his father was happy or if he should feel guilty for putting him there even though it was what his father had asked for. I won't be a burden to you or Mary, he said. Bad enough I'm a goddamn burden to myself.

*Mary'd cried the day they left him there. Red was standing in the bed of the truck. But then she'd wanted him in the cab with her so they drove home that way with her arm resting on the dog's back and the dog's head sticking out the window, squinting at the wind in his face, the wind ruffling his hair.*

He was walking beside a wooden fence now, white birch trees on the side of the road opposite and low rolling pastureland on his side just beyond the fence, all of it grey and lovely in the moonlight like a pastoral black-and-white photograph taken in another age and a simpler one.

He walked. The pain came and went. He didn't mind. The pain reminded him that, remarkably, he was still alive.

He saw shapes in the field ahead.

Horses grazing. Six of them.

He wondered why they had not been put up for the night and thought that perhaps the horses were wondering too. He stopped and leaned heavily on the fence and decided to catch his breath there. He watched them step forward now and then and lower their heads to crop the grass beneath them. He could hear the sounds their teeth made plucking the grass reluctant to be parted from the earth and then their chewing. He could not make out their color in the moonlight, whether black or brown, though one horse was a spotted paint. He heard them snort in satisfaction as they ate.

*When he was a boy of six or seven his Uncle John Fry owned a dairy farm with a couple of horses in the barn and Ludlow had never ridden. Fry decided it was high time that he did. He saddled the big brown mare and hoisted him up onto the saddle. Ludlow complained that his feet didn't reach the stirrups but Fry said,* Doesn't matter, you're only going for a little ride is all.

*Fry was a big man given to pranks that were often cruel pranks and this one on this day was certainly in character.*

*Ludlow could remember his own surprising pleasure at finding himself sitting astride the horse, the sheer enormous size of the animal and the musky scent of her as he patted her and stroked the coarse* short hair of her neck and then brought his hand to his nose to smell it, the feeling of hugely muscled power beneath him that seemed to him a wholly benevolent power and almost instantly his own, a newly discovered part of him. He could remember staring out from her back across the yard to the fields beyond, hoping they would head for that, that his uncle would lead the mare into the field and then just let him ride.

Instead he swatted her rump with his big calloused dairy farmer's hand and shouted.

The mare bolted forward. Ludlow flew off her and landed in back of her in the dust while his uncle roared with laughter. Ludlow's mother came out of the house and called his uncle a damn dumb son-of-a-bitch farmer and they hadn't talked for months thereafter.

Ludlow had never blamed the horse, only the man. When he grew older he'd ridden her again and again.

He plucked some grass beneath him and held out his hand.

The paint horse was watching him. She hesitated a moment and then walked over.

The long prehensile lips took the grass. The horse allowed him to touch her forelock and cheek and the cool wet fleshy nose. She bowed her head and let him cup the nose in the palm of his hand, her nostrils opening and closing, a rich bass murmur of warm breath.

Then she raised her head and shook it, her mane suddenly like dark sparks flying, her eyes gone wide. Wild, staring.

She backed away. She turned and joined the rest but continued to watch him carefully and did not continue grazing.

She smells it, he thought.

Of course she does. Something hurt or dying.

*Is that me?*

A man, *but not entirely a man.* Something fled from him now.

He thought of the dog by the side of the road and felt as though the natural world were alert to him. As though his shed blood had made him more akin to them and that both dog and horse were somehow aware of that. His vulnerability to the rough hand of man now very much like their own.

He pushed away from the fence.

He walked.

When at last he came to the dirt road and forest again the moon had disappeared behind a heavy bank of clouds. The stars as well were mostly hidden. He moved to what he felt must be the center of the road so as not to tumble off into a ditch but he could never be sure that it was in fact the center of the road or even near the center. He walked with arms outstretched ahead of him, unsure of what he might encounter in such a darkness.

*Once when he was a boy of twelve he and a friend had discovered a cave along a cliff face which overlooked the sea. They had climbed to the cave and gone inside it while the breakers crashed below. The sunlight illuminated the interior and they saw that it had been used by animals and men. There were bones of birds and larger animals gnawed and strewn all along the floor. There were empty clam shells and the* remains of crabs. On the ceiling they could see where smoke from countless fires had stained the rock face black.

Finally they saw that another cave led off this one to their right.

They had no flashlights. They wore bathing suits and towels draped across their necks. They stood at the entrance to the second cave and tried to peer inside, into a chamber which had never seen the light of day since a shifting earth first had coughed it up. They lifted their arms to the blackness and their arms disappeared entirely. Try as they might it was impossible to see their hands. They could see neither floor nor ceiling of the cave nor the walls on either side.

Only a darkness so profound it stunned the eye.

Ludlow feared the place as he had feared no other place in his life. It seemed to him that the darkness itself was a warning not to enter, that the darkness hid the secret soul of something which perhaps partook more of gods or spirits than of men. All the same he took a step inside. A dare to himself, a gauntlet thrown down to gods and spirits alike. He remembered feeling with his naked foot for the floor beneath him, almost surprised to find it there and not some yawning void. He felt for and then took a second step inside. And to his friend's eyes, disappeared as instantly and completely as though he'd vanished.

He stood still a moment hoping his eyes would adjust.

They didn't.

The cave was silent.

He took a third step and heard something shift in the darkness along what must have been the far wall *perhaps twenty feet away, something he instinctively felt was big, bigger than big, and he felt fear race over him like a cloud of spiders dropped suddenly over his nearly naked body, crawling and biting him, and he yelled and turned and leaped for the outer cave and saw that his friend was already halfway out the entrance ahead of him. And then he was out there too, racing down the steep cliff face as though the claws of demons were at their ankles and reaching out for them.*

*Later when he thought about it and talked about it with his friend he decided that it must have been a man inside.*

*Just a man.*

*Not wolf nor bear nor even some feral dog because they probably would have smelled any such wild animal before they heard it and there was no such smell inside. He tried to reconstruct the sound he'd heard and thought that it was the sound of clothing moving over stone.*

*He thought that probably it was just a man. That he probably wasn't in that much danger.*

*But only* probably. *Because then he thought how the man must have stood there, silent, watching them, able to see them clearly in front of him at the entrance to the cave all the while that they were blind to him. Stood silent for quite some time, his own eyes accustomed to the dark and watching. He thought of what kind of a man might want to do that and then of the bones on the floor and the smell of fire and he thought that he might have been wrong about the danger to them.*

*He'd never felt that kind of fear again. Not even in Korea under ferocious assault, among the dead and* those who were soon to be dead. It was as though he'd seen and recognized his mortality early on when he was just a boy, pressed his frail flesh tight to the great and lethal unexpected, as though he'd seen the face of death in the cave that day.

Death was the inhabited dark.

Compared to then he walked in sunlight now. Under a moon hidden by clouds.

At least he could see his hands.

The moon was a Janus moon, hidden behind the clouds.

Janus. The god of doors and gates.

Through these we pass.

He saw what in reality he had never seen but only darkly and painfully imagined, Mary at the door of their house, rushing out through the doorway, flames about her like shimmering blue-yellow waves in which she was drowning, saw her roll across the dewy grass and smelled the smoke and the smell of her flesh burning, saw her rise again and hurl herself back through the door one final time in futile hope, in instinct, in love and agony, reaching out for her young.

It wasn't fair, Mary, he thought. God it wasn't fair.

He walked on.

The night had grown cooler. He could feel the breeze along his face.

Pain slid through him like the blade of a knife through soft butter.

After a time the moon appeared again.

He realized that he had no sense of time. The clouds might have hidden the moon for minutes or for hours. He didn't know.

He felt the weight of the gun shift in his pocket

and he reached down and felt its shape outside his pants. He remembered how the gun had come to be there. The gun had seemed to call to him from the forest floor. He'd stooped and picked it up.

He saw the house in the distance, pale stark white atop the hill. It looked like a church set on the hill the way it was, a church without a steeple but he knew it was not a church but a place which had almost brought death to him and to which he had brought death himself, carried in his arms.

*The inhabited dark.*

He approached at the same dogged pace.

His feet scuffled across the hard-packed earth. He listened to the sounds he made in the world and knew what he'd come to do.

# Thirty

He saw the boy sitting alone on the porch steps in the dark. The boy was smoking a cigarette and, when he pulled on it, Ludlow could see his face in its glow and thought for a heart-stopped moment that it was his son Tim he was looking at. Tim all grown up now. But it was only Harold, the boy who said he was sorry and lied to his brother about the flies.

The boy saw him and stood abruptly on the path and crushed the cigarette out beneath his foot. He looked around, scared-looking, watching Ludlow as he approached and then looking around again. Then he seemed to make some kind of decision and stepped out to meet him.

'My god,' he whispered. 'What the hell are you *doing* here?'

'I came back for my dog,' he said.

'You *what*?'

'I came for my dog.'

'Oh jesus.'

'I left him here. Up on the porch.'

'They'll kill you for sure if they find you. Christ, they thought they already *did* kill you!'

'I only want the dog. That's all. I asked your

191

mother if she'd cover him up for me.'

'For chrissakes, mister, he's not *on* the porch anymore.'

'No?'

'Why the hell would they leave him on the porch?'

'Why wouldn't they?'

'They threw him around back. Into the woods.'

'They did?'

He felt the hot tight anger in his chest. They'd thrown the dog into the woods. Animals would get to him. Gnaw his bones. They couldn't care less.

He felt a wave of dizziness.

'*It's evidence*, for god's sake. You understand? The dog's evidence of what they did to you. For god's sake we had *cops* up here before, Mr Bridgewater and another guy, asking questions about last night. The dog shows that *you were here too*. Mister Ludlow, please, you got to leave. Right now.'

The boy kept fidgeting, looking back over his shoulder at the screen door. At the windows.

'Take me there.'

'Look at you. You're hurt bad. You don't know what . . .'

'Take me back where they threw him.'

'Oh jesus. Oh god.'

He reached out and gripped the boy's arm and looked him in the eye.

'Don't you worry about god. Just take me there.'

The boy gave him a defeated look.

'You'll go? You'll get out of here if I do?'

'That's right.'

He glanced at the door again behind him and then back at Ludlow.

'You'll get me killed for this.'

Ludlow waited.

'All right. But real *quiet*, okay? Please?'

'Sure. Real quiet.'

Still the boy hesitated. Ludlow released his arm and stared at him.

'Jesus. All right. Come on.'

They walked back across the long broad lawn in the moonlight. Where the grass ended a narrow dirt trail began, cutting between two young stands of beech and maple before leading into the woods.

'Hope I remember where it is,' said the boy.

'You'll remember.'

The trail cut north into thicker forest. Here the light was dimmer. They moved more slowly. Ludlow smelled pine, damp fallen hardwood leaves and raw cooling earth. It would not be a bad place for Red to lie, he thought, were it not for the McCormacks, the ones who'd put him there.

He remembered in bright static flashes, one fast upon the other.

*The truck going over, tumbling, tumbling.*

*The log in Danny's hands coming down on him as he opened his eyes.*

*The shotgun by the river, the dog's head suddenly gone.*

*Carrie Donnel climbing naked out of bed.*

The living and the dead.

*'Harold!'*

It was McCormack, calling from the porch.

Harold froze in front of him.

*'Hey, Harold!* Where the hell are you at, boy?'

'Go on,' Ludlow whispered. 'Keep going.'

'We can't—'

'Yes, you can. Just be quiet about it.'

They made a turn between two tall pines. The path narrowed. Briars clutched at Ludlow's pant legs. A few moments later it opened up into a small clearing bright beneath stars and moon and overgrown with tall still meadowgrass and then it narrowed down into woods again. They went a few yards. Then Harold stopped.

'It's right around here someplace.'

'Where?'

'I don't know, right around here somewhere, off left here. Damn it! I wish to god we had a flashlight.'

'*Okay. Sure. You got one,*' McCormack said.

He heard a click. The light spilled out over and behind them and they turned. The light was on Harold's face first and he could make out the dark shapes of the two boys flanking the man. Then it went to his own face.

'Good flying jesus,' McCormack said.

Ludlow squinted into the beam.

'I said to myself, no way. Can't happen. The guy's dead. But here you are. Here you goddamn well are. You don't stay down, do you old man? You're fucking unbelievable. What the hell are you doing here?'

'I came back for my dog.'

'For what? For the dog?'

'Yes.'

He laughed. 'You want your dog?'

'That's right.'

The light moved off him and into the brush a few feet behind him. Then it settled. Ludlow's eyes stayed with McCormack. He saw the .44 in his right hand and saw that Danny held a rifle. Pete Daoust seemed to have no weapon. He thought about the .38 in his own pocket and wondered did it show, was there any way for them to know he had it there?

He saw Pete Daoust shift uneasily behind him and wondered if he wished he had a gun on him too. Or maybe not. Or maybe he had one tucked away somewhere like he did.

'There's your goddamn dog,' McCormack said.

Ludlow turned and looked where the beam of light was pointing. The dog's body was lying on a flat rock beside a beech tree. The blankets were wrapped over him again. He guessed that would be the woman's doing. That she'd done as he'd asked her to do.

'Tomorrow we were going to bury the damn thing. I guess now we got to do the same for you. You know, you make a whole lot of trouble, old man. You want the dog? Well, he's gonna be all yours. For all fucking eternity. You stupid son of a bitch.'

'Dad—'

The beam of light moved onto Harold again.

'Jesus, Harold, get the hell over here, you damn fool. What the hell is wrong with you, anyhow? Why didn't you just call me, the old man shows up here?'

Harold shifted uneasily behind him but didn't do as McCormack told him to. He stayed where he was. Ludlow wondered why. He thought the boy had a lot of nerve standing up to McCormack even this much.

'Dad, come on, isn't this *enough*? Can't we just quit it here? Look. We can explain that he came here and that then he came *back* here and we—'

'And we *what? Run him off the road and then tried to cave his head in*? You got no more sense than he does.'

'Dad's right,' Danny said. 'Enough with this old fuck. It ends right here, right now.'

In the moment the light shifted off Harold toward Ludlow he went to his knees and turned to the side to make a smaller target and dug in his pocket for the gun. The beam went over his head and then found him and Ludlow fired twice rapidly into the light. His second shot shattered the flashlight as something pounded into his side and spun him down rolling and suddenly there were shots coming from everywhere, McCormack's .44 roaring and rifle fire and Ludlow shooting again nearly blind into the sudden dark at the dim moving figures and bright flashes of muzzle-fire and he fired a fourth time and saw somebody fall screaming to his knees while he rolled again and came up against something soft and moving and wet, smelling of blood.

*Harold's chest, shot open, bleeding hard, heaving against his cheek.*

There was silence. And moaning in the silence. He heard Harold sob beside him.

He smelled cordite rich and thick in the still air.

He looked around.

No one standing. Not one of them.

It took a few moments for his eyes to adjust. When they did he saw three shapes lying in front of him a few feet away. Two of them were moving in the moonlight where they'd fallen, feet scuffling the trail.

196

A third lay still.

The moaning continued. He could not tell whose voice it was over his own labored breathing.

Beside him the boy sobbed again and sighed. After that his chest moved once and then went still.

Ludlow rose on one elbow. Ahead of him somebody was trying to stand. He decided he'd better do that first if it was possible.

When he got to his knees he felt something bite deep into his left side just above the hip. His face was suddenly burning. He felt clammy with sweat *No you don't*, he thought. *You don't pass out. Not now.*

He felt his side for the wound. He found the entrance wound which was small with not much bleeding but the exit wound in his lower back was another matter. It was soft and raw and he could feel a chip of rib bone at the surface like a jagged broken tooth poking out of him.

He put his hand to the cold damp ground and got one foot on up under him and then the other and, with great difficulty, finally managed to straighten his knees. His head swam.

Whole left side of me's a disaster, he thought. Broken head, broken ribs.

He staggered to where they lay.

The one trying to get up was Danny. He was lying on his back trying to make it to one elbow the same as Ludlow had done. Ludlow looked him over and saw the wound and saw that the rifle was well out of reach. He looked him in the eyes. He saw that the hardness in the eyes was gone. He saw only fear and pain.

'You're gut-shot, boy. Stay still. I'll send somebody.'

Somehow that seemed to calm the boy though Ludlow could not imagine why it would, the promise coming from him. Ludlow could just as easily leave him where he lay. He'd be damn well justified in doing so and the boy would know that. Maybe the boy was tired finally of hauling around that much baggage of manly responsibility and wrongheaded virtues. Maybe it was good to hand the burden of his life to somebody else. Even to him. Even at the cost that Ludlow might be lying to him.

The moment he saw the father's face he knew he had only a few moments left to disgrace the earth he lay on. Ludlow looked him over. From what he could see, McCormack appeared to be shot twice, once in the chest just below the shoulder and once lower down near the lungs. He lay face-up, half on his side, with his gun arm pointed out toward Pete Daoust who lay sprawled on his belly beside him.

Half of the back of Pete Daoust's head was shot away.

Brain matter glistened in the moonlight and oozed down his neck and pooled at the back of his collar.

Ludlow couldn't possibly have done that with the .38.

McCormack had kept on firing even after he was down. Firing wild.

The boy had been in the way.

Ludlow saw he'd been right, that Pete hadn't been carrying a weapon.

McCormack's eyes flickered.

Ludlow kicked the .44 out of his hand, just in

case. You could never tell what was left in a man or a snake. The gun skittered down the trail. He reached over to McCormack's head and turned it to the side, pointed it towards Pete Daoust.

'You see what you did?' he said.

He let the man look, saw him blink and thought he saw comprehension there but only that.

'And somebody, either you or Danny, shot your boy Harold too. I don't think it matters which one of you. Do you?'

The eyes flickered up at him.

'You had yourself quite a day.'

He stood and threw down the .38 well away from the man and limped slowly back the way he'd come. He passed Harold and, as he did, leaned over and closed his eyes. He thought that the boy hadn't been half bad and that this was a damn shame. He thought that sooner or later Harold would probably have gotten away from his father and his older brother, might have even made a life for himself. And that Pete Daoust probably didn't deserve this either. For all the mouth and swagger on him.

Guns didn't give a damn, one way or another.

He walked back into the bushes and a moment later found what he was looking for.

He lifted the dog up into his arms.

He felt very weak. He hoped he had strength enough left in him to make it to the house and to the mother to tell her about her boy still alive back here and not instead go wandering off the trail, delirious with shock and loss of blood into the deep woods. Which today seemed to want to claim him somehow.

He lifted the dog and, for a moment, felt a strange clarity of thought and feeling wash suddenly over him, its access striking him just as the phantom pain had struck him on the way to this place. He knew then what would only be confirmed by others many days and weeks from now, that something was happening inside him he had not forseen, that in a way he and the dog were one flesh now, one spirit, alive yet not only alive, dead yet not only dead, part of a process decreed by earth and flesh that was fierce and steady and implacable, beyond all knowing of life and all of human reason. He knew that the only counter-measure to this was gentleness and he was content with that.

She met him in the clearing.

He saw her and sunk to his knees. All the strength gone out of him.

The clearing spun. His arms felt cold and hollow. He closed his eyes. It seemed he could see himself from the height of one of these tall old oak trees that surrounded them, there on his knees in the moonlight in the clearing facing a woman who had once been pretty he felt certain but who now looked only horrified and anguished at the sight of him, at Ludlow holding the dog out in front of him like an offering as though she were the mother of earth and of the tall waving grass he knelt in, the sad broken mother of creation.

'Help me,' he said.

*Part Four*

# GENERATIONS

# Thirty-One

The day he got out of the hospital his daughter was waiting for him with the wheelchair. He didn't want it. Ten days lying on his back was plenty of inactivity, he thought, but Allie was insistent. Ludlow yielded. It was a small enough thing to do for her and Allie had flown in from Boston and sat with him every day for hours on end doing crossword puzzles and talking since the morning after they admitted him.

Ludlow thought that the only good to have come out of this was getting to know his daughter again.

She wheeled him out into the bright afternoon sunlight. Halfway across the tarmac she told him she had a confession to make. She said that she'd been holding out on him.

'What do you mean, holding out on me?'

'I'm pregnant, dad.'

'You are?'

'Uh-huh. I'm two months gone. You're going to be a grandfather.'

Ludlow had all he could do to stay in the chair.

'That's wonderful, Allie.'

'We sure think so.'

'Pregnant. Hell, *I* ought to be pushing *you*.'

She laughed.

'Really, that's wonderful, Allie.'

He reached up and gripped her hand on the wheelchair, gave it a squeeze.

'I was waiting till you got out to tell you. I didn't want to be telling you in some hospital. I wanted it special. I wanted it out here in the sunlight.'

'You're damn right it's special. Do you know if it's a boy or a girl?'

'We don't want to know. We'll be happy either way.'

'So will I. I only wish your mother could've known.'

'Me too.'

They'd talked a lot about Mary over the last few days once he'd recovered from the concussion and then got off some of the pain-killers, about how she and Ludlow had met and courted and married. It helped pass the time and it served to draw them together. They talked about Allie's childhood and Tim's.

They even talked about the murders.

They'd never done that.

It pleased him that she hadn't brought up the subject of his getting in touch with Billy again. Maybe they were finally beyond that now.

She'd driven his father up from Pinewood one afternoon to visit him in the hospital. The old man wanted to know everything that had happened that night and listened without interrupting once and when it was over he said, *You did fine, son. I just didn't know you had that damn hard a head, that's all.*

She stayed at his house three more days until she'd pleased herself that Ludlow was capable of taking care of himself, despite the pins and the metal rod that held one of his ribs together. He told her to get on back to her husband. He could tell that she wanted to as much as she was reluctant to leave him. He drove her to the airport in the rental car he was keeping until he got the truck replaced. They hugged at the gate and Ludlow thought how like Mary's hair his daughter's smelled.

He called the hospital the night she left to see how the McCormack boy was doing. The attending nurse said he was finally out of danger. Sam Berry had told him they were going to charge the boy with attempted murder and assault with a deadly weapon. Sam said he'd have to testify against him.

He didn't mind if he did.

Ludlow felt bad about the woman though, about his mother. The woman had lost everything. He didn't know her history or how it all had come down to that for her but he doubted much of it was her fault, other than marrying wrong. She'd raised one son who'd seemed to be working his way towards decency.

She'd helped him. Probably saved his life.

And she'd covered Red.

He hoped the maid with the withered hand was sticking by her.

In the month that followed he had his hands full, what with buying himself a new truck, arranging with contractors to rebuild the store and arranging deals with his suppliers. He and Bill Prine were going into business as co-owners this time because Ludlow thought he needed a younger man in there, what with all the doctors had told him. Plus it was time he gave Bill his due. So there were lawyers to talk to and papers to approve and sign. He had therapy three times a week for the broken rib.

One cool clear night in the first week of September just after he'd finished dinner he heard a knock at the door and, when he opened it, there was Carrie Donnel. She was wearing faded blue jeans and a tight green sweater and held a bottle of Moet in either hand.

'Miss Donnel,' he said smiling.

She laughed. 'Carrie, remember?'

'Won't you come in?'

'Why, thank you.'

She walked past him the way she always had, like she belonged there, and set one bottle on the table and put the other in the refrigerator.

'You're looking good,' she said.

'So are you.'

'How'd you like the broadcast?'

'The broadcast? Carrie, the broadcast was over a month ago. Hell, I thought you'd never ask.'

'Sorry. It's just been busy as hell down there. Staff cuts all over the place. I didn't even know if you'd actually seen it. You were in the hospital. I didn't know if you'd be up to watching television.'

She pulled out a chair and sat down at the kitchen table.

'I heard you had your daughter here with you.'

'I could hardly get her to leave.'

'Good. That's good, Av.'

He sat across from her.

'But you did get to see it, right?' she said.

He nodded.

'So? What'd you think?'

'You were good. You were fair. You didn't make me out to be some kind of damned hero. I think I'd be ashamed to show my face around here if you had. You didn't make me out to be a lunatic either. No, you did a fine job, Carrie. Just what I'd expect of you. Are you going to be covering the boy's trial?'

When she looked at him her eyes were sad. He knew what her answer would be.

'I got a job back in the city, Av. A really good job. A network station.'

'New York? But I thought you hated it there.'

She shook her head. 'No, Boston.'

'When?'

'Starting next month. I leave a week from Saturday. I have to find an apartment, settle in. You know.'

He heard what she was saying. That there'd be a lot she'd have to do before then in Portland.

This was the last time she'd be coming through his door.

*Like she owned the place.*

'Well, hell then,' he said. 'Pop the damn champagne, will you? Sounds like we should be doing some celebrating.'

'I think that's really the reason I didn't call, Av. You know. The fact that I was leaving.'

He nodded. 'I figured.'

'You did?'

'Something like that.'

'You hate me, Av?'

He squinted at her.

'*Now* who's talking like a young fool, Carrie.'

He got up and walked over and put his hands on her shoulders and then leaned down and kissed her cheek and her forehead and then he kissed her mouth.

'I couldn't hate you if you got it into your head to smash me with that bottle,' he said. 'To me you've been nothing but a blessing. Going away isn't going to change that. See, I've got this crazy old man's feeling that you love me a little. You suppose that could be true?'

She nodded and began to cry. 'Yes, goddamnit. Of course I do.'

'And I think that's amazing. You sit here asking, Do I hate you? Some observer you are. Shame on you.'

She smiled.

'Now do me a favor and open up that champagne.'

When she left him in the morning he watched her through the kitchen window. She waved to him once and smiled before stepping into the car and he saluted back to her with his steaming mug of coffee.

In that instant he memorized her.

There had been talk the night before of his taking a trip to Boston one day to visit his daughter, that perhaps they'd see one another when he did. But he knew it would never happen. She would disappear deep into her own life and he into his. Now he froze her, car, bright morning and all, so that if she never came back to him again at least her image would.

He hadn't told her about the slow quiet war going on in his bloodstream, the one he'd inevitably lose. The one he'd somehow sensed that night, battered and shot, alone on the trail with Red.

He couldn't see any reason to do so.

He thought about what the doctors had said, that lymphoma could take years to kill you. He was figuring to make it do exactly that.

He could see no reason for Allie to know either. She was busy making a baby inside. He'd made the doctors promise not to say.

He'd do it himself, when the time came.

Ludlow sipped his coffee and watched the car drive down over the hill and disappear. He walked through the kitchen and out the back door to the wooden porch and closed the door behind him. In the waving field of goldenrod that rose gently from the porch up the hill to where Red lay, he was able to imagine that he could see the rolling sea, that he stood on the deck of a schooner in a fine steady wind, alone but for a crew of ghosts forever silent.

He busied himself with papers, with purchase orders and medical bills, and in the waning of the day heard a truck pull up beside his own.

He looked out the window and saw that it was Emma Siddons. She was holding her bright red sweater tight together with both hands and walking with a purpose toward the door, which was Emma's way. He thought she looked older than when last he'd seen her. He guessed that probably so did he.

He opened the door for her and the russet scruffy dark-eyed head of the dog peering out from beneath her sweater was the first damn thing he saw.

He laughed and put out his hand and the dog sniffed it and began licking, squirming in her arms with excitement.

'My god. Is this who I think it is?' he said.

Emma grinned. 'You're darned right it is.' She shook her head. 'That old dog of yours, up to no good to the very end. Evangeline had herself a litter of four. Two of them black like her and two of 'em red. Dropped the three females and then, finally, this guy here.'

She opened the sweater and handed the dog to Ludlow. The dog licked his face and then went back to his fingers again.

'What is he, six weeks?'

'Uh-huh. And high time I got him off my hands.'

'What? You're giving him to me?'

'No, Avery Ludlow. I drove over here just to show you what a pain in the butt your dog turned out to be. Of course I'm giving him to you. Who else in the world should have him?'

'Emma, I hadn't planned—'

'I don't give a damn what you planned. Just look at him.'

The dog had stopped squirming. He lay content and quiet, folded in Ludlow's arms, and slowly licked his fingers.

*Red had always watched his hands.*

*As though the hands and what the hands could do were what made them different, creature to creature, and that was all.*

'Look at him. This little dog *knows* you. I think he knew you the minute we stepped in through the door.'

He put the dog down and petted him and he and Emma sat and talked a while and Ludlow watched the dog go off to explore his surroundings. The kitchen, the bedrooms, the living room, the stairs.

210

He heard the dog's toenails on the wooden floor. After a while the dog returned and sighed and lay down at Ludlow's feet.

Emma laughed.

'I guess you just got your plans changed for you,' she said.

He told her about the lymphoma. That he could very well be dead soon. It seemed important that she understand that for him, taking on an animal was a pact that time and illness could easily break.

'Anything happens to you, Av, I'll make sure he's treated just as you'd want him treated. You have my word on that. But you can't think about things that way or else there's nothing in life you can have that's anywhere near worth having. You give him what you can and give him what time you can. He'll do the same. And you'll both do just fine.'

She left him with some food for the dog from out of her car and Ludlow fed him and played with him and found himself smiling, his heart opening to the dog so rapidly it astonished him. When he went to bed that night the dog followed him, crying out to get on the bed with him, so Ludlow lifted him up. The dog curled at his belly and slept. Ludlow stroked his smooth shiny fur for a very long time until he was suddenly assaulted by tears, not for Red this time or for Mary or for any of his lost loved ghosts but for this new life granted him, for the world of souls that went on and on and of which he and the dog were a part.

'What'll we call you?' he whispered.

Embraced by him, the dog slept on.

# THE PASSENGER
## by Jack Ketchum

# The Passenger

### by Jack Ketchum

It wasn't the best of days even before her car died.

She'd fallen asleep the night before at her desk in the study and awakened from a dream of Micah Harpe, all three-hundred-plus pounds of him, crashing through the picture window and spraying her with shards of glass, slamming up against her desk and scattering papers and cigarette butts everywhere and then laughing, leering up at her, saying, *troubles, counselor?* and she rode that sudden wakefulness for a moment like a bucking steer.

*Then Alan walks in from his shower wrapped in a towel, carrying a manila file folder, drops the folder on the end table and asks her not to let him forget these briefs tomorrow, please.* Sure, Alan, thanks, no problem. It took him a full two minutes to really see her there, pale as chalk, and yet another to ask what was wrong.

1

"Dream," she said.

He glanced at the desk littered with paperwork.

"You been down here all night?"

She yawned, nodded.

"So? How'd it go?"

"So I think I'm screwed without Micah Harpe, that's what it comes down to."

"I could have told you that."

"All I can do is argue insufficient evidence."

She watched him throw the towel over his shoulder and turn and walk toward the kitchen.

"Uh-huh. You want some coffee? I need some coffee."

"I want some sleep. I want a case I can win, goddammit."

He said, "Settle for the coffee."

Then later she and Milton Wendt, the prosecutor, before the bench and Judge Irma Foster—*another* stunning excuse for a conversation.

"We're not arguing," she said, "that my client wasn't at the Willis home that day, your Honor. They were old friends and he had every reason to be there. The prosecution has placed my client in the house and we allow that he was, in fact, present. But Big was there too and there is nothing . . ."

"Big?" Judge Foster squinted at her.

"Micah Harpe, your Honor, the defendant's older brother."

The judge looked past her to Arthur "Little" Harpe at the defense table. Arthur was looking pretty good today, Janet thought, all told. As good as he *could* look, anyway. A new suit and tie off the rack at Burton's and

2

a shoeshine in the courthouse lobby. But Janet still knew what the judge was seeing—a chubby pasty-faced country-ass snake watching them through idiot eyes. She just hoped he wasn't using the eraser end of the pencil to clean out his earwax again.

*"Big* and *Little?"* she said.

"Yes, your Honor."

"Good God."

She tried to move on.

"The prosecution has presented no physical evidence whatever to suggest that it was my client and not, as we contend, my client's brother, who was responsible—*without* my client's knowledge or cooperation—for the murders of these two people. I move to dismiss."

"He confessed, Counselor." Wendt sighed.

"He's since recanted and implicated Micah as the shooter. That confession was taken under duress and you know it. The police went at him for over twenty-two hours. All because they couldn't find his brother."

"They still can't."

"That's *simply not true,* your Honor."

Then the judge sighed too. "Let's take this into chambers," she said.

In chambers she fared no better than expected. The trial was set for Monday morning. She had the weekend to prepare. But to prepare *what?* She certainly wasn't putting that little weasel on the stand. The best she could hope for was to shake the detectives who'd handled the interrogation, or to pull off a miracle in summation. It wasn't very promising. Harpe had confessed to the shotgun murders of Joseph and Lilian Willis over a drug deal gone bad and that was probably that. In the hallway she gave it one last try with Wendt, though.

"It should have been postponed," she said. "It should never have come to trial."

"Come on, Janet. We don't know Big's even in there."

"And you don't know he isn't."

"Nobody's placed him there. Not even his *brother* has definitively placed him there. What do you want the cops to do? Remember *probable cause,* for god's sake? We've gone onto that estate half a dozen times. The place is an armed camp—safe house for half the psychos in the state. But every gun in the place is registered to its owner. *You* know what the locals call it."

"I know. Hole-in-the-Wall."

"That's right. We're talking Butch Cassidy and the Sundance Kid right here in quiet old Adderton County. But it's still *private property*. These guys have influence. They've got bucks. Big bucks. With a cleanup crew to dispose of their *disposables* as good as any in the U.S.A. And we don't have probable cause."

"He's in there. And he did the crime."

She stopped and opened her briefcase and pulled out the folder second from the top. She handed it to Wendt.

"Look at this."

"Big's rap sheet. I've read it."

"Read it again. Arrests for arson, rape, armed robbery, another rape—this one a man, sodomy—murder, attempted murder, assault . . ."

She was aware that her voice was rising, echoing through the nearly empty halls, turning a head or two. She didn't give a damn.

"You can *do something*, Milton. You can send them in there after him."

Wendt shook his head. "Wish I could. Look, no-body's saying Big's a sweetheart, Janet. I'll even grant you that they could have done it together. But the point is we've already got your boy. So I think I'll go right ahead and fry him if that's okay with you."

The Turtle Brook Inn was all amber lights and dark wood paneling and tables and chairs upholstered in bur-gundy—a steak joint with romantic aspirations. Seven-thirty on a Friday night and not half the tables full, nor even half the bar, a testament to northern New York State's fundamental lack of any real trickle-down pros-perity. She was halfway through her second glass of wine when Alan finally made his appearance. There was no point scolding him. Alan was late. Fact of life.

"So?" he said.

So again. She took a sip of wine.

"Alan, you can be boring as spit sometimes. You know that?"

"It didn't go well."

"No, it didn't."

He reached across the table and gave her hand a squeeze. His own hand was warm and dry and despite herself she always found comfort in his touch.

"I love you, honey," he said.

"Alan, you damn well *cheat* on me."

"That doesn't mean I don't love you. Don't worry about the case. You'll think of something. Listen, I'm staying at the apartment in town tonight. I have to take a deposition first thing in the morning. You mind?"

"No, that's okay."

Behind him their young pretty blond waitress was approaching.

"I do," he said. "I mind. I may be boring as spit sometimes but I know one or two sex crimes we haven't committed yet that I'd rather try tonight."

The waitress froze.

"It's all right," Janet told her. "He's an officer of the court."

She was on her way home when the Taurus started shuddering and then died, cresting a hill on the dark slice of two-lane country road that was Route 605 northeast of Meville. She managed to pull over to the shoulder and tried to start it up again but the ignition only screeched at her like an angry cat. She stepped out onto black macadam and a warm still moonlit night. Below and far away across the valley she could see the lights from a single farmhouse. She walked to the front of the car and then the back and looked at emptiness in both directions.

She'd been meaning to get a new cell phone for nearly a week.

*This could take a while,* she thought.

It did.

Nearly twenty minutes passed with her standing there smoking Winston after Winston and listening to the frogs and crickets and she was seriously considering the trek down to the farmhouse before she at last saw a pair of headlights moving north in her direction. She was relieved but apprehensive too and wondered why in hell she hadn't had the sense to take the tire iron out of the trunk when she had a chance to. It would be nice to have it on the car seat where she could reach it through the window in case of trouble.

6

Especially when the moonlight revealed the outline of a pickup with a wooden frame.

By then it was too damn late.

She thought of the old joke, *What's the difference between a good ol' boy and a redneck? A good ol' boy throws his empty beer bottles in the back of the pickup— a redneck heaves 'em out the window.*

She was hoping for the former.

The headlights washed over her. A pickup wasn't what she had in mind. Not at all. She waved anyhow.

And the truck rolled right on by.

"Jesus!" she said.

She couldn't believe it. How the hell *dare* he?

She whirled and ran to the front of the Taurus. "You *asshole!"* she yelled.

The truck slowed.

Stopped.

Sat there idling thirty feet away.

*Oh, shit,* she thought. Now you did it. He fucking *heard* you.

*You better get that goddamn tire iron after all,* she thought, and started digging in her purse, watching the compartment of the cab, a man's silhouette inside, waiting for the driver's door to open and the light to come on, which would mean he was coming out to god knows what purpose and praying that he'd just start moving again, get moving and go the hell away and then she had the keys out and was headed toward the trunk fumbling for the right one. As the truck moved slowly into reverse and started rolling back, taillights stalking her like glowing eyes.

And then suddenly she was stabbed into bright light again and a horn blared long and loud behind her.

She turned to see a station wagon in the process of slowly passing, pulling up alongside the Taurus and stopping, and she glanced at the pickup and saw it start to roll again—this time forward, this time in the *right* direction. Inside the wagon the driver leaned over and pushed open the passenger-side door and she saw that the driver was a woman smiling at her and she damn near leapt inside.

"God! Thanks!"

"No problem. Car died on you, huh?"

She shut the door. "That truck. He was coming after me."

"He was? The sonovabitch. You want to go after him?"

"God no."

"You sure?"

"I'm sure."

"Okay. We'll just drive."

Janet looked at her. A woman of about her own age. Tight jeans and a tight pale yellow short-sleeve blouse, braless, her long hair pulled back in a lush dark ponytail. Rings on every finger of her right hand and hooped costume-jewelry bracelets, at least half a dozen, dangling from each wrist. A good strong profile, a little too much mascara maybe but still, she thought, quite attractive in her way. And then the woman turned to her and smiled again as they pulled away, and she saw the slightly crooked left incisor.

"Marion? *Marion Lane?*"

It was the woman's turn to stare now.

"I'll be good-goddamned! It's *Janet,* right? Janet . . . wait, don't tell me. Don't tell me. I can't *believe* this . . . hold on a minute . . . *Harris!* Janet Harris!"

"Close. Morris." She smiled.

"Morris! You lived . . . ?"

"Plainfield Street."

"That's right, Plainfield Street! Up where the money was. Hell, where the money *still* is. God! I mean, look at you! Jesus, what's it been?"

"Since high school? A long time. A very long time."

"No, really . . . I guess it's got to be, what . . .?"

"Seventeen years."

She laughed. "Oh my god. Seventeen years. Seventeen goddamn *years!* You know how *long* that is? Hell, we were only what? *eighteen* when we graduated? I mean, that's half a lifetime ago!" She laughed again. "Damn! I think I need a drink," she said. "Maybe a *few* drinks."

She gave Janet's leg beneath the skirt a light slap. "Hey, it's good to see you!"

"Good to see you too. You don't know how good. That guy was starting to scare me."

"Forget the bastard. Someday he'll pick up the wrong lady, know what I mean? Where we headed?"

"You know Ellsworth Road? Just outside of town? I'm living over there now."

"Sure, I do. No problem."

She watched the road ahead wash away beneath their wheels. The pause between them was only momentary but still a little awkward. She really hadn't known Marion well in high school. They'd traveled in wholly different circles. Janet was definitely college-bound. Marion hadn't been. She wondered whether or not she'd ultimately made it there anyway but decided that at least for now it would be wrong to ask.

"Listen. There really is half a bottle in there." She

pointed to the glove compartment. "That jerk give you the willies? Open it up and have a hit or two. Good for the nerves."

"No, thanks."

"Go on."

"Honestly. I'm fine."

"You sure?"

"Yes, really."

"Well, dig it out for me then, okay?" She laughed again. "Seventeen years! Jesus!"

She really didn't want to. Not only was it against the law but it was dangerous as hell. She'd seen the results of drinking and driving plenty of times. Enough to know what a fundamentally stupid thing it was to do. But Marion was saving her ass here, for all she knew in more ways than one. And she hadn't smelled any liquor on her breath thus far so this one might well be her first. It was still illegal but she guessed it was safe enough so long as she kept it down to one or two. She pressed the button to the glove compartment and watched the door fall open and the light come on inside.

She saw the flat pint bottle of Kentucky Bourbon.

And behind it the .22 revolver.

When Ray Short leaned back in his chair and neatly lifted the wallet from the baggy jeans of the passing Saturday Night Cowboy, Emil Rothert was almost finished with his fifth beer and just drunk enough not to be seriously pissed at him for waving it around the table like some kind of goddamn trophy, smiling, looking for Emil's approval, and Billy's too, he guessed. Even though the barman could have seen him or any one of the five guys sitting at the bar or the four in back by the pool tables. Not seriously pissed but still pissed.

He had to give him his due, though. Ray was good with his hands.

"Put that goddamn thing away," he said.

"Yeah. Jeez, Ray, you want to get us *comprehended?*"

Rothert sighed and shook his head. Sometimes Billy amused him and sometimes not. Sometimes he thought Billy Ripper was a spaceman only just learning how to appear human.

Ray's smile faded. "You guys are no damn fun at all."

"We're drunk, Ray. What do you want from us?"

He finished his beer.

"I'll have another, though. You're buying."

Rothert watched him walk to the bar. Sitting to his left was a guy in a rumpled gray suit drinking what looked like whiskey neat. The guy was facing straight ahead into the rows of bottles but he still hoped Ray had sense enough not to pay out of the stolen wallet.

"Three more," he heard him say to the bartender, and then the bartender said something back that must have been *three more what?* because Ray said *beers* and then the bartender must have asked him *what kind of beers?* because Ray turned around with a look of annoyed confusion just as the girl walked in. He saw her register on Ray's face—*one helluva looker*—and he turned and she was a looker all right and too young he thought to be walking into a place like this alone, probably underage in fact, long blond hair and cutoffs and tank top straining across her tits. Yet here she was, alone, moving past his table toward the back like she owned the joint.

Willie Nelson stopped singing "Blue Hawaii" and the

place went silent so that he could hear the bartender and Ray.

". . . we got Bud, we got Schlitz, we got Miller, we got Miller Lite. We got Heineken, Heineken lite, we got Coors. We got Tuborg, Becks and I can piss in this bottle for you if any of this don't interest you."

"Huh?" Ray still had his eye on the girl.

"Forget it."

The bartender started to move away and Ray finally got it together.

"Buds. Make it Buds."

"Three Buds."

And then it was Elvis singing "Blue Hawaii" good god as the bartender opened the beers and put them on the bar and sure enough, Ray pulled out the stolen wallet and started counting out the bills. I got me a reckless fool on one side of me, Emil thought, and a *complete* fool on the other.

Ray handed them their beers and sat.

"See that?"

"I'm still seeing it," Emil said.

"I think you should go over," said Billy. "Buy her a drink. Talk to her. I think she looks like someone who'd appreciate to talk to you."

"I'm thinking about it." He drank from the bottle.

Billy smiled. It wasn't a nice thing to see.

"I've always liked a girl like that. Y'know? Somebody who can exist themselves to a function where they can manipulate."

Emil and Ray just looked at him.

Emil thought that sometimes this boy just plain *scared* him.

\*   \*   \*

The pint bottle rested between Marion's legs and she'd only had two sips, but Janet still wished she'd put the thing away. She was driving slowly though, and carefully. She had no real reason to complain.

"Your parents still live in town?" Marion asked her.

"No. Florida. My dad retired, sold the house. My mother says she's a golf widow now. Yours?"

"Passed away."

"I'm sorry."

"Thanks. It's okay. They were never much with us anyhow. So who do you still see? Anybody?"

"Nobody. I used to call Lydia Hill once in a while."

"Lydia Hill?"

"Tall? Blond? Always wore long-sleeved white cotton blouses and minis? You know, the kind with the button-on suspenders."

Marion laughed. "Sure, I remember them. Ran along the sides of your boobs and made 'em look bigger. And I remember Lydia Hill too, I think. Wasn't she a cheerleader or something? Prom committee or something?"

"Lydia? No, she was more debating team. We both were."

She drank from the bottle. "You were popular though. You weren't just some damn egghead."

Janet shrugged and smiled. "I guess."

"Sure you were. You dated that guy Wilder for a while, and Kenny Whatsisname, big Irish preppie. What was his name?"

"Coughlin."

"Coughlin. Kenny Coughlin. Right. Real *sonovabitch* that guy was to me. You know that?"

"No. I didn't even know you'd gone out with him."

*Kenny and Marion?* Before or after us? she won-

13

dered. Kenny was about as straight arrow as they come.

"See, you and me didn't hang out with the same crowd. Guys I hung with, they expected you to put out, and maybe at first you didn't and maybe later you did. And that was *seriously* fucked because as soon as you did their friends would know, so from then on you pretty much always did, and by the time a guy like Kenny comes along your cunt's Grand Central Station and everybody knows it. So what's Kenny do? He comes on like he's going to *save* me. You believe that?"

Marion drank again. *Not good,* she thought. It was starting to worry her. That and the fact that she was accelerating now, just a bit over the speed limit. But the woman would be in trouble if some cop pulled her over.

Then she thought, *what cop?* We're out here in the middle of nowhere.

"At least with one of those other guys it's right out front, know what I mean? At least he doesn't do the movie-and-dinner routine so he can excuse his own sorry butt for wanting to screw you in the backseat later on. And then never *calling* you again. At least with those other guys, they call again. Kenny Coughlin. What a bastard."

She's using the *present tense,* Janet thought. Like she's still there. Back in high school. She knew that some of them got stuck in time—she'd seen it before. The same old town, the same jobs, the same old friends growing older. Some simply got trapped there and it looked as though probably Marion was one of them. She was starting to get very unhappy about the whole conversation and it didn't help at all when Marion pounded at the steering wheel.

"Who the *fuck* is Kenny Coughlin not to call me?"

She watched her take a deep breath and hold it and expel it slowly, and then she seemed to calm again.

"I mean, you *dated* that guy?"

Janet nodded.

"How'd he treat you?"

"Okay I guess. It didn't last that long, not really."

In her look Janet seemed to read a barely concealed hostility. And not toward Kenny, but inexplicably, toward *her*. As though this whole business with Kenny Coughlin were somehow Janet's fault. And she held that look too long—considering she was the one doing the driving. And then she reached suddenly for the glove compartment and Janet couldn't help it, she jumped.

She glanced down and saw the gun in there and then she saw her slide the bottle in and slam it shut.

Her heart was pounding. She wondered if Marion had noticed the overreaction.

*For a moment I thought . . . my god . . .*

But no, Marion had done the right thing—not the crazy thing. She'd put away the bottle. And maybe it was the bottle that had been talking all along. Maybe there was nothing to worry about here at all.

"Not too long, huh?" she said. "Well, good. Good for you. Myself, I could have killed the little prick."

She laughed. "Don't mind me," she said. "I was always too serious. Y'know?"


Emil watched the girl take her beer back into the poolroom, stand and watch one of the games. From what he could see the game wasn't much. The players were just a couple of skinny kids in their twenties who thought that if you didn't hit the fucker hard you didn't hit good. He got more interested when he saw her reach into the pocket of her cutoffs and pull out a quarter and set it down by the left corner pocket.

The girl was a player. Or wanted to be.

He was surprised the bartender hadn't carded her. She was just a kid.

"How's your game these days, Bill?" he said.

"Oh, imperative, Emil. Imperative."

"Fine."


"So I guess you got married, huh?"

"No," Janet said.

They were about twenty minutes from home now. Still in farmland, all gentle rolling hills and dark two-lane blacktop. They'd be coming up at a Kaltzas's service station soon though, in about ten minutes or so. She wondered if she should tell Marion to stop there instead of taking her home. It was probably a good idea. If Dean was on, he'd give her a lift the rest of the way, drop her off and then go deal with her car. Dean had a massive crush on her that she didn't exactly discourage. It helped if your local service-station guy happened to like you.

Besides, there was the matter of that gun.

"You got a boyfriend?" Marion said.

"Yes."

"Fiancé, right?"

"That's right."

"Been together a while?"

"Almost eight years, believe it or not."

"What is he? Doctor? Lawyer? You got a congressman tucked away somewhere?"

"Lawyer, actually."

Interesting, she thought. She hasn't asked me what *I* do for a living.

"Lawyer. *Actually.*" She nodded. "Well, I guess you really made something of yourself then, didn't you."

And the hostility in *that* little zinger was loud and clear. Jesus! It was definitely going to be the service station now, even forgetting about the gun. She didn't want this woman in her life any longer than she needed her to be.

"So how come you don't marry the guy? What is he? Lousy in bed?"

"Marion . . . listen . . ."

"What? I can't ask a question, now?"

"I'm not up to having a personal discussion right now, that's all. My car's dead, I'm exhausted, I've got work to do. You know what I mean?"

She laughed. "You're not up to it. Having a hard night, are we?"

"Now that you mention it, yes. I didn't need a broken-down car right now, that's for sure, and . . ."

"And you don't need me asking personal, friendly questions of an old girlfriend, right? Well, pardon *me!*"

"God, Marion. I only said . . . look, there's a gas station coming up on your right. Why don't you just . . ."

"You want out? Is that it? You fucking want out? You want out of the car right now?"

*Where the hell is all this coming from?* she thought. What in god's name did *I* do?

"Okay, yes. I think I do."

"You *think* you do?"

"I think that'd be best."

"Right here."

"You're angry and . . . yes. I think that'd be best."

"It would, huh?" She looked at her, lips pressed tight together. "Yeah, maybe it would at that."

Her foot went to the brake and the car slowed and Janet could finally breathe again. Then she hit the accelerator. Tires screeched beneath her and jolted her back in her seat. Marion was grinning.

"Nah," she said. "I want the company."

They were standing behind her a little to the left by the jukebox along with three other guys watching her make her shot, the girl leaning way over the table to reach the cue ball so that her ass punched the cutoffs from within like a blast of helium into a balloon. She was wiping the floor with this kid. She made the corner shot and then lined up the seven to the right side pocket and sunk that too. Gently easing it in so that the eight ball was directly opposite. The kid was shaking his head and scratching distractedly at his pimples while Patsy Cline sang "Faded Love."

"Side pocket," she said.

Her voice had a hint of country twang to it.

Not a New York State kid.

She took her time. Aimed low for the backspin and got it right. The eight clattered home and her cue ball stopped on a dime directly in front of the pocket. She smiled and the skinny kid smiled and shook his head again and somebody applauded and Billy and Ray and one of the other guys across the room laughed along with the kid's former partner. She picked up the quarter off the table. Her fingernails were cut short and flat.

"Who's next?"

"Me," Billy said and stepped over with his cue.

"You any good?"

18

"I am the best."

Emil couldn't help it. With Billy sometimes you just *had* to smile. She put the quarter in and when the balls dropped gathered them to the table and racked them efficiently and perfectly over the head spot while Billy chalked his cue halfway to death. She rolled him the cue ball over the foot spot. *Directly* over the foot spot.

"Your break."

"Side wager, miss?"

"Sure. Ten?"

"Ten will be fine. May I buy you a beer?"

"Thanks. I got one already."

She lifted it and drank.

By the time she sank the fifth ball he was ready to make his move. Billy's break had sunk nothing but scattered everything as was typical of Billy, who was decidedly *not* the best and she was popping them in all over the place. Guys were hollering encouragement. The girl was smiling. Billy looked like he was about to blow any minute but you had to know him like Emil and Ray did to see that.

He moved behind her and when she drew back the cue took hold of the hilt and held it. The girl turned around. Annoyed with him.

"Guess that's it," he said.

"Huh?"

He reached into his back pocket, fished out his wallet and flashed her the phony shield. Then returned it to his pocket.

"Got any ID?"

"Hey, come on. What is this?"

"I think you're underage. I think you're drinking in

a public place and hustling my buddy here for pocket money. I'll take the cue now, miss."

She handed it to him and he set it against the wall.

"Lean over on the table. Hands on the table. Spread your legs, please."

And yeah, he'd been right all along. She *was* underage and she was scared now and humiliated and she did as she was told so he proceeded to pat her down, thinking it was too bad about the cutoffs because he'd have liked to give those good smooth thighs a squeeze but there was no excuse for that with the girl bare-legged, though the ass was fine and the tits were especially fine and those he *did* squeeze and when she gasped and the two burly men who saw him do it started forward he reached for the pool cue and pointed it at them.

"Don't even *think* it, gentlemen."

The room was quiet now except for Patsy Cline and the girl, who had started to cry. Emil stepped away from her toward the men and watched them back down in front of the cue and move silent and sullen back to the wall.

"Okay, miss," he said. "Get your purse. Officer Short here and I will escort you to the station. Billy? Officer? Let's go."

Again the girl did as she was told and bent and retrived her purse, and Ray had her by the arm and was starting to move her along when the kid she'd just beat muttered something to his buddy across the room.

"What's that?"

"I said you guys ain't cops. You didn't read her her rights."

"You're interfering with an officer of the law, sonny. Put your quarter on the table and let somebody else whip your ass before I take you along and read *you* your rights."

He took her other arm and Billy trailed along behind while they marched her out of the room and into the bar, weaving their way through the tables and only then was he aware that the barman and some of the guys at the bar were watching all of this, so he stopped in front of the barman and pointed at him.

"*You* I'll be seeing a little later, friend," he said. "Don't go anywhere."

The barman frowned and turned his head away, all of a sudden paying very close attention to the glasses in the sink.

Offensive action. Worked every time.

Lieutenant Paul Wellman picked up his Dewars and finished it and turned to the bartender.

"You know those guys?" he said.

"Nope."

"That's interesting. Neither do I."

He tapped the three singles in front of him. "Yours," he said. "And thanks. They're right about one thing though. You shouldn't have served her."

He got off his stool and walked out of the bar, stood on the porch steps and lit a smoke. They'd moved fast. He could hear them laughing across the lot, but at first he couldn't spot them. If they were cops at all, which he doubted, they were not from around here and thus had no jurisdiction. He knew that because he *did* have jurisdiction. Then he heard more laughter caught in the warm summer breeze and muffled screams and protests from the girl and by the light of the moon saw them standing in a tight half-circle around her behind a beat-up Jeep.

Christ, he thought. *Right here out in the lot.* When he was a boy his dad had talked about how stupid criminals were, but he hadn't really believed him because there had always been their behavior on television and in the movies to contradict him. It was only when he followed in his footsteps and became a cop himself that he realized what he should have known all along.

Father knows best.

He moved off the stairs and casually across the lot as though he were headed for his own car, the Colt unholstered and held to his leg slightly behind him. He tossed away the Marlboro, wondering why in hell he'd lit it in the first place. Nerves, he guessed. *At cigarette prices these days I can't afford nerves.*

The guy who'd spoken to the bartender had one hand inside her tank top and the other cupped over her mouth and must have been squeezing pretty hard because she was wriggling and pushing at him and trying to yell, her back arched against the hood of the Jeep and the other two were watching, leaning against the Ford Maverick parked beside it as he approached them. Waiting for sloppy seconds, he guessed. So that at first they didn't see him. And then of course they did.

And then everything went to hell all at once because a car pulled into the lot and flooded all five of them with sudden rolling light.

"Police!" he said and raised his shield and Colt together.

The one with the girl grabbed hold of her by the hair and threw her headfirst into the passenger-side window of the Maverick. He saw blood splash the window and the girl slam down to the tarmac like a sack of rocks and the other two men were piling into the Jeep when he fired his warning shot into the air. But that stopped none of them—nor whoever had pulled into the lot, because the car stopped right the hell *between* them.

He ran around behind it and saw the fake cop lurch into the driver's seat and heard the Jeep turn over and saw it start to pull away and fired for the left rear tire and fired again. Sparks scattered across the tarmac, but marksmanship had never been his strong suit so he ran to the driver of the car, an old guy in T-shirt and suspenders who from the look of him finally was aware of what kind of shitstorm he'd just driven into. He pointed at the girl.

"Go inside and call Nine-one-one. Tell them you need an ambulance. Tell them it's an emergency!"

*Get to your fucking car,* he thought. And then he thought, *Where? Jesus, where? Where the hell did I park it?*

Inside the Jeep Emil was having his own goddamn problems. The piece of shit kept slipping out of gear, lurching forward, stopping, lurching forward. Through the rearview mirror he saw the cop running around through the parking lot like a confused dog who'd lost the scent and wondered briefly what the hell *that* was all about.

"Better move it, Emil," Ray said.

Emil shot him a look in the mirror and tried again.

Wellman flung open the door to his car and slapped his cherry on the roof, hit his siren and slammed the door. He knew something was happening with the Jeep. He had that window, thank god. The Jeep kept stopping and starting and then as his own car roared to life he saw that the driver had finally got it right. He was headed for the exit and seconds later they were out on the road together and Wellman was riding up his tail pipe.

Emil felt the jolt from behind and then something went terribly wrong and he was swerving back and forth from one lane to the other, the Jeep nearly impossible to control and he glanced into the rearview mirror and saw the cop fishtailing all the hell over, their rear and front fenders locked together.

Then ahead of him he saw the headlights.

Wellman saw them too, headlights coming on fast, much *too* fast goddammit and reflexively hit his brakes. His tires locked, screeching, the car whipping back and forth like a trailer gone berserk. *No belt again, you fool,* he thought, smelling rubber smoke off the braking Jeep ahead as it veered suddenly and finally into the oncoming lane.

*"Marion!"* Janet screamed.

Her hands slammed the dash and the harness scraped her breastbone as Marion hit the brakes and wrenched at the wheel but for a moment she was absolutely certain it was much too little much too late, the headlights were almost on them, so close she could see the Jeep's tires smoking and then it jerked suddenly off to the right and they were tumbling down a low shoulder, Marion struggling for control, and the last thing she saw was the tree.

The cop's car hit them like a cargo tank on a tanker braking without baffles, when what's behind is a shitload heavier than what's in front, jackknifing ninety degrees and slamming into the driver's-side door and throwing Emil clear across the seat. He was aware of Ray and Billy piling out of the back on the passenger side and through the webbed broken window of the cop's car could see him slumped against the wheel, bleeding from a head wound but at just that moment beginning to move.

He opened the door and got out onto the tarmac, sprinted to the passenger side of the cop's car just as the cop's head disappeared from view and thought, *Gun, you want to bet he's going for his goddamn gun?* and pulled open the door and there it was, tumbling out onto the scruffy grass in front of him. He picked it up. Pointed it at the cop. The cop was mopping blood out of his eyes with his fingers.

"Head wounds," Emil said. "They're a bitch."

Marion watched him pull the cop from his car and drop him to the ground. She knew it was a cop because she'd registered the cherry. Her tits hurt like hell from the steering wheel but otherwise she was fine. Poor Janet seemed to have bumped her head. Poor Janet wasn't moving. She just lay back in her seat with her head lolling and except for the nasty cut across her forehead you'd have thought she was sleeping.

Well, she'd said she was exhausted.

She saw the three men surround the cop and the gun glint in the moonlight and then heard him howl and yelp as the smaller of the men began kicking him in the shoulders, in the legs and ribs. She could hear muffled voices.

She watched all this with interest.

Then the man with the gun looked up, looked directly

at her. *Stared* at her in fact, directly into her eyes.

Marion looked right back.

Behind them she saw headlights coming up fast, bathing them all in light. She watched the three men freeze, trapped there beating on a wounded cop for godsakes should the driver decide to play Angel of Mercy and stop. The car slowed, the curve of the road throwing its lights on her too for a moment. Then it accelerated and moved on. She realized she'd been holding her breath all the while.

*"What . . . ?"*

Beside her Janet was moving, pressing her hand to her forehead, aware of the wetness there and looking down into her glistening hand.

"Shhhh," she said.

"What . . . ?"

"Shut up."

The man with the gun had returned his focus to the cop. She saw the little guy kick him in the ribs again and heard him cry out and then moan and she guessed that got Janet's attention too.

"Marion . . ." she said.

"I told you to shut up."

"Marion, get us *out* of here!"

But by then the man had raised the gun to the cop's head and she watched and saw him fire and heard the flat report of the gun, felt its impact deep within her, and the cop jerked to the side and rolled over on his back and lay there and the man looked up and over at her again and she looked back.

"My god, will you get us *out* of here?"

"We're fine. Relax."

And they *were* fine, she knew that, but she guessed

Janet didn't believe her because she turned and reached for the door handle and Marion had to grab her by the arm and haul her back.

"You try to leave here and they'll see you. And you'll be dead. You get that? Look. Watch."

They were piling into the Jeep. The man with the gun was trying to key the ignition but all he was getting was a metallic grind. Obviously the cop's car was useless—there was smoke pouring out from under the hood. She could see the two men in back were starting to panic now, could hear their voices raised and the little one hopping up and down in his seat and then the driver turned and looked at her a third time.

That was when she smiled.

The man stared back, expressionless.

*"Oh my god,"* Janet whispered beside her.

Then her hands were at the glove compartment, bloody palms pounding at the button, leaving bloody palm prints all over the thing. The compartment popped open and she pushed the pint bottle aside and groped for the gun. Marion waited until she had it out waving around in front of her and then reached over and simply wrenched it from her slippery hands.

*"Unh-unh,"* she said. "Nope. Not today you don't."

She leaned out the window.

"Guys!"

At first they just sat there watching her. Then she turned the ignition key and the car fired up nice and easy, so she backed away from the tree and shifted and pulled forward to the roadside and waited.

The driver got out first and started across the street. The others followed. And that was when Janet went for the door again so she had to whack her on the head with the gun barrel and hit the automatic lock.

"Hey, prom queen. Stay the hell put."

He was a good-looking guy, this one with the Colt. Reminded her of some actor. *Scott something.* Craggy face, thin sandy hair, deep blue eyes that stared at them now through the open window. And then moved down to her gun.

"Oh, this?" she said. "It's not loaded."

She handed it to him and he broke it open, inspected it and handed it back to her. She hit the automatic lock again.

"Hop in, fellas," she said. "My friend and I were just out for a little ride."

Alan didn't know why he was doing this. He was younger than Janet by nearly five years—too young, maybe, to be stuck with just one woman—and he guessed that was one reason.

Though being stuck with Janet was hardly being stuck.

He'd have to cut it out though once they got married. He'd emulated his father by going into criminal law but he didn't have to emulate the rest of his behavior.

*Does the word* satyrasis *mean anything to you, buddy?*

She was a cute one, though, this little blond waitress from the Turtle Brook. Cute and so young and firm he'd lay odds her breasts didn't even bounce when she jogged and he'd lay more odds she *did* jog, and if her apartment was the kind of godawful mess a high school kid would be proud of, you didn't notice that under the sheets where he was, doing what he was doing. He listened to her groan and then suddenly he remembered.

*"Shit,"* he said into her pubic hair. He threw off the sheets.

She sat up against the headboard. He looked at her and guessed he'd been pretty good so far. Her breastbone was glistening with beads of sweat.

"I'm sorry. I don't believe it."

"What's the matter, honey?"

"I left my briefs at the house. They're sitting on the goddamn table."

"So?"

"I can't stay. Sorry."

"I don't get it. Who cares where you leave your underwear?"

Yeah, he thought, he was going to have to cut this out.

She felt as though she were trapped inside a kind of living thing, Jonah in the belly of a speeding whale that hurtled through a lonely electrified night. She couldn't seem to wrap her brain around the fact that a trio of killers were riding along behind her or that Marion was doing this or that she'd just watched one man kill another the way you'd put down a wounded dog. She'd represented killers before. She was representing one now for godsake—Arthur "Little" Harpe. Yet she'd never seen or felt the impact of what they did.

She was feeling it now.

The little man—the one sitting in the middle—seemed nervous, the others calm. *How could they be calm?*

"Where we going, Emil?" he said.

"Don't know."

*The killer's name is Emil,* she thought. *You remember that.*

"I could use a drink I guess."

"There's a package store ahead," Marion said. "Or do you want a bar?"

"Package store will do."

He was sitting directly behind Marion and she saw them exchange glances in the mirror and Marion's was amazing and simple to read. She's *turned on* by this, she thought. *Jesus.* She's crazy. Hell, they're all crazy. Either that or stupid as they come. Driving around like nothing had happened back there at all. When a cop was dead. It frightened her but it made her mad too. Stupidity disgusted her.

"You're going to a *package store?*" she said. "What about the car? I can't believe you people."

"What car?" said the man sitting behind her.

"The Jeep you left behind. Don't you think somebody might be *looking* for you?"

"Well, that Jeep ain't actually ours, ma'am. Sort of a loaner. You don't have to worry about the Jeep. It was nice of you to ask though."

"Your fingerprints will be all over it."

"Fingerprints don't work. They never get anybody on fingerprints. That's TV."

He wasn't exactly right there but he wasn't exactly wrong either.

"I've got a police band here," said Marion. "We can turn it on if you want. Just in case."

"Later, maybe," the man called Emil said. "Police band's a godawful noisy thing."

Marion slowed and turned into a gravel lot with two cars parked in front of a squat stucco building and a neon sign saying WILEY'S LIQUORS over the door and even before they stopped Janet wrenched at the door handle, her heart racing as the door opened and the impulse was irresistible, the gravel was going to hurt like hell but damn the gravel she was about to leap and roll when a hand gripped the back of her neck and pain shot through her head like a sudden migraine.

"When you got up this morning," the man behind her said, "did you get up this stupid?"

She could barely hear him, the pain was so bad. Some pressure point or something.

*"Please . . . let . . . go."*

"You gonna scream?"

"No!"

"Nobody around to hear you anyway. Couple frogs maybe. They build these stores like concrete bunkers. I guess I could let up a little."

"Pu . . . please do."

The man did but still held on to her with one hand so that the pain wound down to a dull throbbing ache while he leaned over and closed the door with the other and settled back in his seat.

"Better?"

"Y . . . yes."

"You're welcome."

The man called Emil opened the door on his side and climbed out of the car.

"Ray, stay with her. What's your name again, honey?"

"Janet."

"Stay with Janet here. Billy, come on along with me."

*The man who had her was Ray and the little one was Billy.*

He turned to Marion and smiled.

"C'mon," he said. "You'll see something."

"Wait here," Emil told her so she stood by the counter like she was interested in the magazine rack and listened to some old duffer in a white T-shirt and suspenders bend the balding store clerk's ear with some ragtime about plaster dust and sawdust just *pullin'* the moisture right out of his hands, *just pulling it outa my hands, look at them hands, just pullin' it right on out, i'nt that awful?* and the clerk looking at the upturned palms of his hands and saying *Yeah, Bob, that's terrible,* the customer paying for his bottle of Old Times and the clerk brown-bagging it while Billy set the two six-packs down on the counter just to the left of her and Emil his fifths of Makers Mark and J&B next to that.

The old man shoved his wallet into the front pocket of his baggy tan pants, hefted the bag into the crook of his arm and started to leave.

"Excuse me? Sir?" Emil said.

The man stopped and squinted at him.

*You'll see something,* he'd said. She guessed this was going to be it. She had to work to keep from smiling.

"Pay for this for me, will you, friend? I'm short on cash."

The man glanced at the whiskey and the beer. He shook his head.

"Crazy sumbitch," he muttered.

He moved toward the door again, and Emil flung his arm across her shoulders from behind and pulled her between the man and the door. When she felt the gun against her cheek the gasp was real.

"Pay for it. Or I shoot the lady and then I shoot you."

32

"He means it," Billy said. "He's not facetious."

"And you behind the counter. Don't move."

You could see the old guy sizing up the situation. She wondered what war he'd served in. He wasn't particularly rattled. Tough old bird.

She was doing all right so far though, she thought, playing the victim, eyes wide and mouth hung open in what she hoped looked like sheer terror though she was practically coming in her pants here for god's sake— and then Emil made things worse by sliding his hand down over her breast and squeezing and the old guy seemed to get the picture all at once. His face changed, hardened. And Emil must have seen that too because that was when he turned the gun and fired and the old man dropped to the floor howling and clutching his left foot, the Old Times bursting beside him.

"I forgot to mention that I could just as easily do it reverse order," Emil said. "Bag it. Ring it up," he told the clerk. He caressed her breast and she couldn't help it now and didn't try, she moaned. "Soon as he can, I know he'll be happy to pay up."

Which was exactly what both of them did.

They'd come whooping out of the package store like schoolkids at a panty raid but she'd heard the muted gunshot and now Billy was driving, with Emil and Marion in the back with Ray and she glanced around and saw the two of them kissing and his hand between her legs, so that she wasn't at all surprised when he told Billy to pull onto the narrow dirt access road and then to stop and cut the lights. They got out, a bottle of scotch in Emil's hand, and went running, laughing, for the woods.

They didn't go far. Just behind a stand of pines. She could hear them over the drone of crickets through the open window. Marion giggling and then groaning. Emil grunting like a goddamn animal. Brush crackling beneath them in the still air.

They *were* animals. So was the one Ray with the gun against her cheek, running it along first one side of her face and then the other so that each time she had to pull away and finally rapping her head with the barrel to make her sit still—rapping her lightly but her head was taking such a beating tonight it still hurt like hell—and then she could feel him lean over her, could smell the beer on his breath as he ran the barrel down over her neck and collarbone, heading for her breast and she could feel Billy's eyes on both of them.

You've got to stop this, she thought. *Now.* Already she felt bathed in filth.

"You'd better be ready to kill me," she said. "Just one more inch."

"Who says I'm not?"

"You didn't do the cop. *He* did the cop. You get caught, I can say that. You kill me, I can't. You've heard of state's evidence?"

"Uh-huh."

" 'Course he has," Billy said. "Everybody has. It's where you angle in on somebody and you get impunity."

The little guy was short a few major cable stations. She'd keep her pitch to Ray, who at least *appeared* to be somewhat sane—and she'd damn well have to hurry. The sounds from the bushes had all but stopped now.

"If you don't hurt me and you don't abuse me I can

help you. I know what I'm talking about. I'm a lawyer. It's my job to know."

"A lawyer?"

"A defense attorney."

"Bullshit."

She'd expected that. She dug into her purse for the wallet, opened it and flashed the laminated card at him.

"See that? That's a court pass. They don't come in cereal boxes, Ray."

He took it from her. The gun no longer pressed her flesh.

"I'll be damned."

He studied it a moment and handed it back to her.

"Well," he said, "I probably wouldn't be the one to shoot you anyway, truth be known. 'Less you started something. I'm a family man, you know. Want to see?"

She heard him digging into his back pocket, pulling out his own wallet and flipping through the plastic inserts. He couldn't seem to find what he was looking for.

"I had a lawyer once," he said. "I kinda liked the man. I appreciated his efforts on my behalf."

Then she heard him slap the wallet closed and abruptly shove it back into his jeans and turned and saw Marion and Emil come thrashing through the brush. Marion leaned in through Janet's window and smiled.

"Nothing like the great outdoors, hon. Shove over."

Alan was already thirty yards past it and headed along the downslope, briefs for the Mohica case foremost on his mind, when he registered Janet's blue Taurus, warning lights blinking like fireflies, dark and silent by the road. It wasn't safe to pull a U-turn here on the hill so he continued to the bottom and turned and drove back up again. He crossed lanes and parked into her dead headlights and got out of the car and peered in through the window. He didn't know whether to be relieved or not to find that there was nobody home.

He got back into his car and tried her on his cell phone but all he got was the machine and that *definitely* didn't relieve him. The gas station, maybe? Arranging for jumper cables or a tow truck? Could be. He got Kaltzas's number from Information but when he tried it the line was busy.

The anxiety really didn't hit him until he reached the roadhouse and saw the side of the road swarming with cops, saw the jackknifed car and the Jeep and the crime-scene tape and the forensics team working over the body of a man and then it *really* hit him when he saw the paramedics wheeling a woman into an ambulance. *Janet? My god,* he thought. He didn't know why he thought it—the woman could have been anybody—but it came unbidden and pounded through his blood. He slowed and then stopped even as the officer waved him on. He flashed his ID. The officer frowned at him anyway.

"What happened? Accident?"

"Shooting. One dead. One of ours, dammit."

"The woman?"

"Girl. Can't be more'n seventeen. Concussion, fractures, god knows what else. It's a helluva mess."

He nodded. "Thanks, Officer. Good luck. Hope you get the bastard."

"Bastards," he said. "Three of them."

Alan guessed it was just his night to be corrected. He pulled out and tried her again on the cell phone.

*"Leave a message,"* she said.

* * *

"Vehicle described as a late-model four-door Buick station wagon, light blue. Suspects are assumed to be armed and . . ."

"Dangerous," said Emil.

Billy reached over and flipped off the police band and pounded once at the steering wheel. "Shit," he said.

"How'd they make the wagon?" said Ray.

"The car that passed us by back there. While Billy was toyin' with the Man."

"Shit!" He pounded the wheel again.

"Called us in as an accident, probably. Good citizen. Well hell, we *are* an accident. An accident waitin' to happen!"

It seemed to break the tension and they laughed. Broke it for them, anyway, if not exactly for Janet. They were all too damn matter-of-fact about this. It wasn't right. It wasn't normal. And Emil. Couldn't *anything* shake Emil?

"We'll just find us another car, that's all," he said. "Meantime we better get off the road awhile." He turned to Marion. "You know a place?"

She looked at Janet.

"Do I know a place? Hell, yes."

She draped her arm over Janet's shoulders and gave her a squeeze.

" 'Course I do," she said.

She'd chosen the house because, unlike the Justice Building, where every footfall echoed like pistol fire across the marble floors, where even the walls were polished on a weekly basis, where the air was processed and always traced with disinfectant, the house was as much of nature as in the midst of it. Over 120 years old, it stood surrounded by tall untended grass atop a hill at the end of a two-lane dirt track that wound past a small country graveyard and an abandoned church of even earlier origin. Its beams were hand-hewn. Both fireplaces worked. The occasional bat still fluttered upstairs in the attic.

Her nearest neighbors were over a mile away. The house was quiet. It was private.

*Now it was remote.*

"How many phones?" Emil said. He'd walked in with his gun drawn. He shoved it in his belt.

"Just the one in the kitchen."

"Truth, now."

"Just the kitchen."

"Ray? You want to take care of that?"

"Sure."

Ray walked into the kitchen, put the paper bag containing the whiskey down on the counter and the beer in the refrigerator and unplugged the wall jack. The blinking light on her answering machine blinked out.

"Any guns?"

"No."

"You sure?"

"I'm sure. You want to hide the carving knives? I promise not to look."

Emil smiled. "I just might do that."

Billy plopped down in her armchair like a man after a hard day at work. Emil went to the refrigerator to get himself a beer. He popped one for Ray and handed it to him, then another for himself and closed the door.

"Hey," said Marion.

"Oh, right."

He got her a beer, opened it and stepped out of the kitchen and handed it to her.

"Sorry, Marie."

"Marion."

"Sorry. You care for one?"

"No," Janet said.

*She needed something a whole lot stronger. Not too much, god knows she had to keep her wits about her. But Jesus, something.* She went to the kitchen cabinet and took down the fifth of Glenlivet and a glass and uncorked the bottle.

"Scotch?" Ray said.

"Uh-huh."

"Hey, we got scotch too. Have some of ours. Be our guest."

"No thanks. *This* is scotch. You bought rubbing alcohol."

She poured herself a double. Ray took the bottle from her hand.

"So educate me," he said.

She got him a glass. He poured and drank.

"Smooth. What is it?"

"Single malt."

"Good stuff," he said.

"Where's the bathroom?" said Marion.

Janet pointed. "Through there. Through the bedroom."

"What's over there?" Emil said.

He was pointing to the closed door to the study. Neither Emil nor Marion knew what she happened to do for a living yet and for some reason she didn't want them to. So far the others hadn't said anything. But if he went browsing around in there he could probably figure it out for himself.

"A study. Books and papers."

He moved to the door and opened it and flicked on the wall switch and his eyes went to the cluttered desk.

"You work here?"

"Sometimes."

"You some kind of writer or something?"

"I write."

She walked over and as she turned the light off again and closed the door in front of him she saw Alan's forgotten briefs on the end table.

*He needed them tomorrow.*

*He's supposed to be staying in town tonight.*

"Please," she said. "This room's private."

He shrugged and smiled. "Sure. Okay. You figure on writing about me?"

"Would you want me to?"

She glanced at Billy, slumped in the armchair, opening and closing a big sharp-looking folding knife, his brow furrowed as though deep in thought. *Billy's got a knife,* she thought. *You damn well remember* that *too.*

"Sure I'd want you to. Farm boy makes good, right? You know I'm the seventh son of a seventh son? Supposed to be magic or spiritual or something, real powerful. Now Billy here's a preacher's son. A very spiritual being in his own right. And Ray . . ."

He turned to Ray, who was drinking Glenlivet straight out of the bottle.

*So much for a second one for me,* she thought.

"Hey, Ray, what's your story anyhow?"

"No story, Emil."

He laughed. "That's what I thought."

40

Then the door to the bedroom opened and Marion appeared and her anger at all four of them flared from dull to blazing. *She was wearing the black Versace nightgown, the one Alan had more than splurged for in Manhattan last Christmas, the one she'd worn just four times since—that night and then on his birthday, her birthday and the Christmas following and the garter belt was hers too and the panties and the black silk stockings.*

"I borrowed some things," she said. "Hope you don't mind."

Oh, I mind, she thought. You bitch. You bet I mind and you damn well *know* I do.

"Lord, Maria! Look at you!"

He went to her and Janet had cause to wonder exactly how much jealousy was floating around here in the room just then between these guys because Ray moved toward them too from the kitchen, the expression on his face unreadable as Billy stood up gawking while Emil ran his hands over her, showing off for them and for Janet too, Marion laughing and wrapping her arms around him as he dragged her back through the doorway to the bedroom and pulled her down on top of him across the bed, hips already grinding.

She saw Marion break the kiss, his big hands roving her breasts, and saw her turn and stare at her and knew that Marion was showing her something at that particular moment too. It was something about power and spite, she thought, that the girl from the wrong side of the tracks was all grown up now and somebody to be reckoned with. She got that message clearly. And never broke the look as she purposefully and calmly walked over to the bedroom and closed the door.

Billy slumped back into his chair. Began fiddling with his evil-looking knife again. She crossed to the couch nearby and sat. He wasn't going to scare her. Damned if he was. In the kitchen she could hear Ray swilling at the bottle. In the bedroom she could hear *them*. They all could. She had the feeling that it bothered each of them in one way or the other. She reached into her purse.

"You mind if I smoke?"

"Unh-unh. It's your domesticity."

She lit it, crossed her legs and tried to relax.

"Your TV work?" he said.

"Remote's right over there."

He took it off the table and pushed the POWER button. Some innocuous family comedy sprang out at them and the sounds from the bedroom disappeared beneath canned laughter. He started surfing the channels. His attention span seemed to be just about what she'd expect it to be: nil.

"Cinemax? HBO? Showtime?"

"No."

She saw him take in the furnishings—the Boston rocker, the rows of hand-carved decoys, the country primitive desk and pie safe and chairs and table, the 1821 children's sampler, the hundred-year-old map of the Hudson River, the heavy carved-oak shelving, the Tiffany-style lamps.

"I wouldn't think you were that penurious," he said.

"Excuse me?"

"I wouldn't think you were that penurious. That you'd just have basic cable, I mean. You have so many encumbrances here."

She sure did.

\*   \*   \*

It seemed forever sitting there with Billy flicking his goddamn knife open and shut with one hand and the channels with the other but it was probably no more than fifteen minutes because she was only on her second smoke when the bedroom door opened and there was Marion, this time draped in a bedsheet. *Her* bedsheet.

"Janet? Come on in a minute, would ya?"

Her bedroom seemed sullied to her now. Foreign. Enemy territory. She didn't care for the notion of going in.

"Why?"

"Got to ask you something."

"Ask me here."

"It's *girl talk,* honey."

She stubbed out the cigarette. As she passed she saw Ray seated in the kitchen, the bottle in front of him, pulling cards out of his wallet and shoving them back again, frustrated. Still looking for that family photo. She wondered if it even existed.

At the door Marion took her arm and led her into the room and there was Emil on the bed lying sprawled beneath her coverlet. Marion closed the door behind her and stood there and Emil smiled.

*"Next,"* he said.

It was a gut punch that turned instantly to rage and fear.

"Fuck *you!*" she said, and turned and saw Marion blocking her way and didn't hesitate for a moment— her two elder brothers had taught her to fight way back when and damned if she'd forgotten. She threw her right to the side of her jaw and Marion went down against the pinewood door like so much raw meat. She shoved her out of the way and her hand was on the doorknob when Emil lunged naked off the bed and she felt the warm sweat of his arms around her waist straight through her clothing. He pulled her down on top of him and she turned in his arms, kicking and squirming and trying to pull free but he was too strong. He shoved and rolled her so that he was on top of her straddling her hips, his hands pinning hers to the mattress near the foot of the bed. Then she felt other hands on her wrists, not as strong but strong enough and she heard Marion spit the word *bitch* and looked up at her naked and looming over her and holding her down, Billy and Ray standing in the doorway behind her and she knew she'd get no help from either one of them.

"Don't do this. Please, Marion!"

Marion smiled. And there was so much wrong with that smile that she knew she'd never understand it as long as she lived.

"Oh, honey," she said. "It ain't nothing. I had boy-friends used to give it to me rough all the time. You lay back, watch the ceiling. You'll get used to it."

Emil's fingers went to her blouse, to the buttons. Billy had his pocket knife in one hand and was poking its tip to his opposite thumb as though *testing* it while he and Ray moved to the bedside, watching them, an impossible drift of soulless motion and for the first time she really did fear for her life, knew that this might be the end of her right here on this bed, knew it so deeply and well that when her skirt went down and her panties went down and she felt his cock, hard and still beslimed with Marion against her thigh the room swirled and she nearly fainted in the knowledge, but she didn't, she wasn't going to be that lucky. She just looked away from them, from all of it and heard him spit on his hand and felt him wipe it across her and then the bright pain of entry like a thousand needles sinking all at once into her flesh and she cried out and heard the drone of Marion's voice above.

*"There, there, darlin'. You might as well know it. Life's nothing but a trail of tears for us girls. You might as well know."*

And then later, Billy demurring but not Ray. Ray the family man, solemnly stripping off his clothes. She turned away again.

And again that voice above her. Dreamy and cooing evil at her.

*"You've never seen what I've seen. There's so much you've just been protected from. Had a guy once, beat me morning, noon and night, regular, pretty much every day. And people used to say, why do you stay with him? He beats you! And I'd say I love him. He's mine. And I did, and he was. He may be crazy drunk nights but days he's mine, I said. What's a woman to expect from a man, anyhow? So don't you worry about any of this, honey. A woman can get over near anything. And I'm the living proof."*

When it was over they left her alone but did not completely close the door and she knew they could hear her sobbing so she stopped sobbing and wiped away the snot and tears and got up and used the bathroom, gave herself a whore's bath in the sink and washed away the blood across her face and hairline, then left the water running so they could hear and went back to the bedroom and opened the bedside drawer and silently as possible took out a pen and notepad, thought hard and began to write.

Emil leaned into the room just as she was zipping up her skirt and asked if she was ready. She said she was. She guessed they weren't going to kill her quite yet. He looked strangely hesitant for a man who'd just finished raping her.

"You're pretty much okay, right?"

"I'm . . . *(going to fucking get you)* . . . yes. *(Somehow I'll see you dead for this.)* I'm all right."

"Good. That's good."

She walked past him, fists clenched, on into the living room and saw the other three standing set to leave but ignored them and walked straight to the kitchen, took the half-empty bottle of Glenlivet off the counter and poured all that was left into a tall tumbler off the dish rack and drank prodigiously—*an old magician's trick, a little slight-of-hand, fellas*—because as she drank they were watching that and trying to gauge her. So that they did not see her set down the bottle on the small square of paper she'd slipped onto the counter beside it.

She drank most of what was in the glass. It wasn't only to complete the illusion. She needed it.

She slammed the glass to the counter.

"Let's go."

"Janet!"

Ever since the crime scene back on the highway he hadn't been able to shake the feeling that something was seriously wrong. Something wrong with Janet. He'd phoned Kaltzas's garage and got through this time and nobody had heard from her. It was the most likely place to go for help and she hadn't.

*Why?*

Inside the house was silent. Living room, study, silent. Just as he'd left them.

But not the bedroom.

The sheets were stripped off the bed and piled on the floor and that wasn't like her at all, they'd be in the hamper if she was planning to do a laundry when she came home tonight and that was troubling enough but then he saw the pair of beer cans on the dresser. She *never* drank beer. Hated the stuff.

So that now he was *really* worried.

*Phone the police.*

In the kitchen he saw more beer cans in the garbage and two more on the counter along with the empty bottle of Glenlivet.

*Jesus.* The Glenlivet was fucking *empty.* That was wrong too. They'd had a nightcap last night before bed and the bottle was still nearly full when he put it away. Then he saw the scrap of paper beneath it and pulled it out from under.

*NY TA45567*
*blue Dodge wagon*
*regist Marion Lane*
*Emil? Ray? Billy?*
*murder, Rt 605—8:30 p.m.?*
*HELP!*

The handwriting was shaky but hers. He reached for the phone and heard nothing but dead air so he followed the line down to where they'd pulled it out of the wall socket—*Who? Emil? Ray? Billy?*—plugged it back in and dialed 911. What if I hadn't come back for the goddamn briefs? he thought. What in god's name if I hadn't? Then the cop was on the line.

"Officer Hutt speaking. How can I help you?"

He put on his most businesslike, no-nonsense voice. A little amazed that he could do so.

"Listen carefully. My name is Alan Laymon and I'm an attorney. I have specific information regarding the murder of a police officer on Route Six-o-five at approximately eight-thirty this evening. I have a plate number for a blue Dodge wagon. The killers are holding at least one hostage, maybe two. I have names or partial names for all of them. Do you understand me?"

He did.

All told, Emil thought, things were looking good. He'd had two pieces of ass in a single night. He more or less preferred the one he hadn't raped. Which was fine since it was simpler. He had both of them here in the front seat beside him right where they ought to be.

He'd shot a cop—dangerous as hell, sure, but something he'd seriously wanted to do since fucking prison.

Not a bad night at all.

They were headed along a narrow dirt access road toward a farmhouse. Margaret or whatever her name was had spotted it, one light burning in a window in the valley below. She'd killed the lights when he told her to but the moonlight was plenty bright enough.

"Go easy," he said.

To the side of the farmhouse he saw a rusted-out Ford pickup that looked like it hadn't been on the road in years but beside it in front of the porch, a light-colored, four-door Chevy. It would do.

"Pull up here," he said. "Keep her running." They were about three car lengths away.

"Chevy looks just the ticket. Ray? You want to do the honors?"

Ray, the one with the hands. He nodded.

"Billy, go along and keep an eye on the house. Real quiet."

They opened both doors and stepped outside. He didn't have to tell them not to shut them. He turned to the woman beside him.

"You too," he said. "*Real* quiet. Are we clear about that?"

"Yes."

He watched them move to the driver's side of the Chevy and saw Ray open the door and duck in, Billy a little in front of him watching the house and already jittering like he had the shits, looking back at Ray as though willing him to hurry. He heard the engine sputter and die and sputter again through the still night air and thought, *damn!* just as the living room window flew open and the shotgun appeared and let fly and the Chevy's windshield exploded. He saw Billy hit the ground and start crawling toward the back of the car, Ray nowhere in sight.

"Get outa there! Goddammit! I'll blow your goddamn ears off!"

An old man's voice. One very *pissed off* old man.

The shotgun sparked and roared again and punched a hole in the grille. The car shuddered and the hood flew up as he fired a third time and then the left front tire was down and hissing. He saw Ray bail out of the seat and stumble for cover toward the rear of the Chevy and crouch beside Billy.

"Aw, shit," he said.

He put his arm out the window and fired at the same time the old man did and this time the blast kicked the hood off its hinges entirely and back against what was left of the windshield. *The bastard's sure doing a fuck of a job on his own car,* he thought. *Doesn't seem to give a fuck either.* Only now he'd discovered that there was somebody in the station wagon firing back at him, and Emil saw the shotgun glint and shift in the moonlight.

*"Hit it, Maggie!"*

He got off three fast ones toward the window and saw wood fly off the sill as she slammed her foot to the gas pedal and sent the car screeching into a turn behind the Chevy, spraying dirt and gravel as the goddamn woman beside him tried to haul herself over the seat, making for the open rear doors so that he had to reach for the back of her blouse and grab hold of her with one hand and fire at the farmer with the other and the farmer was shooting back. He felt the impact thump and quiver through the right rear body of the wagon. Ray and Billy were up and running for the wide-open backseat doors as she pulled the car through the full 180-degree turn, *getting them the hell out of there, yes!* and picking up speed, the two of them racing for the car and catching it right and left just as the shotgun roared a final time and they finally slammed the doors.

"Whew! That was one single-minded guy," Ray said.

"Disreputable," said Billy.

\* \* \*

The detective—the bigger of the two, Frommer his name was—was seated on the couch flipping through his notepad, frowning. Alan sat across from him on the edge of the armchair and waited. He heard the toilet flush and finally the smaller cop came out of the bathroom so that then they could begin.

"What we've got here's kind of unusual, Mr. Laymon," Frommer said. "Three out-of-staters and a local girl."

"Why unusual?"

"The boys turn up easy on the computer. Emil Rothert, Ray Short and Billy Ripper. Rothert and Short originally from Dead River, Maine. High school buddies, what little they had of it. Mostly they had Juvenile. Assault, arson, skin the neighbor's cat, that kind of thing. Graduated to armed robbery, rape and aggravated assault. No convictions. Both did time in Jersey—armed robbery again. And we figure they linked up with Ripper there because next we got all three of 'em booked for auto theft in Bristol, Connecticut, charges dismissed. This Ripper's a total fruitcake. Went after his mom eight years ago with a straight razor and damn near killed her. Lady sixty-six years old. Imagine that? But the real puzzler's this Lane woman."

"How come?"

"Let's just say the consensus is that she ain't got all her cookies in the jar," the smaller cop said. Frommer shot him a look that went from hot to cold. Then he shrugged.

"It's true," he said. "I wish I had a buck for every time she's called the station with some lame news or another. First she says she's being followed by some guy in a white Mercedes. Then she's getting obscene calls every night and she can't be sure but she thinks the caller's a *woman.* She can tell by the breathing. She calls us at least a dozen times on this one. Then somebody breaks in and cuts the wire to her window fan in the dead of summer. Then somebody breaks in *again* and cuts her phone line. Finally somebody sets fire to her garage.

"Well, there *was* a fire. Burned up an old sleeping bag and some old clothes and papers. We got no proof but two guesses who set the thing. She was all right I guess until her boyfriend ran off and dumped her. Since then, whacko."

"So you're saying . . ."

"So I'm saying we don't know if she's with 'em or against 'em. We figure she wasn't in on the killing. The driver who called it in said their car was off the road trying to kiss a tree. But other than that? Could easily be the one as the other. So the point is . . ."

*He knew what the point was.* "Jesus," he said.

"Right. We could be talking three bad guys and two hostages, or three bad guys, one hostage and one crazy. And I got to be honest with you. Either way it could get very nasty here."

They're up against it now, she thought. The police band had them *made.* Not just the car but *them.* She didn't know whether it made her feel frightened or elated. Maybe both.

*". . . suspects identified as Emil Rothert, thirty-four, white male, six feet two inches, two hundred fifteen pounds . . . Ray Short, thirty-four, white male, five feet eleven inches, one hundred seventy pounds . . . William*

*Grant Ripper, thirty-one, white male, five feet nine inches, one hundred forty pounds. . . ."*

Emil reached over and turned it off.

"I don't like this," Ray said. "This ain't good at all."

"We're fine. All we need's a car."

His voice was different though. Maybe she was seeing the first cracks in the great Emil Rothert bravado. She could hope so.

"They got the names, Emil, they got the plate number, the registration . . ."

"Which is why we need the car."

"And maybe here she comes," said Marion.

Headlights gleamed in the rearview mirror.

"Go for it, Mags," Emil said.

Marion got out and slammed the door and Emil reached across and locked it. His look said she had better not move, locked or unlocked. He turned and offered Marion's .22 to Ray and Billy.

"Who wants it?"

"I'll take it," Billy said. "Thank you very much."

"Everybody down."

In the mirror above she could see Marion waving frantically at the car's approach and she thought how she'd been doing exactly the same thing a few hours ago, *just looking for a lift* and then watched the car slow and stop directly behind them, the driver, a man in jacket and tie, leaning out and Marion walking over and leaning down, pointing back at the wagon, the man opening his door and getting out and his car's courtesy light blinking on so that she could see that there were other people in the car too, a woman in the front passenger seat and two smaller figures in back, Marion gesturing with fake exasperation as they walked toward the wagon, heard their footsteps approach and stop and the man say *what the . . . ?* in surprise as the two left-side doors swung open and Emil and Billy stepped out. She sat up. The man's eyes were going back and forth from gun to gun.

"Oh god. Oh, Jesus. Listen, please . . . my family. Whatever you want. Anything you want. Please . . ."

"Sir," Emil said. "We won't hurt your family. Just walk back to your car nice and slow. We're not gonna hurt anybody. Just take it easy, now, okay, sir?"

The man was clearly terrified but he did as he was told, turned and started walking. Emil, Marion and Billy followed.

Emil called over his shoulder, "Hey, Ray!"

"Yeah?"

"Bring her."

"Ray, you don't have to do this," she said. "Let me help you. Remember our talk? I can *help* you."

He sighed. "Listen, lady, I don't *want* your help. And I'm not so stupid that I'm gonna trust you either. Now get out of the car. Nothing's gonna happen to those people except we take their wheels."

"You can promise me that, Ray? Really?"

He couldn't. Only Emil could.

"Damn right I can promise you."

He dug into his shirt pocket and pulled out a wallet-sized snapshot, creased and worn. He handed it to her.

"Look," he said. "I found it."

She was looking at a color photo of a scrawny dish-water blonde and two scrawny kids of indeterminate sex, barely smiling, standing in a miserable yard in front of a broken swing.

His family.

"Now would you please get the hell out of the car?"

He held out his hand and she gave him back the photo and opened the door. He got out behind her.

"Listen," he said. "I want you to know I feel bad about . . . what happened back there. At the house I mean. Sometimes a guy . . . you know . . ."

"I know," she said and started walking.

She guessed the man and woman to be in their late twenties, early thirties. The woman had seen the guns and was out of her seat already and had gone around back to the little girl. The woman was pretty and her left eye had let go of one long tear that streaked her cheek but her arms were around her little girl and you could see she was trying to be brave and stay calm so as not to panic her and you could see that it was working. The girl was only five or so and looked confused by all this activity and her mother's sudden urgency but she didn't cry but only sat silent, wide-eyed and tense.

Beside her sat a teenage girl who looked much like the woman. She guessed they were sisters because the girl was too old to be the woman's daughter. At first glance she seemed frozen with fear. Then Janet saw something pass across her face and her lips set tight as she took the girl's hand in both of her own.

A family with grit, she thought. They don't deserve this.

"Let's go," said Emil.

He waved them out of the car. She noticed that it was another station wagon. Another fake "woodie" like Marion's, only a later model.

"Like I said, it's just the car we want, ma'am."

The man's arm went around his wife's waist and his

hand down to his daughter. The sister held the girl's other hand as Emil and Billy walked them back to Marion's car. Marion lit a cigarette with a wooden match that flared brightly in the still air and then diminished. She leaned back against their car.

Somewhere in the distance frogs bellowed out their longing.

"I think you can all squeeze together in the backseat there, right?" Emil said. She could hear every word. "I mean, for all I know, your wife might be an expert at hot-wiring. This is your wife, right, sir?"

He was trying to be reassuring. Janet wasn't reassured.

"Yes," the man said.

"Your daughter?"

"Yes."

"Kid sister?"

"Yes . . . well, no. My wife's sister."

"Well, sir, you've got a real pretty family here."

"Thank you."

"What I want you all to do is to stay in the back right where you are till we're ready to leave, okay? Then I'll toss you the keys as we go. Oh, and I might as well take yours now, sir. Good now as later, right?"

The man dug into his pocket and handed him the keys.

"What we're going to do is, we're going to have a little conference, the three of us, and then we'll be moving on."

They walked back to Ray, Janet and Marion.

"Give Margaret the gun, Bill," he said. "I don't see any problem coming from these people, Maggie, but you might want to watch your friend here. Ray, let's us talk."

They went off onto the shoulder a bit. Janet nodded toward the gun.

"Would you really use it on me?"

She seemed to consider.

"I don't know. I might. I think, probably. I mean, old times only goes so far, you know?"

"Jesus, Marion. He can't even get your *name* right!"

And then she shut up because she could hear what *they* were saying, talking the way other men might discuss some ad campaign or product or corporate merger, the way she'd heard *herself* talk in conference rooms and chambers with judges and lawyers and witnesses, all matter-of-fact and bottom-line and so much more terrible for that to hear *hell, they'll remember all of it, everything . . . how many guns we've got, what we look like, what we're wearing . . . sure they will . . . I don't see that we've got a choice, then . . . neither do I . . . we have to kill them . . . we've got to kill 'em . . . okay then, so what about the kid?* because if Janet could hear, then *so could the people in the car,* the windows were all wide open and they could hear their deaths discussed like three guys splitting the check in a restaurant and she could see them all huddled together, heard somebody openly crying now, saw them through the rear window embracing tight and frantic and the woman stroking her sister's hair and thought, *so tender! my god! this can't be happening!* and the man leaning over and wrapping his arms around them as though to ingest and swallow them up safe inside him and his back moving, sobbing or trying not to sob, she couldn't tell which and then she looked at Marion.

Marion standing there still and cold as a snake. The gun pointed casually in her direction.

Marion, who could and would let this happen.

*She might be the worst of them,* she thought. At least the others have their twisted evil reasons.

Then the men were moving, Billy toward Marion, taking the gun from her hand and following Emil who was headed straight for the car and Ray stopping beside Janet saying, *you want to be very smart now* and then watching them walk to the wagon and Janet watching too still unbelieving and wholly unable to speak as though that power was shut down tight in her as Billy and Emil turned their guns to the backseat of the car, flashes of muzzle fire and raw sharp clapping in her ears and bodies jerking, twisting, falling inside the car, blood and glass suddenly everywhere and the sharp tang of cordite assailing her and she turned and tried to run, *needed* to run, run anywhere, fighting Ray with all her strength and Ray simply *turning* her, his grip on her arms shearing deep into her muscles, turning her and forcing her to see the final volley, the sullen punch of bullets into limp flesh.

"Bless our loved ones," Billy said.

*And when she heard the whimpering into the silence that followed, the little girl's voice, the first she'd even heard that voice take breath, her legs gave way beneath her. Oh dear god no, she thought. Alive. Amid all that frightful death.*

Ray held her to her feet while the firing began again and Janet closed her eyes.

When she opened them and cleared them of tears the first thing she saw was Marion, her hands clutching hard at her breasts, the sheen of perspiration on her face and the wild light skittering in her eyes—a woman shattered in the wake of revelation and probably the orgasm of her life. She saw the men staring through the window, watching for further movement. She turned and saw Ray. And there was nothing there to see at all.

In the distance behind them headlights crested a hill and began to roll toward them deep into the moon-drenched valley.

Emil held up his brand-new set of keys.

"Let's *move!*" he said.

They'd driven a mile or so before she thought of it. Until then she'd felt empty inside as a propped-up wooden manikin sitting between Billy at the wheel and Ray riding shotgun, aware only of the straight smooth tarmac hissing beneath their wheels, the sound of flight, of movement. And maybe it was that which served to bring her back to herself and back to what she'd actually seen these people do just moments before. Because finally she thought of it.

She reached over past Ray to the glove compartment. Popped it open and reached inside. A can of de-icer. A pair of sunglasses. A cracked plastic windshield scraper. Half a roll of Five-Flavor LifeSavers.

The papers were scattered at the bottom atop the owner's manual. There weren't many. Insurance papers for the car. A dog-eared state map. Somebody's old shopping list on folded paper. Penciled directions to somewhere or other torn off a yellow legal pad.

That was all.

She almost wanted to laugh but laughter was still not even remotely possible.

"He was one of those," she said.

"Huh?" said Ray. "One of what?"

"He was somebody who kept his license and registration together. In his wallet. Did anybody get his wallet?"

She sat there and let that sink in.

Emil pounded the car seat behind her. It didn't even startle her. She'd figured he'd be the one to get it.

"God-fucking-*damn* it!"

"I didn't think so. So it was all for nothing," she said.

"What?" Ray said. "What the hell are you talking about?"

"Shit!" said Emil. "God*dam*mit! We gotta go back now."

*"What?"*

"We gotta go back!"

"Are you fucking out of your *mind?"*

"You wanted to get lost again," she said. "Switch cars. Lose the APB. Problem is, as soon as they find him they'll find the registration for *this* car in his wallet. So you didn't get lost again, did you? It was all for nothing."

"Jesus H. Christ."

"You killed a five-year-old girl for nothing."

"Turn here!" said Emil.

They were coming up on a turnoff to the right, a narrow strip of two-lane blacktop winding higher up the mountain. Billy slowed and made the turn.

"Pull up some and kill the lights, Billy. I want to see that car go by. Whoever it is can't be very far behind. There weren't any other turns off the road between here and there. If they didn't stop they'll pass us real soon. We've got to go back there but I want to see them pass first. That's it. Kill the goddamn lights."

They waited and Billy fidgeted beside her, tapping at the wheel with his thumbs to some music unheard by them while Emil, Ray and Marion watched through the rear window and Janet sat there staring straight into the dark, feeling strangely calmer now as though something had changed between them, some reconfiguration of their tableau and the odds against her. Though nothing had changed, really.

They waited and nobody came. The road behind them dark and silent.

"They stopped, didn't they," said Billy. "They stopped back there. They're viewing the whole image."

"Shut up, Billy."

"Shit! Shit! Shit!"

"I said shut the fuck up, Billy."

"He's right," said Marion. "They'd have passed by now if they hadn't stopped. Billy's right."

"I know he's right for chrissake. I just want a minute to figure this thing, okay?"

"What do you suggest, *Counselor?*" said Ray.

*"Counselor?"*

"She's a lawyer."

"What?"

"She's a lawyer. She told me."

"No shit. And you knew this how long?"

"Since before we went to her place. While you and her lady friend here were out in the bushes."

She could feel the rush of anger behind her, then just as quickly sensed him gain control again.

"You ought to have told me, Ray."

He sighed.

"Well, we got maybe two more hours till dawn, three to the state line. So I figure the state line's out for tonight. And yeah, she's right. We've got to assume they'll make this car once they find him. For all we know whoever the asshole is is already calling it in. So we need another car or a place or preferably both. Maggie's is out because they know she's with us and her place is probably out for the same reason. So your question's pretty good, Ray. What *do* you fucking suggest, Counselor? And don't say give yourselves up or I'll figure you're too damn stupid to be a lawyer."

"You think I should *help* you?"

"I'd say it's in your goddamn best interests, yeah."

And she knew he thought she was considering his threat. But she wasn't.

She was considering something else entirely.

So that when she spoke the hesitancy in her voice was phony but not the least *untrue*. She was a trial lawyer and part of lawyering was about performance and the correct and useful stance so she knew damn well it wouldn't show.

"Okay . . . all right. I know a place. It *might* work anyhow."

"So tell."

"You ever hear of a place called Hole-in-the-Wall?" she said, and then turned toward him.

He was smiling.

The night was awash in artificial light. Police flashlights slow-arced through the scrub and field along either side of the road. Flashbulbs burst sudden and stark against the human ruins in the wagon. Six sets of headlights set to high poured off the cruisers and the Volvo of the guy who'd called it in. Alan leaned against one of those cruisers and tried not to puke.

He'd seen what was inside.

He was shaking like it was zero degrees out, clammy with sweat at the same time. All he kept thinking was *at least she wasn't one of them*. At least that.

Frommer stubbed out his cigarette on the center line of the tarmac and then carefully policed his butt into his jacket pocket and walked over.

Alan shook his head. "I never . . . Jesus, Frommer, that little girl . . ."

"I know," Frommer said. "But I'll tell you, I think we can still hope for the best here, Mr. Laymon. I don't think we'll find her out there. I think she'd have been in the car with these poor people. These guys don't seem to take too much trouble hiding what they do."

He glanced toward the car and then back to Alan.

"I told you you shouldn't have looked," he said. "Hell, I shouldn't have either."

"How far?" Ray asked her.

Ray was nervous, Emil could see that—almost as nervous as goddamn Billy driving. It wasn't like Ray. It wasn't the guy who could lift a wallet in plain sight or steal a car in broad daylight on a busy street. Billy, on the other hand, was probably born nervous. He wondered if maybe he should be doing the driving but then thought no, it was better back here with his arm over whatsername's shoulder and his hand playing with her tit. Irresponsible but what the hell. They'd be all right.

"Just a few miles or so," she said.

"They're not gonna do this for free," he said.

"I know," Emil said.

"So?"

He'd already thought that out. He didn't answer

though. There was no way he was going to let *that* out of the bag just yet. But he knew about Hole-in-the-Wall from the joint and didn't think it was going to be a problem. Ray obviously did. He dug into his pocket and pulled out some wadded bills and change and counted it. Emil watched him and almost had to laugh.

"I got a total of seventeen dollars and seventy-eight cents."

He grabbed the lawyer lady's purse out of her lap and flipped open her wallet and started counting the cash inside. She didn't make any effort to stop him.

"She's got fifty-nine. Makes sixty-six, seventy-eight. What about you, Billy?"

"Exactly twenty-five dollars. Exactly what I came out with—you and Emil being kind enough to entail me my drinks for free."

"That's ninety-one, seventy-eight. Shit. Not even a hundred bucks. Emil? Maria?"

"Marion."

"Marion, sorry. What've you got?"

Emil pinched her nipple and she jumped and smiled, then reached over for her purse.

"Forty-three dollars, fifty-two cents, hon."

"Okay, okay. Shit, forget the cents. Forty-three dollars. Forty-three dollars and . . . what?"

"I believe we were up to ninety-one, Ray. Ninety-one dollars, seventy-eight cents, when you bash your groupings," said Billy.

"Forget the seventy-eight cents, all right? Forget the goddamn cents! That's . . . one hundred thirty-four. Emil?"

"Don't worry about it."

"Huh? Don't *worry* about it? Jesus, Emil! We're asking them to get us outa state here, you know? And so far we haven't got fifty bucks apiece!"

"Don't worry about it. I've got plenty."

"You got plenty. Fine. What's plenty?"

"Your turn's right here," the lawyer said. "Road to your left, just ahead."

"Goddammit, Emil," Ray said. *What the fuck's plenty?*

She'd driven by one day, curious, but as an Officer of the Court and "Little" Harpe's attorney of record, she'd been restricted from going any farther or seeing any more than she was seeing now—a wide dirt strip maybe twenty yards across cut through open, uncultivated fields on either side, rising up the slope of a mountain. No house in sight and no gate. No structures at all. But any approach observable from above.

They drove slowly and in silence until they crested the hill and that was when the first guard appeared along the side of the road, a big man almost comically dressed in nightfighter makeup and combat gear, his assault rifle held at port arms. There was nothing comic about the rifle.

"Slower, Billy," said Emil. "Stop if he tells you to."

But he didn't. He didn't look interested in them at all. Didn't even bother to wave them on.

Nor did the second guard a quarter-mile up, the field narrowing around them by then, gradually being swallowed by scrub and pine.

At the top of a rise, with dense forest pressing close now on either side, narrowing the road to a single lane funneling them up the mountain, she saw a third guard dressed in biker's colors talking into his cell phone, saw him shove the phone into his utility belt and raise his automatic rifle. The guard checked their license plate but didn't even glance at them.

It was eerie. As though they didn't matter.

And maybe they didn't.

The road narrowed even more. The woods drew closer.

At the top of another rise two more guards in military gear stood across from one another on either side of the road, one black man and one white. Each had a sleek black Doberman on a short leash.

"I hate those doggies," said Billy. He pronounced it *dawgies*.

"Shut up," said Emil. "Slow down."

Because this time the guards were stepping toward them. The men stopped and turned their flashlights into the car and then the black guard on Billy's side motioned them on.

"This is pretty fucking weird," said Ray.

Nobody contradicted him.

The road sloped downward and narrowed yet further as though the woods were a fist closing in on them and at the bottom of the hill stood a tall bald black man in dark neatly pressed suit and tie with his hand raised and his assault rifle cradled in the crook of his arm. Billy stopped the car. The man walked over to his side, taking his time. He stooped and peered in, smiling.

"Welcome to Hole-in-the-Wall, gentlemen," he said.

The man had no trace of an accent at all. *The black man in the dark expensive suit was from Anywhere, U.S.A. Their welcoming committee. Very civilized. Uh-huh.*

"Directly on top of the next hill there. Can't miss it.

You can state your business to the gentleman at the bar. Have yourselves a pleasant evening."

He stepped aside and watched them pass and Janet turned and looked back.

The man was following them on foot, his rifle slung over his shoulder, moving at a graceful, easy pace.

Marion thought, *Humpty Dumpty.*

*Humpty Dumpty sat on a wall, Humpty Dumpty had a great fall. All the king's horses and all the king's men, couldn't put Humpty together again.*

It was something about the tree, something about the huge ancient solitary oak tree in front of the house— the mansion, really, Hole-in-the-Wall was a three-story, gabled, corniced, fucking bay-windowed porched-in old mansion, *some hole! some joke!*—something about that tree and the tire hanging from the chain that depended from a limb, the skeleton of a big openmouthed dog or maybe a wolf, the wolf-dog grinning, arranged seated on the tire with hind legs dangling, another fine joke, the four thick nooses swaying in the wind hanging from another limb higher up, the nooses not so funny, something about the tree had put that stupid old nursery rhyme into her mind.

*Humpty Dumpty sat on a wall. . . .*

A marching song. A drum cadence. Her dad had been VFW all the way. *Dat*-da-*dat*-da-*dat-dat-dat-dat* . . .

As Marion herself marched along behind Emil, as they all did, past the hogs and pickups and Land Rovers and Jeeps and Mercedes and black stretch limos and Rollses. Marched up the stairs to the porch, the suited black guard with the rifle ambling along behind, *dat*-da-*dat*, to the dimly lit porch with heavy chains hanging

67

from the eaves like a thick metal curtain, parting them, chains ringing in her ears like strange dull wind chimes and the scent of oil and metal on her hands as she touched them, stepping onto the porch hung with mobiles—inverted bone crosses and rusted knives and studded belts and weathered leather collars—where six wooden barrels filled with what looked like old automobile and motorbike parts stood in an orderly row to her left and a smashed-in Wurlitzer jukebox lay on its side to her right beside a broken plough propped up against the siding, its handles carved into knobbed human phalluses and flanked by two painted wooden signs—TREE FROG BEER and DWARF SNUFFING STATION NUMBER 103.

Somebody around here's got a real strange sense of humor, she thought.

She saw Emil hesitate at the door and heard the black man behind them tell them to *go on in, folks* in his calm soft voice and so they did.

They walked into a fucking *party* is what they did.

She could feel her heart thud all of a sudden fast and heavy, making her tits tremble, was aware of her eyes going wide and her lips pulling up into a smile she had nothing to do with at all.

*Daddy,* she thought, *if you could see your little girl now. You'd be fucking floored by this.*

Beyond the heavy oak door was an enormous open space and the goddamn place was swarming. Motorbike headlights slung from the rafters handled the lighting, streaming down on them like spotlights. She saw bikers, skinheads, longhairs straight out of the goddamn Sixties, men in tuxes and women in gowns all mingling and laughing. She saw a male tattooed hand go to a female pearl-draped breast. She saw steroid freaks dressed for combat and guys naked and limp-dicked and emaciated all to hell. She saw martini glasses and Budweisers and joints and in the corner to her left, the sharp glitter of needles. She saw crude prison tattoos and elegant multiple piercings. They had weapons all over the place. Handguns in shoulder holsters. Shotguns and automatic rifles propped against the wall while their owners roamed and drank and did whatever the hell they were doing.

The whole first floor had been completely gutted, the walls knocked down to expose rough support beams that reached twenty-five feet all the way to the ceiling—a ceiling draped and webbed thick with a canopy of chains. At intervals they dangled to the floor. Six feet or so up one of the support beams a naked brunette dangled too, suspended by ropes wrapped around her wrists and elbows. She looked drugged out of her fucking gourd and like she'd been up there quite a while. There were bloody welts along her tits and thighs and the blood was already drying. Everybody just ignored her.

They moved through the crowd toward the bar, Emil first with her behind him and then Ray and then Billy behind Janet bringing up the rear. Some asshole headbanger music was pouring off the speakers. The floors were long wide slabs of polished hardwood, expensive as hell she bet. By contrast the bar was crude and cut of rough naked oak with the bark still attached where it wasn't planed down smooth and it crawled the whole length of the room all the way to the open staircase in back like a living thing. The six beefy guys who were working it were dressed in formal white starched shirts and black ties. Directly across from the bar a fire blazed in an open stone grate cut into the wall like the huge open mouth of hell. It must have been over a dozen feet across. Considering its size it didn't seem to throw much heat, just the smell of wood smoke.

She guessed that on the air-conditioning bill alone this place could probably buy and sell her.

She saw bright primitive murals on the walls, scenes she recognized right away from Revelations. *Daddy? Momma? You'd just* love *this shit! The Dragon. The False Prophet. The Great Whore. The Beast. The Woman in Scarlet.* Religion? In *this joint?* Between the murals meat hooks polished to a high sheen, dozens of them, substituted for what—in someplace less bizarre than this—might have been stuffed moose or deer or bobcat. Somebody'd painted the words BILGE RAT next to one of them. Under another, MEN ARE NECESSARY FOR THE GODS. *Huh?* Beside a third, the numbers 666. She sure as hell knew what *that* meant.

Jesus, she thought, who *are* these people?

She glanced back at Janet. Janet was looking decidedly twitchy and tense, eyes darting around the room as though she expected somebody to come out after her with a goddamn meat cleaver. Poor baby.

Their bartender was a neatly dressed Jabba the Hut made flesh.

"Heineken," said Emil. "Five of 'em."

The bartender reached for the beers and popped them.

"We need a car," said Emil. "First we need a place to stay tonight and tomorrow we need a car."

The bartender shrugged. "You don't get anybody too pissed off at you, you can stand right where you are till

70

you drop dead or hell freezes over, whichever comes first. I could give a shit."

"What about the car? We need a car."

"You can pay? Got money?"

"We can pay."

She wondered how much Emil *did* have. Billy and Ray seemed freaked about the whole money thing.

She watched the bartender walk the length of the bar and stop in front of a black man who looked like the twin of the suited guard who'd pointed them toward the house—right down to the shaved bullet-shaped head and the assault rifle slung across his shoulder. The bartender spoke to him and the man nodded and turned toward the staircase and the bartender waddled back to his post.

"You're Rothert, right?" he said.

"How the hell do you know that?"

"You're the news tonight. Shot a cop. That gives you three whole minutes of glory. Enjoy yourself. I could give a shit."

She heard a sudden commotion behind them, raised voices and heavy footfalls and clanking, grating sounds and felt the crowd shift around her and turned and saw two big men in studded boots and leather pants and vests hauling a woman off the floor by a chain attached to a pulley twenty feet away. The woman wore police cuffs and nothing else and the look in her eyes was drugs and fear and then pain shooting through her wrists as the men tugged the chain through the pulley and she could see that somebody'd shaved her completely, both head and cunt too.

They hauled her five feet or so off the ground and then slipped a link of the chain through a hook set into the floor and she hung there and the men were smiling and saying something to one another and then they *weren't* smiling, they were all pissed off all of a sudden. With the pounding tide of music she couldn't hear what it was they were saying but they were pissed off all right and the crowd was moving back in her direction even though some were laughing as though the two men arguing were the center of an oncoming twister.

One guy had a short goatee kind of thing and the other didn't but they were matched pretty well physically, she thought, big raw biceps and beer bellies so goddamn hard that when the bearded guy gut-punched the other she could hear it over the music like a basketball smashed down from a hoop. He doubled over and the man kicked him in the face and sprayed the crowd with blood and spit. The man went over backward and scrambled across the floor and came up with a length of chain, stood and started flailing, catching the bearded guy across the back and then the shoulders and then the head as he fell, going for the head over and over again—and the crowd was wild by then and so was she. She could barely fucking breathe. The bearded guy's head was a mess but he must have had something amazing left inside him because his hand swung up from the floor and he took the other guy's balls in his great big hand and squeezed. Then they were both rolling groaning along the floor.

*Humpty Dumpty sat on a wall*, she thought and she couldn't help it, she giggled like a goddamn little kid and as the pair of guards in combat gear parted the crowd and dragged the two men away across the bloody floor a skinhead with tattoos of a swastika and a bolt of lightning on his arm prodded the shaved naked woman

72

hard in the ribs with his rifle as though it were her fault all this had happened so that she jerked away in pain, more pain, and Marion finished her beer and set it on the bar and turned toward where she hung and started forward.

Janet watched her move through the crowd. The others didn't seem to notice she was gone.

"You want this?" Emil said.

He pointed to her beer on the bar. She shook her head. The last thing she wanted was a beer. He upended it and she watched his throat move. The man is nervous, she thought. Fine.

"Just four this time," he said to the bartender. The bartender set them on the bar. He passed one to Ray and one to Billy and only then did he realize they were missing somebody.

"Where's Whatsername?"

He sounded more annoyed than she'd have expected and there was something else there too. Fear? From Emil? If so, fine again. The only question was as to why.

"Let's go," a voice behind them said.

*The black man in the suit. The first guard's twin.*

"Where to?" said Emil.

"We got to go deal for your transportation, my man." Not quite so well-spoken, she thought.

"Wait a minute. I can't . . . listen . . . just hold on a second, okay? Have a beer."

He handed the man his beer and started pushing his way through the crowd.

"Hey! *What the fuck? Fuck you, asshole!*" The man slammed the beer down on the bar and moved after him.

Ray took her by the arm and then they were moving through the crowd too with Billy trailing behind. They heard somebody scream ahead, throaty and then shrill. *Marion?*

I should be so lucky, she thought.

She spotted Emil and the guard at the edge of the crowd and then saw Marion standing beneath the woman, staring up. A thin line of blood ran from the woman's rib cage to her navel. The neo-Nazi skinhead had his arm around Marion's waist boyfriend-and-girlfriend-style and was gesturing toward the woman with a broad, sharp-looking knife like an instructor working a blackboard with his pointer. Like the woman was some sort of math problem.

"See?" the Nazi said. "You cut her here and it don't hardly hurt."

He sliced the top of her foot just above the second toe.

"You cut her here though . . ."

He moved the knife across the sole of her foot and the woman screamed again. Emil grabbed Marion's arm.

"What the hell you doing?"

She didn't answer. Just stood there watching the blood drip off the woman's foot along either side.

"Hey, Maria. We got to go."

"Damn right," said the guard.

"Fuck off," said the Nazi. He pointed the knife at Emil. Emil let go of Marion's arm and backed off, hands in the air.

*Now this was interesting.*

"Got nothing to do with you, friend," he said. "We got business, that's all."

74

"I told you, fuck *off!*"

He jabbed with the knife and as Emil darted back and away the black guard stepped forward easy as you please. He placed the tip of his index finger against the tip of the blade and smiled.

*"Play nice,"* he said.

The Nazi didn't seem to know what to make of that.

"Like the gentleman says, it's business. This what you came for?" he asked Emil.

He nodded. The guard looked at Marion.

"Come on, sweetcakes," he said. "She gonna be hanging around awhile."

"Not yet."

She turned to the Nazi and put her hand out, palm-up. The Nazi didn't seem to understand at first and then he did. He handed her the knife. Marion looked at the guard.

"Is this okay?" she said. "I can do anything I want, right? I mean, that's true, isn't it? Hell, I can kill her if I want, right?"

*"Excuse* me, lady?"

"Suppose I killed her, is anybody going to mind or what?"

"Jesus, Marion!"

"Oh, shut up, Emil."

She turned back to the guard. He smiled again and shook his head.

"Nah, can't kill her, honey. She belongs to somebody. You could hurt her a little, though. Nobody going to bother you about that."

You don't need to see any more of this shit, Janet thought. You can just turn away. But it seemed important to know exactly how far this goddamn woman was willing to go. So she watched her as she reached up and traced a slow deep line across the woman's thigh from hip to knee with the point of the knife, the woman trembling and moaning, and watched the blood well up thick over the blade of the knife onto Marion's white-knuckled hand. Watched the hand draw away and poise to cut again and then the black man's bigger hand close over it gently and take the knife away and hand it to the Nazi.

"Come on, baby," he said. "Leave a little somethin' for later."

As he moved her away she was smiling.

"You're not entirely a real nice person," said the guard as the music welled and boomed again. "You know that?"

They followed him through the crowd to the stairwell at the end of the bar.

At the top of the stairs he led them down a long dark oak-paneled hall, empty but for half a dozen vases on pedestals from which dozens of long-stemmed red roses sprouted and scented the still air, rioting away the odor of cigarettes and stale beer below. He opened a set of double doors to a stark, brightly lit room with a single long table and chairs around it the only furnishings—a boardroom not unlike those back at the courthouse except that this table and these chairs must have cost a lot more than the taxpayers were going to put up with. Closed glass doors beyond the desk led to an open porch—a widow's walk. Beyond them she could see moon and stars.

The man at the head of the table was middle-aged and small and thin, his wrists wiry in his rolled-back shirtsleeves. He looked like a businessman who'd just spent a rough but eventful evening coming up with whole new ways to hammer the competition. Papers fanned across the desk in front of him. Behind him stood an immaculate gentleman with manicured fingernails and a rose in his wide lapel and the word *thug* writ plain all over him.

"Mr. Thaw?" said the guard.

"Fine. You can leave now."

He backed out of the room and closed the door.

The man looked up from his desk.

"Harold Thaw," he said. "This is my associate, Mr. Coombs. And you are Rothert, Short and Ripper. You want a car, I'm told. Is that all?"

"That's all, Mr. Thaw," Emil said.

"Fine. Ten thousand cash."

Ray looked stricken. "Ten *thous* . . . ?"

"You killed a policeman, Mr. Short. It's a very good price."

"I was thinking of something else, sir," Emil said.

"Were you."

"Yes, sir."

"What were you thinking, Mr. Rothert?"

"I heard that . . . I understand you do . . . a certain business. With certain parties. Foreign investors, sort of . . ."

For the first time Thaw smiled. "What business would that be, Mr. Rothert? I have any number of businesses and you're interrupting all of them. Please do get on with it."

She saw that Emil was distinctly uncomfortable now but determined to do as the man said and *get on with it*. And even before he opened his mouth again she knew exactly where he was going with all this. It was rumored at the courthouse. She'd heard it a dozen times. You goddamn son of a bitch, she thought.

*"Women,* sir," he said. "I understand you . . . that you deal in women sometimes."

For a moment Thaw just stared at him as though he was speaking in some unknown tongue. He looked at Marion and then at Janet and when his eyes went back to Emil again he laughed and his hands went wide and spiderlike across the table. Behind him, Coombs smiled.

"You're offering me *these?* In exchange for a car?"

"Uh, yes, sir."

Thaw laughed again and shook his head.

"Rothert," he said, "these *parties* you're talking about are interested in twelve-year-olds. Twelve-year-olds, Rothert. Do you understand me? Do you see the problem here?"

Emil nodded toward Marion.

"Sir, this one in particular. Have somebody try her out, that's all I'm asking. She's a little crazy, see? She'll do anything. You don't think you can use her? Fine, no car. We'll figure out something in the morning."

"Hey, Emil," Marion said, "screw you!"

"That's all I'm asking, sir."

"Fuck *you,* Emil!"

She turned on her heel and went for the door, turned the knob. Twisted it. Shook the door and pounded it.

"What have you got to lose, sir?" Emil said.

"You fucking prick! Open the fucking door!" she yelled to the guard outside. She turned to Emil. "Tell him to open the *fucking door!"*

Thaw leaned back in his chair and sighed. Marion twisted at the knob one last time and then she was moving fast across the room to the glass double doors to the widow's walk beyond, and to Janet it looked like she just might kick the damn things in in order to get out of there. Thaw stood up from his chair and shouted.

*"Big!"*

The glass doors parted and Marion stopped dead in her tracks. The man standing in front of her was big all right—as big as a goddamn bear and looked easily as dangerous. She recognized the long square jaw and scraggly beard. The arms beneath the cutoff sleeves of his faded denim shirt were easily as wide as her thigh. A massive chest tapered down to an almost graceful waist. *Six-foot-six, 320 pounds,* she remembered. *"Big" Micah Harpe. In person.*

He didn't move.

He didn't have to.

And seeing him there finally after having searched for him ever since arriving scared the hell out of her and made her heart leap all at once. With Micah Harpe it would be all or nothing. She'd known that from the very start.

Thaw sat down again and leaned back in his chair.

"You heard?" he said.

"I heard a talking asshole, sure. How about you?"

Harpe's voice had a Kentucky twang to it that surprisingly was not at all unpleasant.

"About the same, Big. About the same. I'm wondering, though. Is Mr. Harrison still here?"

"Downstairs, I think."

"Downstairs?"

"Think he was planning to stay awhile."

"You might try him, then. If he's happy, perhaps we can accommodate these gentlemen. If not . . ."

"Will do."

He took a single step toward Marion, reached out and wrapped his huge hand in her hair and pulled her toward him. Then he turned to Emil, released her hair and shoved her at him like a kid would pass a basketball and with no more effort.

"You're the one trading here," he said. "You handle her."

The waiting was making Alan crazy. He guessed it wasn't doing Frommer a lot of good either. The man kept lighting one cigarette after another. A couple of puffs and he'd stub it out and a couple minutes later light another. It was as though he *wanted* to smoke but was determined to be smokeless if and when any news came through. The roadblock was one of dozens throughout the area but standing at this one felt like being all alone in the world, cut off from everybody and everything, waiting for a train that was never going to pull on in.

"I don't get it," Frommer said. "Homes are pretty few and far between around here and we've pretty much covered them all. We've got the roadblocks set and we've checked the access roads for miles damn near to the state line. We've got enough highway patrol units working these mountains to flush out a jackrabbit. They can hide overnight in the woods but the car sure can't. So how come I'm doing everything right and they're still not showing?" He lit another smoke. "You maybe thinking what I'm thinking?"

*He was.*

"Hole-in-the-Wall," Alan said.

"We'll need a warrant. Know any judges who are early risers?"

"As a matter of fact I do," he said.

A year ago he'd slept with her. Janet never knew.

*Now,* she thought, *it's got to be now.*

Ahead of her on the stairs Emil was hauling Marion down, cursing and fighting him all the way but Janet knew his strength firsthand and knew it wasn't going to do her a damn bit of good. Billy was smiling, having a fine old time with all this, laughing and poking her with his index finger from behind. Ray ignored him but seemed to consider Marion with something like regret.

In one way or another each of them was focused on Marion. She stopped and turned.

"Micah Harpe," she said. "Big."

He looked puzzled. *How would this woman know his name?* So did the black guard behind him.

"Yeah?"

"Two things. My name's Janet Morris. Does that ring a bell?"

"You been on the bands all night. I know who you are."

"You don't understand. I'm a lawyer. I represent your brother. And our defense is based solely on you, Mr. Harpe. We're saying it was you who killed George and Lilian Willis and not Little. That's the first thing."

She was talking for her life now and she knew it. She also knew learning of her defense strategy wasn't going to make him happy.

"I'm interested. The second?"

"I read your rap sheet. The attempted murder, the one in prison."

"Uh-huh."

She glanced down the stairs. The others had reached the bottom and Emil was staring hard at them, suspicion knotting his brow.

"The man was your cellmate. He'd been there just three days. You beat him into a coma. Why?"

"I didn't like him."

The guard was smiling.

"You didn't like him because he'd murdered his wife and children. His *children*. You seemed to feel very strongly about that."

"Nobody on the inside likes a baby-killer. Maybe me less than most. So what?"

"What if I told you what you *haven't* heard on the police bands yet?"

She looked over her shoulder. Emil had handed Marion off to Ray now and was climbing back up the stairs. He was already halfway there.

"What if I told you I just saw these people shoot a four- or five-year-old girl to death in her parents' car, just to *steal* the car? Would you still let them walk on out of here? Because that's what they did. A man, a woman, a teenage girl and a five-year-old *child,* Mr. Harpe."

She was aware of Emil right behind her now and knew he'd heard that last part but she didn't give a good goddamn what or how much he'd heard and her anger was real when she whirled on him.

*"Tell him!"* she said.

Emil looked too damn surprised to answer.

"That true?" said Harpe.

Emil just looked at him.

"You a pimp *and* a baby-killer, asshole?"

Then suddenly his confusion seemed to resolve itself. He threw his arm around her neck and yanked her off the stair she was on and slid the gun out of his belt and jabbed the barrel to her forehead, his breath hot and sour against her face.

*"Fucking bitch!"*

The guard behind them raised his rifle.

"Go ahead," said Harpe. "Shoot her. And then I guess you're gonna shoot your way outa here, right?"

She glanced down at Billy and saw him draw Marion's .22. Harpe saw it too.

"Looks like you are," he said. "You are one bunch of stupid people, you know that?"

"Back off!"

He slammed her forehead with the gun barrel. His arm was choking her. She saw stars and tried not to fall.

"Back off, goddammit!"

He hit her again, harder this time, exactly where she'd hit the windshield hours ago so that she was bleeding again, yet even through the bright spreading pool of pain she could feel him trembling, fear or anger or both, and that drove her own anger, keeping her afloat above the pain. She was aware of all the people watching them below and that the place had gone practically silent, that somebody had finally killed the chaos they'd been listening to all night. So that the third time he hit her it thundered in her ears like a single blow on a drumhead.

*"You want a dead lawyer here? I'll damn well give her to you!"* Emil screamed.

"You already did that, remember?"

"What?"

"I said you already did. You're damaging your own merchandise. Fool."

And that was true enough. She could feel the warm blood crawling down her cheek. Emil didn't seem to understand.

She did, though. Hope seemed suddenly to fly away down those stairs.

"Did I say what you did or didn't do changes anything?" Harpe said. "Mr. Thaw says to try Harrison, I try Harrison. You get it now, you ignorant sonovabitch?"

Then he *did* get it finally and lowered the gun and let go of her and she fell to her knees against the stair. Harpe held out his hand. Emil hesitated and then handed him his pistol. Then turned to Billy downstairs.

"Put it away, Bill."

"I don't have any accord with this man," Billy said. The gun was pointed directly at Harpe.

"The man don't like you either. Put it away."

"It's all right," said Harpe. "Let him hold it if he wants. Don't matter."

He nodded. Just once. And suddenly the room exploded in gunfire, all of it pouring across the floor at Billy, at least a dozen guns at once, Ray and Marion pitched flat-out beside him with their hands covering their heads as Billy danced and twitched like some boneless thing erupting flesh and blood, muzzles flashing and bullets tearing into him from every which way keeping him on his feet until he dropped like a sodden sack, the gun still clenched in his bloody right hand.

She smelled cordite thick and vile for the second time that night and thought of the little girl again. She felt nothing at all for Billy—not even satisfaction. It was no surprise to her at all.

She looked at Emil. His face was white, his mouth

slack. Without his own gun he seemed smaller, diminished down to just another weak aimless man. Harpe moved on past them down the stairs, saying nothing to either of them, past Marion and Ray peeling themselves up off the floor and past Billy's pooling blood, and Emil stooped and helped her up and they followed, Emil's legs just as unsteady as her own, she thought, the guard a step behind them. Followed him as he moved through the crowd and gunsmoke like a walking boulder or some living, breathing god past a biker leg-wounded in the crossfire, patting him on the shoulder, the man grinning at that, followed him to the back of the room where he opened a door and led them down to more stairs and darkness.

Billy was there one moment and *not there* the next and that was the way of it, the way it always was, Emil thought, for the cop and for that family back there and for all the others, nothing too fucking astounding about that, nothing to worry a man particularly. So he had to figure it was the fucking *room* and what was going on in it that was troublesome, the dark of the room and the long moving shadows against the rough stone walls as they came off the stairs, the room dark except for some candles and a flickering fireplace way down at the end. So the *room* was bothering him? The fucking *room?*

Or maybe it was the fucking *altar?*

Because that's what it was all right, a goddamn altar, three long wide slabs of what looked like solid granite— these assholes and these rich bitches gathered around it a bunch of weirdo zombies going about their business crowded around the altar toward the back, the word RISE painted across the ceiling, some dumb-ass pentagram thing on the wall behind them just like in the horror movies, diamond necklaces and formal ties showing above black robes, diamond earrings and Rolex watches, no bikers or Nazis in *this* neck of the woods, no sir, all these rich-fuck weirdo zombies moving along one by one, washing their hands and faces out of a great big copper bowl and toweling dry and throwing the towels in the fireplace.

All *that* was bothering him. Yes it was.

The six big Dobermans prowling around were bothering him too. Their eyes gleaming by firelight, their wet panting. The chattering sounds their toenails made against the fieldstone floor.

And the one he guessed was the Big Kahuna, the only one facing him, the one with the *hooded* robe and the upraised bloody hands and the goddamn blood streaked all over his goddamn bony face, he was *sure as hell* bothering him.

"Who the fuck *are* these guys?" he whispered to the guard.

"Ever hear of the Church of Final Judgment? Meet your basic pastor."

And then he was coming toward them, smiling, face and hands washed and dried now just like the others who parted to let him pass and Emil could see what else besides the bowl was on the altar.

It had been a guy once. Now it was naked body parts. A hand here. A leg there. A cock and a pair of hairy, bloody balls.

"Jesus Christ," he said.

"Healthy, Mr. Harpe?" said the man.

"Depends on your point of view," said Harpe. "Healthy enough, I guess."

And then the goddamn fruitcake was walking around *inspecting* them. *All* of them. He took a while checking out Whatsername's tits in particular.

"Seedy," he said. "I like that."

"The price is ten thousand," said Harpe.

Whatsername had already begun to cry. Fuck her. Two black-robed women took her by either arm.

"All right. They'll do," said Harrison.

"Hey. We're only talking about the ladies here, remember?" Emil said.

"Really?" said Harrison.

He looked at Harpe and Harpe looked at Emil.

"Not really," he said.

She watched them bolt up the stairs and hit the door at a dead run. The door wouldn't budge. Ray stumbled and fell and Emil backed off and tried again.

"This one's excepted," Harpe said.

"Why?" said Harrison.

"She's a lawyer. A defense attorney."

Harrison laughed. "Quite right, Mr. Harpe. No policemen, no lawyers and no Supreme Court justices. I suppose I can live with the other three."

There was considerable strength in numbers and it didn't take them long to pull them off the stairs—Emil's furious terror, his flailing feet and fists be damned. Ray put up practically no resistance at all. Maybe he really *was* sorry about what he'd done to her. Maybe he figured he deserved this. Whether he felt that way or didn't, she couldn't care less.

On the floor they surrounded them and began to kick and as though that was some signal the Dobermans began to bite and growl and shake. *Ray's calf, blood flying off it, his right hand. Emil's arm and then his shooting hand.* Over the howling of the men and shrieks from Marion she heard Harrison tell Harpe he could take her now.

"You want to watch?" he said.

"No."

They started toward the stairs. Behind her Marion screamed her name and she turned.

"Janet!" She was struggling to get free of the women behind her. There were three of them now. One of the women clenched and squeezed her breast, her diamond ring catching the firelight, just as she'd done to herself not so very long before. She wondered what passions Marion was feeling now.

*"Jesus,* Janet! For Christ's sake, *please!* You got to help me! I didn't kill anybody! You *know* I didn't kill anybody!"

"I know," she said.

They'd hauled Ray and Emil up off the floor to the cinderblock wall, to the shackles there. The family man was sobbing. Someone was stripping off Emil's belt and tugging down his pants while another took his head between both hands and pounded it against the wall to make him stop his bellowing. She supposed it annoyed him.

It worked.

She looked at Marion again. The women were already dragging her toward the bloody altar.

"But this way," she said, "you never will."

The naked woman in the main room was still swaying from her chains as they passed. Three men were gambling, throwing dice beneath her. Another was snorting something white—coke or speed or heroin.

At the door Harpe stopped her.

"You want to know," he said. "Little's full of shit. He shot those people and he was all by himself when he did it. My brother always was an asshole. You tell him for me that if and when you get him off he better slit his own fucking throat because I'm coming after him and what I do to him will be a whole lot worse."

She nodded and turned and walked into the half light of the coming dawn.

*Micah Harpe closed the door behind her and thought that you never did know what the day was going to bring. When he was a young man he'd quietly slit some lawyer's throat in his very own office because of a padded bill for services rendered on a chickenshit DUI rap and here he was letting another lawyer go—and this one was defending his idiot little brother. Forgetting the generally damaged condition of her, a damn good-looking lawyer too. Under other circumstances he'd have poked her all night long into the morning. Life was full of surprises.*

*He walked over to the bar and Edwin the bartender—not* Eddy, *never, the man was one vain sonovabitch—looked up at him and smiled.*

*"You guys downstairs missed the good part," he said.*

*"Oh yeah? What part was that?"*

*"Guy got up and walked right out of here. See that trail of blood over there? Guy went for a little stroll."*

She walked slowly, half-dazed in the clean open air and head pounding and reflected with grim humor that her head had taken a whole hell of a lot of abuse for a single night. The dog skeleton on the swing swayed on a breeze that wasn't there and with so little light she saw too late in her approach the bloody hand that moved the chain and saw him slide around from behind the tree, Billy grinning and covered with so much blood that it could only be craziness keeping him alive and standing. The hand that darted out at her and closed over her wrist was cold and slimy red. *All* of him was red. Only the knife blade in his other hand glinted clean at his side.

*"You swayed your charms with him, didn't you?"* he said. "You did."

Blood bubbled over his lips and slid over his chin and she tried to jerk free so that he staggered toward her but somehow kept his stance and pulled her toward him with improbable, impossible strength and then he raised the knife.

And then screamed.

Harpe's hands were over his wrist. She heard it snap like a dry twig in the forest and the knife fell to his feet. Billy clutched at the wrist, wailing, Billy suddenly gone boy soprano as Harpe lifted him off his feet bear-hugging him chest-to-chest and walked him from the swing and grinning remains of dog or wolf and then lifted him high to the first of the nooses hanging beyond and slipped his head through and then dropped him like a log.

The snap of neck was louder than the snap of wrist had been. She could hear bone grind bone inside him. His legs jerked and spasmed and then he was quiet, swaying, drooling pulsing waves of blood and pissing the length of his jeans.

Harpe turned to her and smiled. "Hole-in-the-Wall," he said. "A little frontier justice."

\*    \*    \*

She was nearly to the turnoff to the main road when she saw the headlights coming toward her—on a night filled with blazing headlights searing into her, two more now, like lasers burning through the most awful headache of her life and she fell dizzy to her knees before them.

*Too much,* she thought, *too damn much* and then she heard car doors slam and feet pound the dirt and then he was calling her name.

"So that's it," Alan said. The Turtle Brook was busy with the lunch crowd for a change. He wiped some burger juice off his chin and wondered why they had to make these things so thick no normal mouth could close over them.

"Thanks to you and your late friend Marion they finally got to close the place down. Harrison gets indicted on four counts of murder for the kid, who turns out to be your basic runaway by the way and for Marion, Short and Rothert, with Thaw and Coombs as co-conspirators since they run the place. Thaw and Coombs? They may very well beat the rap or take a plea. Hole-in-the-Wall's a big place to supervise and you can't be everywhere at once. You know, that kind of thing. The Church of Final Judgment keeps no records and it looks like takes no prisoners and nobody thinks Harrison will do a whole lot of talking, so that's probably *all* they'll get. Too bad it took a day to get that goddamn search warrant."

"Why *couldn't* you get the warrant?" she said. "I thought you and Judge Lardner were thick as thieves."

You should only know, he thought. *He hadn't called*

*her in months,* that was why. It pissed her off. Simple as that. She wouldn't even talk to him. And he couldn't do much begging with Frommer standing by. He shrugged and bit into his burger.

"So there's nothing at all on Micah Harpe."

"Nothing," he said. "Vanished."

"Good," she said and smiled.

She looked terrific in the turban, he thought. Hell, she'd even looked terrific in the bandages last night. The bandages and nothing else. Stark white against tanned smooth skin. She was quite a goddamn woman to have gone through all of that and come out of it the way she did. He was going to have to marry her soon before somebody else beat him there. If he didn't know that before, he sure did now.

"Good? Why's that?" he said.

Her smile broadened. "Don't worry. You'll see."

Arthur "Little" Harpe sat on a bench in the hall flanked by guards on either side. He got up when he saw Janet and her new co-council Linda Morrison striding in his direction and smiled that shaky, *snaky* little smile of his that she used to wish she could dissuade him from using in the courtroom.

"Hi, Janet," he said. "Feeling better today?"

"Much better, thank you."

"What was the problem? I mean, if you don't mind my asking. All's they told me was you weren't so hot."

"Nothing to worry about, Arthur."

He didn't need to know about the nightmares. God, no. Certainly not Arthur Harpe. He didn't need to know about that poor little girl twisting in a sudden gale of gunfire.

"Come on," she said. "We're going to see if we can't get you out of here today."

The smile this time was absolutely genuine. The little worm probably had never hoped for such luck. The fact that it *wasn't* luck—that she'd be lying when she got up there on the witness stand and told the jury that Micah Harpe had confessed to the Willis murders to her back in Hole-in-the-Wall—that was something he didn't need to know either.

Linda opened the door to the courtroom for them and they stepped on through.

"By the way," she said, "I have a message for you. From your brother."

The look of alarm on his face nearly made her smile. But it wouldn't do to smile. Instead she put her hand on his shoulder and turned him toward the defense table.

"But that can wait for now," she said, "can't it?"

# BRYAN SMITH

It was known as the House of Blood. It sat at the entrance to a netherworld of unimaginable torture and terror. Very few who entered its front door lived to ever again see the outside world. But a few did survive. They thought they had found a way to destroy the house of horrors…but they were wrong. A new house has arisen. A new mistress now wields its unholy power—and she wants revenge. She will not rest until those who dared to challenge her and her former master are made to pay with their very souls.

# Queen of Blood

ISBN 13: 978-0-8439-6061-7

To order a book or to request a catalog call:
**1-800-481-9191**

This book is also available at your local bookstore, or you can check out our Web site **www.dorchesterpub.com** where you can look up your favorite authors, read excerpts, or glance at our discussion forum to see what people have to say about your favorite books.

> **"If you've missed Laymon, you've missed a treat!"**
> **—Stephen King**

# RICHARD LAYMON

Many people have a hobby that verges on obsession. Albert Prince's obsession happens to be cutting people, especially pretty girls. There's nothing he loves more than breaking into a stranger's house and letting his imagination—and his knife—run wild. Albert's on the run now, heading cross-country, but he's not about to stop having fun....

A pregnant young woman, a teacher, a librarian, an aging Southern belle, a famous writer and a budding actress. All of them have troubles and all of them are looking for something in their lives. Unfortunately, what they'll find isn't necessarily what they wanted. What many of them will find instead is Albert and his very sharp knives.

ISBN 13: 978-0-8439-5752-5

To order a book or to request a catalog call:
**1-800-481-9191**
This book is also available at your local bookstore, or you can check out our Web site **www.dorchesterpub.com** where you can look up your favorite authors, read excerpts, or glance at our discussion forum to see what people have to say about your favorite books.

# ATTENTION
# BOOK LOVERS!

Can't get enough
of your favorite **HORROR**?

Call **1-800-481-9191** to:

— order books —
— receive a **FREE** catalog —
— join our book clubs to **SAVE 20%**! —

Open Mon.–Fri. 10 AM–9 PM EST

Visit
## www.dorchesterpub.com
for special offers and inside
information on the authors you love.

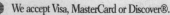